Praise for the previous
Jordan Myles mysteries

BREAKING POINT

"Great fun; intriguing yet accessible and delightfully entertaining. I think what Ms. Navratilova has accomplished is yet another major win."

—PATRICIA CORNWELL

"Wonderful."

—*USA Today*

THE TOTAL ZONE

"An inspired behind-the-scenes look at the world of tennis, with intrigue and suspense thrown in for a grand slam."

—CLIVE CUSSLER

"To read *The Total Zone* is to plunge into the reality of international tennis. . . . The authors set a rapid pace with a swift, sure, original style of writing."

—*The Houston Post*

By Martina Navratilova and Liz Nickles:

THE TOTAL ZONE*
BREAKING POINT*
KILLER INSTINCT*

By Martina Navratilova:

MARTINA*

By Liz Nickles:

THE COMING MATRIARCHY*
BABY, BABY*
HYPE*

Cartoon Books by Liz Nickles:

ALWAYS KISS WITH YOUR WHISKERS
HEAVY PETTING

Published by Ballantine Books

KILLER INSTINCT

A Jordan Myles Mystery

Martina Navratilova and Liz Nickles

BALLANTINE BOOKS • NEW YORK

A Ballantine Book
Published by The Ballantine Publishing Group
Copyright © 1997 by Martina Navratilova and Elizabeth Nickles

All rights reserved under International and Pan-American Copyright Conventions. Published in the United States by The Ballantine Publishing Group, a divison of Random House, Inc., New York, and simultaneously in Canada by Random House of Canada Limited, Toronto.

http://www.randomhouse.com

Library of Congress Catalog Card Number: 97-97101

ISBN 0-345-38876-3

This edition published by arrangement with Villard Books, a divison of Random House, Inc. Villard Books is a registered trademark of Random House, Inc.

Manufactured in the United States of America

First Ballantine Books Edition: June 1998

10   9   8   7   6   5   4   3   2   1

Here's to all the people who try to make the world a better place.

—MARTINA NAVRATILOVA

ACKNOWLEDGMENTS

The authors wish to thank all the people who helped us in the writing and publishing of this book, especially: for medical insight, Dr. Rosemarie Morwessel and Dr. Stanley Liebowitz; Bunny Williams, Missy Malool, "Bunny's Bunch," Goerge Breed, Jr., and Anni Miller at Hilton Head; John McKally and Janet Indelli at HBO; Craig Nelson; John Nelson; Brad Dancer; Ted Walters; and Lady Valerie Solti. Thanks also to Villard Books: David Rosenthal and Annik LaFarge; and at Ballantine Books, Joe Blades. At IMG, we thank Julian Bach, Peter Johnson, and Carolyn Krupp. And, for all her assistance over the course of the entire Jordan Myles series, a particular thanks to Nancy Falconer.

KILLER
INSTINCT

ONE

Gladiators. That was how they seemed to me, although their game was tennis. It was still an unfamiliar angle for a game I knew so well, a sport I knew in my soul. I had faced a similar crowd of fifteen thousand—more, if you counted the television audience—hundreds of times myself. I had faced an opponent, on grass, clay, and compound. I had faced the ball. And I had faced myself. But when I was on the court, I never realized how much I was on center stage. It seemed more private somehow, when I was playing the game, as opposed to watching it from high up in the network commentators' box, giving the play-by-play to the television audience.

I hadn't realized then what an invasion the camera was. Now, sitting in the commentators' booth at Madison Square Garden, looking down at the huge rotunda with its sea of purple seats and the blue-surfaced court, I saw things from a different perspective. As a player, you face your opponent and the crowd, not the camera. The crowd's attention can be on the other player while you prepare for your next shot, unaware that the camera has zoomed in to record your every expression. You're playing, competing; you don't realize that the camera enhances each move as if you are a specimen under a microscope, that it can see the hairs on the inside of somebody's nose, if that's the shot the director wants.

I admit that after almost two years it still feels somewhat strange to be sitting in this booth, wired with earpiece and microphone. I am far more of a naturalized citizen than a native of this broadcast territory. Watching the match action below, I often find myself wishing it were me down there on that court, knowing in my heart I could have beat whoever is winning, but those are feelings I try to hide from the audience, feelings that have no place anymore. Still, I'm much more comfortable in my earlier incarnation as Jordan Myles, tennis player and, on occasion, champion, or as Jordan Myles, physical therapist, my current alter ego. Even seeing myself on the screen is still disconcerting. It's me—with my curly, barely controllable dark hair sleeked back into a braid, my high cheekbones dusted with powder that masks the sun wash of freckles, my athletic figure draped in the requisite navy blue commentator's blazer—but it seems like someone else. Before I went on the air myself, I never gave much thought to the commentators, except to bristle when they seemed to play favorites among the competitors. The people in the booth were just tournament fixtures. Now, however, I've grown to have a healthy respect for anyone who can face a camera and come out looking and sounding coherent.

I've learned, for instance, that the first week of a tournament is particularly tough for the commentators. Superstars like Graf are easy to call, because you know them and their game. But then all kinds of qualifiers whom you don't know very well come out of nowhere and sweep through the field, and you have to pick up on their game very quickly. Sometimes I've found myself talking about a player I haven't ever seen until she (or he) appears on my monitor. Then it's tap-dance time—I have to look at the statistics, the player's record, her three-set win-loss ratio, tie-break win-loss ratio; I have to pick up her game by watching to see patterns in her technique; I'll watch how she strokes the ball, looking to see if she's better crosscourt or down the line, and then use the cues to come up with an analysis that makes sense on the spot. It's a continual process of on-the-job learning. The fun is in picking up what's going on, what's working and what isn't.

During my second match as a commentator, I made a mistake. I talked during a player's key shot, and the director cut into my earpiece and told me to stop. That in itself was bad enough, but then, at the next day's pre-production meeting, which involved the crew and the other commentators—including a roomful of former stars like Billie Jean King—he mentioned that it would be a good idea if I didn't do it again. Since then I've made other mistakes, like the time I inadvertently swore on the air, but I've learned from them and moved on. With that first one, however, I felt as if I'd just missed a match point. But then, I was a beginner, and as I covered more matches I learned it wasn't as personal as playing the game—and tennis is a lot easier to talk about than to play. But I knew I had things to learn. I had to realize that I wasn't the expert on court anymore. I was just a member of the freshman class.

That was why I went into broadcasting two years ago. It seemed like a challenge, something fresh and new and fun. I'd been head physical therapist at the Desert Springs Sports Science Clinic for five years, helping tennis players regain their game. I was a partner, and I enjoyed my work.

I knew I'd never play tennis again myself, much less the Grand Slam circuit—my tumble down a mountainside had shut the door on that. So when the call came from the U.S. Sports Network, I was intrigued. It seemed like a way to stay closer to the game than I'd been, as well as to keep an eye on clients and future clients. And I can't say it wasn't flattering that the media people still thought of me as one of the recognizable names in tennis. It turned out the viewers agreed. In spite of my flubs, eventually my performance smoothed out and, more important to the network, the ratings went up whenever I did commentary. Now things have evolved and I have a new magazine show called *Woman/Sport*. We tape six high-profile specials a year with three segments each.

"How many times did you play the Garden, Jordan? This must feel like old home week to you," said my cocommentator, Jon Wetherill, during a changeover. He squinted at a page of statistics that had been handed to him and signaled his runner to bring him some water. Jon's a nice guy, good-looking with curly blond hair and a perpetual tan, very smooth on the air, but his knowledge of tennis leaves something to be desired. He was never a player himself and basically learned by watching. On the air, he just calls the score and leads us in and out. Then I come on and handle the color and the technical narrative. The audience identifies with his trademark folksy banter, and my technical expertise provides a good counterpoint. The two of us are often paired up, sitting side by side in identical blue blazers at tennis tournaments all over the world. Today, though, would be the last time we'd work together for a while because it was basically the end of the women's season.

The Saturnia Championships, renamed a few years ago after a long association with a tobacco sponsor, were now supported by an international conglomerate that made hundreds of household products. It was the traditional grand finale of the year for women's tennis, and I'd played here dozens of times. The Garden always thrilled me, with its larger-than-life history and heritage.

On the court, Seranata Aziz, one of the all-time great women's champions—"the Lege," they call her, short for "legend"—was dueling it out in the last tournament before her retirement. When I was on the tour, I'd played Aziz many times myself, and she has a huge history to draw on, so it wasn't a tough match for me to comment on. Aziz was due to receive a special award from the sponsors after her final match, but it was a good bet that just as many people had come to see her opponent, Jasmine Li, an exotic young Dutch-Indonesian sensation who'd been sparkling across the headlines for the past season. At the U.S. Open a few weeks earlier, she'd made a strong showing by getting to the quarterfinals. Aziz was blasting away with her famous power game, but Li covered the court like a feather on water, skittering from the baseline to the net with a seeming lack of effort, then exploding with a killer two-handed forehand. Because she had grown up playing field hockey, she had two good hands. Her lithe, almost six-foot-tall grace and exceptional exotic beauty had made her an instant cover girl, and her court sense and ability to return almost any shot, to instinctively be wherever the ball appeared—ahead of the ball—made her a crowd favorite. Even though she hadn't won a major tournament yet, the nineteen-year-old was already being called "ESP Li," the girl with the sixth sense about the game.

Coming up with provocative questions for the interview with Jasmine hadn't been too hard. In addition to her meteoric rise on the circuit, there was her high-fanfare romance. For several months, Jasmine had been seriously involved with Malik, a one-name wonder and transplanted star from the NBA, now dead set on becoming the first black basketball player to win a tennis Grand Slam title. They were the hottest tennis couple—maybe the *only* tennis couple—since Chris Evert and John Lloyd. No, they were the hottest couple in sports, period. Every reporter in journalism had tried to get an interview with them, but they had both steadfastly refused to talk about their relationship. Now Jasmine had agreed to talk exclusively to me.

"So how'd you get to Jasmine?" asked Jon. "She's a brick wall."

I smiled secretively. Very few people knew it, but Jasmine was about to become one of my clients. As soon as this tournament was over, she was scheduled to fly to Palm Springs and check in for a weeklong intensive analysis and training session at the clinic. The clinic was the home base for our magazine show, so it was perfect timing.

"Not bad for a rookie. Lots of people with lots more experience than you wanted that interview," jibed Jon.

I smiled again. That was precisely the point.

"The press has been swarming all over Jas and Malik, but she trusts you," Jasmine's agent, Paul Kessler, had said. "After all, you're not a hard-core journalist like the rest of them. You're a player with a medical background. You're not going to blow this out of proportion or misquote her or run some fucking topless picture or something equally irresponsible."

I always listened to Paul, who was known to players on the circuit as "Pinocchio," with a grain of salt, knowing he would say just about anything to achieve his objective. I knew he wanted to keep Jasmine's image as polished and pristine as possible, so she would have maximum worth to the sponsors he was lining up. He wasn't about to risk an interview with someone he didn't have total confidence in. And so the interview had been handed to me, my first media coup. The buzz on this interview was already incredible. It would virtually guarantee that our ratings would go through the roof, and the exposure would be good for the clinic, too.

The network contract allowed me to continue my work at the Springs, and I was committed to doing just that, although my new schedule demanded that I limit the number of clients I worked with. Now that I was on the air on a regular basis, it seemed that everybody in tennis with a sprain or a pain wanted to work with me, but I traveled so much now that I was forced to work with only a select few.

Down on the arena floor, the match between Li and Aziz seemed to be delayed for some reason. "What's taking so long down there?" I asked, nudging Jon. The huge octagonal electronic scoreboard that hung over the action was frozen; the players were standing on the sidelines; the ball girls in their crisp white polo shirts and navy blue skirts stood at attention.

The director's voice barked over the earphones. "There's a disturbance off court. Security is moving in to remove the players from the area."

With the current security climate, the attitude was get the players to safety immediately, then ask questions later. Looking down, Jon and I could see people suddenly standing in their seats, peering toward a courtside box, as Garden security people ushered Jasmine and Seranata back to the locker room.

"Hold on, we're cutting to Hank on the floor," said the director. "There's some disturbance going on down there."

Scanning the crowd, I noticed a hive of activity now surrounding a box midway along the court, behind the players' seats. The scene appeared on our monitor, then cut in closer. I could see a woman frantically waving an arm and screaming hysterically. She was clutching a limp child in her other arm. The little girl seemed to be about three years old. Her eyes were rolled back in her head, and she was having a seizure.

I ripped off my earphones. "I'm going down there," I said, leaping over Jon.

"You can't do that," he said. "They're not going to leave this on camera very long. The kid probably choked on a piece of popcorn. What if they put us back on the air as filler until they start playing again? Who will I have to banter with?"

"You'll think of something," I said, as I pushed out to the aisle, brandishing my red all-access pass at the guards.

I knew that the Garden paramedics would be on the scene momentarily, but I also knew I couldn't sit up in the booth, watching a child in trouble. I had been trained to respond to emergencies, and this was such an occasion.

I knew a backstage shortcut. Another wave of the pass hanging around my neck, a check of my photo laminated to it, and I was in the bowels of the Garden, running across the gray-painted cement floor, pounding down an inner track that crossed through the rotunda, past the blue-curtained media room. I raced on into the marshaling area, a dark, cavernous space where a fleet of yellow pallet trucks was parked. A guard with a flashlight stared at me curiously as I raced by. "Hey, Mac," he called out. I knew this guard. He called everybody Mac. Farther down the hall, inside the open door of the players' lounge, several women and their families and friends were gathered by the buffet table, and I could hear a television, tuned to our station, and Hank's voice describing the scene on the arena floor.

Usually, when there is an accident or illness in the crowd, the paramedics handle things quietly and efficiently, and most spectators never even become aware of the emergency. Heatstroke, choking, indigestion, and flu are common at tennis events. I had been a physical therapist at the Family Circle Magazine Cup when a man went into cardiac arrest and the tournament doctor and paramedic team leaped into the stands, stabilized the man's head, cleared his throat, strapped him to a board, and passed him literally over the crowd's heads while simultaneously doing CPR. The game had not even stopped momentarily.

But a child was different.

Entering the Garden arena from backstage is like going from black-and-white to color. The gray cinderblock walls suddenly give way to a sea of faces, the bright blue of the courts, the confetti multicolors of the coats and sweaters of the people in the stands. The low ceiling suddenly soars to a huge height, and all this is usually accompanied by the roar of the crowd and the applause.

Now there was a mother out of control, and the mood had spread to the crowd. I could sense it the minute I burst from the tunnel, through the fabric curtains, and

onto the floor. The massive crowd seemed frozen, para-
lyzed, their collective breath hanging in the air. Even the
still photographers flanking the sides of the court, usually
firing off rapid bursts of light-metered flashes, had
assumed a state of suspended animation. The screams of
the agonized mother continued to reverberate, echoing
off the huge structural ceiling, as loud as a crowd roar.

Hank and our network cameraman stood off to the side
as he spoke gravely into his handheld microphone. I
could see the child, a little girl with curly blond hair in
blue denim overalls, lying still, almost dwarfed by the
crew of adults bending over her inert form. Her tiny face
was pale, like a molded wax figurine. An IV had already
been inserted into her arm, and CPR was under way. Several people were trying to calm the mother, who still
screamed and struggled to break free from their grasp.
"My baby! Save my baby! Let me go! Save my baby!"
she shrieked. The child was strapped to a gurney and
quickly wheeled out.

They passed close by me, a phalanx of security people,
doctors, paramedics, and the still-hysterical mother, and I
trotted alongside the procession for a few seconds, wondering how I could be of assistance. Then I caught the
expression of Rachel Allyn, the Women's Tennis Foundation's doctor for the tournament. Over my shoulder, I
could hear Hank telling the TV viewers that the emergency had passed, the match would immediately resume,
the little girl was in good hands, and everyone was confident she would be taken care of. But Rachel looked grim,
and in the set of her jaw I detected not confidence but the
one thing nobody in any medical capacity ever wants to
see: hopelessness.

*   *   *

Seranata Aziz won the Saturnia. It should have been a triumphant exit from her spectacular tennis career, but the fact that the three-year-old girl, Celine York, had died on the way to the hospital dimmed the joy of the occasion. Seranata did not know this until the match with Jasmine Li was over, and when she found out, she burst into tears and was unable to attend the post-match press conference. The next day, she dedicated her finals win to little Celine. The child, the daughter of a friend of a trainer in the Aziz entourage, had been a particular fan; in fact, just before the match, Seranata had been teasing merrily with her and had tossed her a tennis ball to keep. It had been found, still clutched in Celine's hands, at the hospital, and the desolate mother had announced that it would be buried with her daughter.

"The preliminary says it was a birth defect," Rachel said, when we discussed the tragedy two days later. "I had a feeling. When I got to her, she already had no pulse. She wasn't choking; her airway was clear. The mother managed to tell us she had no history of allergies—God knows how, she was so hysterical. Not that I blame her."

After a tournament, I like to get together with my old friends from the tour. In New York, our favorite hangout is Tandoori Rose, an Indian vegetarian place on the Upper West Side. I picked at my curry. "Poor little thing. How's Seranata taking it?"

"She went to the funeral today. So did I." Rachel was still dressed in a black pantsuit. Usually, she'd be wearing jeans and a sweater, her dark hair tucked up in a clip.

"God, what a terrible thing to happen. I wish I could have done something."

"We all do. Some people, unfortunately, are born with

time bombs. A weakness in a heart valve, an aneurysm waiting to burst. Sometimes we just can't play God, no matter how hard we try, Jordan."

I turned to Gale Lieber, who was sitting next to me. We live in neighboring towns in the Palm Springs area, but we've known each other for years. She'd been a fixture on the women's tennis scene for decades, ubiquitous at matches as an umpire until she'd become too friendly with the players to be effective. Now she worked full time for the Saturnia tournament as a player liaison, and she functioned as the den mother to the tour. I liked Gale because she was very funny and told wonderful stories full of amusing details and bits of spicy conversation, but tonight she, like the rest of us, was subdued.

"I heard that the mother was a friend of Seranata's trainer," I said.

"Right, Artie Lutz," said Gale. "Actually, they were dating. I went to see him the day before it happened. He was looking for some circus tickets, and I was able to locate them. The little girl was there then, playing around in his hotel room. He told me he was baby-sitting, and obviously the circus tickets were for her. He was really sweet with her, too—you should have seen the pile of presents he'd bought her at FAO Schwarz. There was ripped-up FAO rocking-horse paper all over the floor. He must have bought out the stuffed animal department, but what the kid really seemed to like was the toy tennis racket he'd given her. She was running around swatting at everything in sight."

"Poor Artie. He was wiped out at the funeral," said Rachel. "Very stoic, like Artie tends to be, but totally devastated."

"How's the mother doing?" I asked.

"You can imagine. She's sedated, but she's still in shock, I think. I mean, seeing your child die before your eyes; it must unhinge you. I can't imagine the devastation." Her mouth tightened. "Anyway, she's saying her daughter was murdered. She kept breaking down and crying that somebody killed her."

"But everybody saw it happen," said Gale.

"Well, it's her only child. She's grasping at anything to make sense of something that's senseless," said Rachel. "People do that." She sighed and pushed her food around her plate, eating none of it.

Nobody felt much like either talking or eating. Earlier in the tournament, there had been talk of planning a group vacation, maybe renting a sailboat in the Caribbean, but the mood was hardly conducive to discussing it. As soon as the dishes from the main course had been cleared, I found myself pushing my chair back from the table. I had an 8 A.M. flight back to Palm Springs the next morning. I'd been on the road for most of the past year, hurtling from Paris to Wimbledon to New York and many points between, and now—especially now—I couldn't wait to get home.

TWO

    Walking into my house, I encountered a unique experience: the smell of food cooking. At first, I almost went back outside to recheck the address. Let me put it this way: The only appliance in my kitchen that ever gets used is the can opener, which I use for the dog's food. Yes, it was my house in the Sandstone Canyon Villa complex—white stucco, terra-cotta roof, rock garden flanking the door. I dropped my bags in the front hall and headed for the kitchen, where I found Gus whipping up something on three burners at once.

    As long as I've known Dr. Augustus Laidlaw, he's been brilliant at anything he ever tried, and that includes cooking. He's been my partner and my boss at the Springs, and he's been the most important person in my life from the day he saved it, which was the day I met him. After my accident, I opened my eyes, which had been shut tightly in the blackest despair I have ever known, to see this tall, sandy-haired man with hazel eyes looming over my bed. Gus was the insightful psychologist who brought me back from total emptiness when I learned I would never play competitive tennis again, that my body would never be the same and could no longer support me, and I would literally have to find a new life for myself. And he helped me find it, as a physical therapist. Then, when he became a founding partner of Desert Springs, he invited me to join the clinic professionally and provided me with the security of a home base.

I'd like to say that Gus was always there for me, that he was my anchor, my platform. Maybe he might have been—if I hadn't made the mistake of falling in love with him. Well, it was my mistake because Gus was too much of a professional to fall in love with a patient, even a former patient, which I was at the time. My fall from grace had been quite literal: One minute I was a top-ranked tennis player, at the peak of my career, enjoying an exhilarating day of rock climbing—and the next thing I knew I woke up in a hospital bed with a broken body, a broken marriage, no career, and no prospects. Physically, I managed to heal, but it was Gus who pulled me through emotionally. The fact that he was an eminent sports psychologist was less important than the fact that he was, simply, there for me. He believed I could not only start over, but succeed at something other than tennis. And because he believed in me, I learned to believe in myself again.

We grew so close, we became each other's alter egos. It was Gus who guided me to the right schools to become a physical therapist, and when he and his partners opened the Desert Springs Sports Science Clinic, he made sure there was a partnership slot for me. I liked to think that I helped him learn to love, to have a warm and giving relationship. Because that's what we had, for a while.

There was a time when each of us knew the other's thoughts and bodies as well as our own. Sometimes, I look at Gus and flash back to a cold, clear desert night, lying in each other's arms in front of the fire, full of dreams and languid kisses. But our life together at the Springs was a double-edged sword. The details of working together, being together every day, gradually eroded our relationship. Philosophical discussions became squabbles. Squabbles deteriorated into icy silences. Maybe the pressure of being a protégée was too much for me, or my emotional expectations were too high for him—or vice versa. Maybe it was just that we are very different, and we'd lost the arc of my recovery that had held us together. I don't know. But I do know that when the romance faded out, I lost the lover but kept the mentor; at least, that's how it was until just last month, when Gus and I found ourselves drifting back together again. I had vowed, Never again, but then Gus made me dinner one night, and the fact is that his cooking is very seductive. I don't know what he does with the spices. And now, here he was, continuing his relationship with my underutilized oven, tempting my equally underutilized sexuality.

"I thought you'd be hungry after a day of airplane food," he said, his back to me as he chopped at breakneck speed. His sleeves were rolled up, and I could see his tan arms. "I've got a risotto going here." He turned around, wiped his hands on a towel, and took off his sunglasses.

"Cooking incognito?" I asked, as I reached down to scoop up Alice Marble, or A.M., as everyone calls her.

"They form a shield if you're chopping onions. So your eyes don't tear up."

"Of course. Silly me." I kissed him, and he rubbed my back. It felt good. I laid my head on his chest, rather squashing poor A.M. between us—luckily, Jack Russell terriers don't take up much room. There was a solidity to Gus that I'd always responded to, a presence in his face, with its strong features, and in his bearing.

"Your girl didn't win," he said.

"Well, her shoulder has been giving her so much trouble. And then there was this horrible tragedy, the child who died right there at courtside. It had nothing to do with the game, but of course nobody could concentrate afterward."

"Seranata could."

"Seranata could concentrate in the middle of a nuclear attack. The woman's a machine." I leaned down and set A.M. back on the floor, where she immediately began scouring for scraps of fallen food. "It was pretty bad, Gus."

"A tragedy, like you said." He whisked the stock.

"The little girl really got to me," I admitted, lowering myself slowly onto a bar stool by the kitchen island. "I can't forget her face." I felt as if I'd aged ten years since I last left this house. Maybe I needed a good steam. I wondered if I should tell Gus that, for most of the plane ride home, I'd been thinking about children—or, specifically, the lack of them in my life. Maybe it was the little girl at Madison Square Garden, maybe it was my biological clock ticking. Whatever, I was well into my adult life without any personal roots, or even a reason to put them down. The closest I was to having a baby was A.M.

I decided not to mention it, at least not right now. But the fact that I was suddenly thinking about children made me consider that Gus might have something to do with a train of thought that was, for me, borderline radical. The relationship was definitely restarted. I told myself it was totally normal to wonder where it was headed.

"So when does Jasmine arrive?" Gus asked. He handed me a glass of mineral water, without ice, as I like it.

"Tomorrow. We'll do the baseline physical, get her

into diagnostics, and let her settle in, and then the network crew will arrive to put down the *Woman/Sport* segment."

" 'Put down the segment.' God, you even sound like one of them now." His face was expressionless, but then that's one of Gus's specialties. I can never read what's behind those steady eyes, with their striated irises, hard as cracked marbles.

"It really bothers you that I'm doing this media thing, doesn't it?" I asked.

"Not at all, if you don't walk away from your work here, which you've been doing since summer."

"I've brought in some very high-profile patients."

"Yes, but I hate to see you give up what you trained so hard to do. You're not just a tennis player, you're a trained physical therapist with a major facility behind you. Any monkey can sit in front of the camera and read from a cue card." He touched my chin. "I just don't want to see them turn you into a talking head. It's so mindless. You're much too smart and have worked much too long and hard to have that happen."

"Well," I said, "first of all, you should try getting in front of the camera before you criticize me. It's not that easy, believe me. And there's not much danger of me turning into a talking head with you around as my reality check."

It didn't surprise me that Gus had never been excited about my on-camera work. He was a doctor, after all, and I could see how it must have seemed frivolous to him, compared with serious medical issues. Even I certainly didn't put the commenting and interviewing in that league. My work was fun, a new experience, a learning opportunity, and I was being paid for it as well.

"Maybe after we shoot the Jasmine Li segment here at the Springs and you get a firsthand look at the process, you might give it a chance," I said.

"If it weren't for you, I'd never let them on the premises," Gus said sourly. "They're going to be dragging those cables everywhere, tripping everybody, making a mess, disrupting our clients and our schedules."

"It'll be good press."

"God knows what they'll end up running. They can shoot anything and put it on the air."

"Gus, it's a scripted interview. I'll know every question in advance, and every camera shot and angle. If there's a problem, I'll catch it. And this is tape, not live. We have control. But relax. I really think this will be good for the Springs. I hope Bill's still okay on this." This was a rhetorical question. Bill Stokes, president of the clinic, thrives on the press; when it comes to publicity, he's the polar opposite of Gus, but that's probably because Bill, a former Olympian, really understands the role of the media and how it can help your business. Gus, on the other hand, is dedicated to medical development, the kind of man who by choice would spend all his time with his patients or behind the clinic doors.

He spooned the risotto out onto my best plates, and we sat at the breakfast bar.

"This is great," I said. Gus is an amazing cook, and the kind of person who can eat anything without gaining an ounce. "I really appreciate it."

"You know, Jordan, I hope you don't get so carried away with this media thing that you throw away what you've worked for here."

"I can't imagine why you would say something like

that again," I said, putting my fork down. "You know what the clinic and our work here means to me."

"I know, but it's just that when I brought you in, I envisioned a partner who would be on the scene one hundred percent, totally accessible to our clients." Gus fiddled with a button on his shirt. He looked uncomfortable, but then, Gus has always shied away from confrontation.

This was clearly a difficult speech for him to make, but I could understand it. From the day I left the hospital after my accident, I had been focused on physical therapy and the clinic. Gus had never even known me as a tennis player. This was a new role for me, a fresh dynamic in our well-worn relationship.

"I'm not going to become inaccessible to our clients, Gus. In fact, with the show I'll be able to share our work and philosophy with people who can't even come here. I don't think this is any different from when the resident pro at a tennis club or golf course also travels on the tour to play or to coach."

"Well, we'll see how it pans out. I trust your sense of these things. It's just that we have a group of people here, and it wouldn't be fair to the others if they had to juggle your share of work in addition to their own."

"Don't worry about it. I'll handle it, okay?" I didn't need Gus to help me run my life, but I realized he was right; I did seem to be spreading myself very thin these days. That was something I was going to have to deal with.

Gus shrugged. "Just a hint from a friend. But that's not the main thing. I'm also concerned about your private life. And our life together."

I looked up. Gus rarely used words like "together" that implied commitment.

He smiled softly. "Don't you ever wonder about the future? About having a family?"

"These days, I do. When I saw that little girl, and I knew she was dying, it ripped me apart. You can't imagine."

Children were on my mind now, more often than I would want to discuss, even with Gus. When a woman reaches her thirties, that has a way of happening. Family, children, relationships—these were all issues I'd managed to avoid since my brief, disastrous marriage. But now they were resurfacing, in spite of myself. One thing about my impossible schedule I found appealing was that I rarely had the chance to dwell on my personal life. It was easier that way.

I sighed. "It's late, Gus. We'll talk more about this later."

"Later. Fine. There's always later, isn't there? That is, until it's too late."

We ate in silence for a few minutes, both of us concentrating purposefully on the food. "This may be your best risotto yet," I said, finally. "Cooking may be your fall-back career." I leaned down and fed A.M. some table scraps.

"I don't think so. I'm already working on another career. Or at least a major project."

"What's that?"

"Aha. So you're curious."

"Of course I'm curious. Especially when you show up at my stove and talk about 'another career.' Specifically, what 'other career' are you referring to?"

"Well, you're not the only one who can do two things at once." Gus was being purposefully enigmatic.

"And what about focusing on the Springs, like you were lecturing me to do?"

"What I'm doing, Jordan, evolved directly from my work here and would be a great enhancement to the programs we offer. It's totally relevant."

"Oh, of course it is. It's *your* project."

Gus stood up, collected the dishes, and stacked them in the sink. "Can you take a field trip to LA on Tuesday? I have a meeting that will explain everything, and I think you'll find it extremely interesting. It could mean a lot to both of us. At any rate, I'd like your opinion. We could combine it with a stop at the Ivy."

A blatant bribe: He knew that the Ivy was my favorite restaurant in Los Angeles. I wondered what Gus was up to. He was so private, even with those he was closest to, that you never really knew what he was doing until he decided to share it with you on his terms.

"Once I get Jasmine settled in, I think it could be arranged," I said. "I was planning to take Tuesday off anyhow, while she works with Bill. We don't tape the show till Thursday."

Gus held up his glass of Evian in a toast. "To Tuesdays."

The next morning, I met Jasmine in the dining room. The Springs dining room is one of my favorite parts of the complex. The menu specializes in healthful food, which is good, but the chef also knows how to make everything taste and look delicious. The view is spectacular as well, with huge walls of glass looking down across the golf course to the stark profile of the Chocolate Hills looming beyond.

Jasmine sat at the table eating a sliced mango and a bowl of oatmeal. Sitting in the chair next to her was what appeared to be a small rubber penguin.

"Hi, Jasmine. Who's your friend?" I asked as I pulled up a chair.

She laughed. "That's Stanley. Stanley goes everywhere with me. He's quite a traveler. He's been to Indonesia, of course, and all over Europe. He's been at all the Grand Slams and the Olympics, and he's gone on all my vacations, including scuba diving. Last summer, after Wimbledon, I was invited to Elton John's estate, and somehow he fell out of my coat and got lost. I refused to leave without him, and they had to get the gardeners to walk the grounds to find him."

"I understand perfectly," I said. "My dog, A.M., goes everywhere with me." I opened my gym bag, and A.M. poked her head out. "We'll have to be sure they're both in our interview for the show."

"Absolutely!" Jasmine grinned. "Stanley loves being on camera, and we wouldn't want A.M. to feel left out." She blew a kiss across the table to A.M., who cocked her head appreciatively.

"And where's your coach?" I asked.

She looked puzzled. "I didn't ask her to come. You told me you didn't want any entourage. I told Paul to stay away too. I'm here on my own, to work."

We tell every player who comes to the Springs that, but almost none of them listen. Once a player gets to be somewhat of a star, the entourage seems unavoidable; at minimum, we get the involved coach, anxious agent, or pushy parent—all, of course, making themselves indispensable on the star's payroll. Already I liked Jasmine for not falling into that trap.

The young woman sitting across the table from me was also remarkable in her startling, exotic looks, which reflected her combination of cultures. This was a girl who had won the gene pool lottery. She had a Eurasian face, with golden skin and hooded, almond-shaped eyes. The irises of those eyes were a deep, velvety brown, and her hair was honey blond, smattered with sun streaks. When she smiled, deep dimples bracketed both cheeks. Her voice was soft and lilting, with the trace of an unplaceable accent, probably an amalgam of the languages she had been exposed to in childhood. Jasmine's father was a tennis player who had met his wife during a stint in Holland, and Jasmine had traveled with her parents from the time she was a baby. It was no secret that they had put a racket into her hands as soon as she could walk. She'd been pushed from a young age, and although her personality seemed delightfully unaffected, the question was, Could her game ever catch up to her beauty?

"I heard about your big new deal with the car company," I said. Actually, I had seen the commercial, which featured Jasmine driving around in a convertible, her hair blowing in slow motion. Sponsors were lining up, especially now that she was involved in a high-profile relationship.

Jasmine looked straight at me. "I know what you're thinking," she said. "You're thinking, 'What's she doing with a big sponsorship contract when she hasn't even won a major tournament yet?' And you're right to think that. I know doors have opened for me because of my looks. But now it's time for me to do something with myself. Those doors are going to slam shut if I don't deliver with my game. I don't want to let these opportunities slip away because I was lazy. That's why I came here to work with your team."

"It's really brave and smart of you to say that, Jasmine.

You're really looking into yourself and taking responsibility for what you see. I know we'll be able to work together."

She smiled, and the dimples deepened. "I know it too. I know what you've done. How you came back from that horrible accident, what it must have taken. I need to take my game to the next level. I know I can learn from you."

"Well, we have a group of the best possible people here at the Springs. You'll have a medical evaluation, and then we'll talk about the results and the options. You'll start with that, in fact. Then Gus Laidlaw, our head psychologist, will talk to you, and then we'll get back together."

"A psychologist?"

"We take a total synergistic approach. Every part of your body is considered here—mental and physical."

"What about the TV interview?"

"That's not till Thursday. We'll talk about it beforehand."

"Good. I told Paul he could come then; I just couldn't stop him from being here for the taping. He's very protective. You know how he is. And it's good that he comes. I feel better about it, less nervous."

"Well, I have to lay down the law on this one," I said, wagging my finger and assuming a stern expression. "Just don't let him give Stanley any off-camera directions."

Jasmine giggled and patted the rubber penguin on its head. "I don't think there will be a problem. Stanley is always in charge."

"Jordan Myles, I haven't seen *you* here for a while!" It was Virginia Jennings, who spearheaded our fund-raising efforts. Ginny worked closely with Bill, on events and in soliciting donations. She also made sure that we donated

money for good causes, like children's charities. Ginny
had soft brown hair that she usually wore in a long ponytail and a deep tan that no sunscreen could suppress. She
had had a major career in academic fund-raising but she
also had an intense interest in outdoor sports, particularly
orienteering. Ginny was the type of athlete who could
find her way home in a forest without a compass, survive
on berries in the wilderness for weeks, or cross the ocean
single-handedly in a sailboat. Her opponent was always
the elements. She now had her own business with an
impressive client roster. For months, I'd been promising
Ginny that we'd go camping, but our schedules never
meshed.

"So what about that camping trip?" she asked, after I'd
introduced her to Jasmine and, of course, Stanley.

I groaned. "I know, I know. I've got to get some time
off. Maybe right after the first of the year."

"I'm thinking, bareboating in the Virgin Islands," she
said. "It's like camping out on the water, and the weather
is right for then."

We shook on it, and she left for her meeting.

"Now that you're out of tennis and don't have to practice, don't you have more time for vacations and things?"
asked Jasmine.

"It should work out that way," I answered. "But in fact
I've managed to fill in about every second on my calendar with work." I thought for a minute. "That's not
good, is it?"

"Anybody in your life at the moment?" she asked.

"One person, in and out—for years." I decided not to
tell her it was Gus. "We go back and forth on things. It's
a pattern. At this point, I'd like to settle down, but then I
think I'm not ready. There's too much I want to do."

Jasmine smiled shyly. "Well, I'm ready. Malik and I are getting serious."

"That's wonderful! You two are an incredible pair."

"He's so gentle, and so exciting at the same time. He loves the same things I do—the outdoors, music, movies, and animals. But there's something I can't put my finger on, something nobody can ever control. Like two people in one. I always thought you couldn't get those two things in the same guy, until I met Malik."

"It *is* rare."

Gus was many things, but exciting wasn't one of them, I thought. He'd never been one to take the big chance, go out on a limb, do the unexpected. He was totally predictable. And maybe that's why our relationship had lasted so long. I'd had enough uncertainty in my life. I wasn't looking for it in love.

"Well, I'm really happy for you."

She suddenly looked worried. "You won't mention this during the interview, will you? I mean, this was off the record, wasn't it?"

"Of course."

She looked relieved. "Malik gets upset when I talk about him. So I'd rather not."

"Fine. Let's talk more about why you're here."

"Well, like I said, originally I wanted to come because I wanted to work on my game as a whole, but what's happened since is I've had a setback. I seem to have developed this wrist problem."

"How'd it happen?"

"It was just after the tournament, only a couple of days. I'd been playing eight hours a day, and at the end of the Saturnia, when I was serving against Seranata, I snapped my wrist and I really felt something give. It ached the rest of the day, and the next time I went out to play I just felt like I had no power, and it's never really come back. We iced it and had it x-rayed, but nothing was broken. I even got an MRI, and my doctor couldn't find anything wrong. But it's still a problem. When I go to whack the ball, I feel a jolt of pain."

"Keep your elbow at your side and turn your wrist so the palm faces up," I said, and she did.

I reached out and gently tried to force her palm up farther, and she winced. I repeated this on the other side, and she did not wince.

"There's definitely some restriction there," I said. "Come over to the medical building after you have your evaluation with Gus, and we'll take a look at it with Max."

Max was actually Maxine Kellerman, an orthopedic surgeon and sports medicine specialist. Although we had five doctors who worked with the clinic, Max specialized in most of the tennis-related injuries and conditions. Jasmine would also have a complete general physical workup as part of her stay, but before I put her on the tennis court and risked aggravating any conditions she might have, I wanted to check the severity of the wrist problem.

Max had been working with the tennis circuit for at least twenty years and knew everybody in the game. She had run a sports medicine clinic in the Carolinas for years and every year generously volunteered two weeks of her time to work at the Family Circle Magazine Cup in Hilton Head. As soon as she finished examining Jasmine, she called me in. "We took our own X rays just to confirm, and I reread her MRI. Nothing showed up in the way of a visible tear. It's a sprain or a slight displacement," she said. "The TFCC."

Jasmine's eyes widened. "What's that?"

"The triangular fibrocartilage complex of the wrist," Max explained. She sat down next to Jasmine and went over the anatomy of the wrist in layman's terms. Max was very small and thin, with delicate hands that seemed to sketch pictures in the air when she gestured. "This can be caused by putting too much strain on the wrist when receiving the ball or in the serve."

Jasmine nodded grimly. "I don't have to stop playing, do I? I have a six-figure exhibition match coming up."

"If you weren't a professional, or if the sprain were a little worse than it is, I'd say to stop and give it a total rest. That's always best, of course. However, you can practice with a volar splint on the wrist. Our first treatment goal is to relieve the pain. Second, get the motion back. Third, get back strength. I'd also like to try a little phonophoresis, which is a steroid cream that penetrates deep to the tendons and ligaments with the aid of ultrasound. I'll put you on an anti-inflammatory and arnica. We can also try icing it down, followed by a strengthening program at night."

"Sure, let's try it," Jasmine agreed.

"It should gradually improve, and you can return to match play in a couple of weeks," said Max. "But overall, I'd say your muscles are imbalanced in your upper extremity. You may need to alter your conditioning program."

"But I play tennis eight hours a day already," Jasmine protested. "I work out all day long."

"That is probably exactly the problem," I explained. "Every muscle in your body has two types of fibers.

There are power fibers and endurance fibers. Aerobic activities like running and tennis work the endurance fibers, but the power fibers only respond to resistance. You need to get on a strength program. So you'll be doing less tennis and more other stuff." I thought back to the Saturnia and Jasmine's match with Seranata. Although Jas had showed great talent, Seranata had been able to wear her down. It was a case of a young woman who'd gotten where she was on pure talent but then ran into problems in an overuse situation due to a lack of strength. "You need to strive for muscle balance," I said, as Jasmine listened intently. "What you don't want is to have one muscle group stronger than the others—that leaves you predisposed to injury, such as what happened to your wrist."

Jasmine looked skeptical, so I continued.

"Studies have shown that if you have, for instance, strong internal rotators of the shoulder and weak external rotators, you can get tendinitis. And the same thing can happen if the dominant hand and arm is markedly stronger than the other. But don't worry," I reassured her. "Once your pain is relieved, we'll work out a conditioning routine that focuses on the upper extremities. Maybe you'll work one day on the upper body and one day on the lower body. You'll want to use weight training to strengthen your wrist, elbow, and shoulder."

"But I can still practice?"

"With the splint. We'll take care of that."

"Okay," she said gamely. "I'll see you on the practice courts, later today."

"It's a deal."

*　　*　　*

"So when's the unveiling?" I said to Gus as we finished our grilled salads at the Ivy. We had driven to LA in record time and arrived on Robertson at the perfect time to sit on the terrace, eating from the oversize pink-and-green china, watching agents, writers, producers, and stars pull up for the valet parking in front and sashay through to their tables. It was quintessential Hollywood.

"My partners are going to do a professional presentation," Gus said. "My part is the development end."

"What, exactly, are you developing? The mystery is making me crazy."

"Well, I'll tell you. It's an endurance package—a total sports system that involves a drink, a power bar, and a vitamin supplement."

"Gus! That sounds wonderful. What a terrific idea." Gus always had brilliant ideas, but they were usually more academic in nature, and this was the first one I knew of that took a form other than a book.

"I'm in partnership with a firm called BioTech. They're very big in this category. Most of their products are natural herbals, more hard core to the health-conscious market. They've done a lot of work in translating ancient tribal remedies into modern formats. You'd be surprised how effective some of this stuff is, in medical terms. Anyhow, they position the product and package, but so far they've really been dealing with niche markets, specialty markets. My system will be their first attempt at a more commercial venture. I've been working on the formulas with their chemists for almost a year."

"A year? And you never told me?"

"Well, you were wrapped up in your own world, Jordan. And I didn't want to tell you until I was sure it was working out myself. Now, where is that waiter? The BioTech people are expecting us at two."

BioTech occupied an entire large black glass building on Wilshire Boulevard, not far from the Ivy. "Of course, the lab's not here," Gus said, as we stepped into the elevator and he pushed the button for the penthouse. A few seconds later, the elevator doors opened onto a luxurious wood-paneled lobby with a travertine marble floor dotted with tasteful antique kilim rugs.

"Hello, Dr. Laidlaw." The receptionist smiled.

"Karen, nice to see you." Gus nodded. "How's your sister?" Obviously, he was a fairly regular visitor.

"She's better, thanks. Trent is expecting you. I'll buzz him."

Gus turned to me. "Trent is president of the company. Actually, he owns a lot of companies. It's a family business. Used to be strictly medical in his father's day— that's why these offices sort of resemble a doctor's office—but Trent and his team are taking a more contemporary mass-market approach. That's why they asked me to work with them on this product."

A massive carved door swung open and a young man in a white lab coat walked out. "Gus! Great to see you! And you must be Jordan Myles. Trent Byers." He shook my hand enthusiastically. It was hard to believe that a person who looked about twenty-two years old headed up this giant company.

Trent led us back through a long hallway lined with offices, most of which looked out over the Hollywood Hills. "I've seen your show, Jordan, and I want you to know I'm a real fan of yours. So is my wife. She thinks you're the greatest thing on TV. You really know how to reach women viewers. That's one reason why we're very interested in your feedback today. The women's market is important to us." He swung a door open, and we walked into a large, state-of-the-art, windowless conference room. The walls were lined with huge color blowups of charts and products. Around a massive oval conference table were five people, whom Trent introduced. Everyone seemed to be a vice president of something or other. There was someone named Joe, vice president of marketing, another one for public relations, another for engineering, somebody else for what they called "R and D."

"Research and development," Gus explained. "The BioTech lab does the actual product formulations, working to my specs."

"And you must know Artie Lutz," Trent said, as we reached a small, dark man with massive hands.

Artie Lutz. Seranata Aziz's trainer. "Artie," I said. "How goes it?" I wondered what role Artie played here.

He leaned in and kissed my cheek. "We can talk later," he said. "Catch up, you know."

Gus and I joined the group at the table, and Trent stood at the front of the room. "It's wonderful to see everybody together," he said. "This has been a real team effort. I must say, Gus, that at first we at BioTech had only a small idea of the potential of this product. But now I see it can play a very very significant role in the sports marketplace. Which is why the company has invested so heavily in its development. Joe will explain where we are at as of now."

Joe stood up and pointed to a time line. "We are now in the process of final adjustments to the product before we submit it to the FDA. Some of our focus group testing has suggested that we expand our line of flavors—"

"Excuse me, Joe," Trent interrupted. "Could you back up and explain the basic premise of our product to Jordan?"

"Happily." Joe nodded. "What Dr. Laidlaw has developed, what we plan to merchandise and market, is a product called Duration. But Duration is more than a product. It is a unique total system for increasing athletic endurance. Gus has completed performance reviews of twelve sports to analyze their nutritional and supplemental requirements. Gus is truly the biomechanist of the future, and Duration is the system of the future. Our package includes a sports drink, a vitamin, and a power bar. There will also be an explanatory videotape, Gus will be writing a book called *Go the Duration*, and we will produce thirty-minute infomercials in a talk-show format with guest sports celebrities who have used the system and can recommend it. This will be an important element of our marketing plan."

Trent handed me a glass of orange-colored liquid. "Try the drink," he said.

I sipped it. It tasted pretty good. "Not bad," I said. "Very nice flavor, in fact."

Gus nodded. "I've found a way to make it taste more like real fruit juice."

"Consumers loved that aspect," Joe added. "That's why we want to expand on the flavors, Dr. Laidlaw. We're thinking strawberry, kiwi, lemongrass . . . go more gourmet, so to speak, than the traditional sports drink— which will, by the way, help justify our premium price point."

"How soon can we do those kinds of flavors, Gus?" asked Trent.

"I'll start right away, working with R and D," he said, taking notes on an index card.

"We're working on the packaging, but the design group came up with some sample designs for the logo." He pointed out the boards along the wall. "This one's too hospital." He threw one board onto the floor. "This one's striking, but too cola-esque. We're a serious product, with a purpose. It's wrong for us." That board joined the discard pile. "We like this one. It has a sense of purity to it. Like a bottled water, but with clinical imagery plus subliminal taste imagery."

Everyone at the table nodded. "If we add more flavors, maybe you'd want to boost the specific taste component on the label. Maybe show real fruit," Gus said.

"Brilliant," said Trent. "I totally agree. Joe, get the designers on it. And now, Jordan, we'd like you to see what we call our sizzle film. It's just a short piece the ad agency worked up to help explain the concept to people involved at the preliminary stages." He cued a videotape.

After a fast-paced montage not unlike a music video, Gus appeared on the screen, with a super at the bottom that gave his name and his position as founding partner of the Desert Springs Sports Science Clinic. He spoke briefly about the product and what it could do in helping athletes develop greater endurance when they needed that extra strength to push them over the top.

Then the tape cut to Artie Lutz and some footage of him working with Seranata. His super identified him as a "trainer of world-class athletes." He enthusiastically endorsed the product. A voice-over explained how the Duration system worked. Then there was another quick montage, and the tape ended.

"Obviously, this is a work in progress," said Trent. "But it sets the top-tier professional tone we're after."

"What do you think, Jordan?" asked Gus.

"I'm totally impressed," I said. "It looks like you're going to have a real winner. This must be very exciting for all of you."

"In a few weeks we'll have our package designs," said Trent. "Then you'll get a real sense of how it will look on the shelves." The meeting adjourned, and as Trent cornered Gus for a private discussion, I found myself talking to Artie.

"So now you're into marketing, Artie," I said.

He gave a lighthearted shrug. "Aren't we all. Well, it's something new for me. Speaking of getting into new things, I hear your show is doing great."

"So far, so good." I touched his arm. "How's your friend doing, the one who lost the little girl? I think of what happened all the time. I felt so badly for her—and for you too."

"I don't see much of her anymore," he said sadly. "She took it real hard, and so did I. I think Celine was the glue that kept us together. She went everywhere with us. I haven't ever had any kids, so she was like my own. Me, Mr. Independent, at my age—well, there I was taking Cellie to the park, to the toy store, teaching her tennis, the whole bit. And loving it." He had to stop, to regain his composure. "I was heartbroken, Jordan, and that's a fact. But Anna, her mother—well, she kind of went off. She's under a doctor's care, you know. Half the time she's raving. She thinks Celine was murdered as part of a conspiracy."

I looked at him sympathetically.

"Of course, she's irrational; who would conspire against

a kid? She's suing Madison Square Garden for millions of dollars for not providing proper security."

"She thinks the Garden was part of a conspiracy?"

"Like I said, Anna's not rational. I tried to talk to her, everybody has. . . . She'd like to think Martians were responsible. Anybody, at least so there's a reason. But I understand. It's hard for me to be rational too." His eyes filled with tears. "Poor little kid. What a bad break to be born with a bum heart." He rubbed his forehead distractedly.

I squeezed Artie's hand. "Hang in there, buddy," I whispered. "And if there's anything I can do to help, please let me know."

He nodded bleakly. I stood staring after him as he wandered out of the room.

Gus's hand gripped my elbow, steering me firmly toward Trent.

"It's such a thrill to meet you," the head of BioTech enthused. "I used to watch you on the circuit. You were a great player."

"And now she's a great physiotherapist," Gus noted. "There aren't many players who've done so well with their lives after tennis."

Trent put his arm around my shoulder, a gesture I despise from strangers. "You know, Jordan, with your background and your show, you'd be a terrific addition to our team."

"It's a very interesting product—"

"Interesting is not the word," Trent interrupted. "It's a breakthrough."

"Well, as a novice in your field, I can only see that you've clearly done a quality job, and Gus would do nothing less, but to be honest, products just aren't my thing. *People* are. I don't know anything about products and marketing."

"Ah, you said the magic word, didn't she, Gus?" said Trent. "People. That's what the Duration system is all about. Enhancing people's capabilities, expanding their limits, pushing the envelope. Yes, we're on the same wavelength."

"We *are*?" I had no idea what he was talking about.

"We are. And the fact that you communicate with millions of people, particularly women, would allow you to bring our message to them very effectively, don't you think?"

"I'm flattered to hear you say so, but I'm over-committed right now. The show, the Springs—there's a lot on my plate."

Trent patted my back. "Well, think about it, Jordan. We're still in development; there's plenty of time. But you'd be a tremendous asset. We'll be sure to keep you in the loop."

I shrugged off his arm and stepped back. "I appreciate your confidence, Trent."

Everybody shook hands, and the meeting was over.

On the drive back to Palm Springs, Gus was quiet until we got to the expressway, playing one CD after another to mask the fact that he wasn't talking.

"So what did you think of Trent?" Gus asked finally.

"Well, I suppose he's a good businessman, but personally I found him a bit touchy-feely."

"He likes to reach out. I'd already told him so much about you, he probably felt he knew you. But underneath it all he's a good guy. Very committed. You can't imagine the amount of time and money BioTech has put into this project. I could never have done it on my own, and all the major companies in the business turned me down. Trent has vision, I'll say that for him. He has vision, and he's not scared to take a risk."

"Now I see what your secret project has been," I said. "It looks great. Really great. It's a wonderful concept."

"You really think so?" Gus said. "Then why don't you want to get involved?"

"It's just not my thing, Gus. And I really have no time to learn a new business."

"You don't have to learn the business, Jordan," Gus said, speaking slowly, his tone implying he was lecturing someone with a learning impairment. "But Trent thinks you'd be very effective as a spokesperson, to do an infomercial for the women's market and use the product on your show. That's all."

"That's *all*? You spring this on me now?"

"Well, it wasn't the original plan, but there have been developments. Artie was supposed to be our main promoter within the sports community. You saw Artie. He's a mess. I feel for the guy, but he's not very effective. How can he represent a product like this, something BioTech has put so much money behind? They are very risk-averse regarding their investments. Trent wanted to fire him, say he couldn't fulfill the contract, but I said no, let's just add another spokesperson. It's not like we hadn't planned to do it from the beginning of our strategic discussions. The issue just came up a bit more quickly." Gus gestured nonchalantly. "I thought—forgive me if I presumed—I thought you'd be happy to step in. I thought you'd be thrilled to be involved in something so cutting edge in the bioengineering field. It would mean a lot of money to you. And ultimately to everybody involved."

"Well, I can't do it, not right now, so you'd better not

offer me up on toast to Trent." I decided to soften it a bit. "Maybe later, okay? We'll see."

Actually, hawking a product in any way was the last thing I wanted to do. As I saw it, my impartiality and distance from the marketing swirl was one of the things that made me effective. And though I'm sure the fee involved would have been tempting, I didn't need the money; *Woman/Sport* was a franchise with its own potential, and I wanted to concentrate my efforts there and on the Springs. Gus should be the first person to understand that, I thought, considering how he had verbally slapped my hand last weekend. And while a case could be made that there was a link between the Duration system and Gus's work with athletes at the Springs, I didn't see myself as part of the chain. I had learned years ago, however, that arguing with Gus was futile. A former champion student debater, he could always win any argument. I reached over and turned up the volume of the CD, drowning out the possibility for rebuttals, but I had a feeling this discussion was far from over.

THREE

I had too much going on to be distracted for long. Gus and I spent the night apart, ostensibly so both of us could catch up on paperwork, and first thing Wednesday morning I had to meet Harrison Barber and the crew from my *Woman/Sport* show to go over pre-production details for our taping the following afternoon. After that, it was straight to the therapy room to work with Jasmine, and then we went to the practice courts.

"I saw Artie Lutz yesterday," I said, as we walked along the manicured gravel path past the nutrition center and the running track. The sun was high and it was hot. A.M. trotted at my ankles, panting. "He's in bad shape."

"I heard he and his girlfriend broke up after her daughter died at the Garden," said Jasmine.

She pushed her long braid up under her baseball cap, and I could see a small tattoo of a bat on her upper arm— no doubt for Malik, who was called "the Bat."

"It was just too much pressure, I guess. I can understand it, though. The tragedy made her insane. She wrote me, you know."

"She did? Why?"

"Because I was on court playing when her daughter

got sick and passed out. She wanted to know if I had seen anything. You know, from my vantage point."

"What was there to see?" I asked.

Jasmine twirled her racket. "The poor woman. She thinks it was a plot, or at least that's what she said in the letter."

"Did she say what kind of plot?"

"No. She just said someone would pay for implicating her innocent daughter in this evil plot, that her daughter's death would be avenged. I was very upset. I couldn't even answer her."

"Did you keep the letter?"

Jasmine shook her head. "No, it was so disturbing, I immediately sent it on to Paul." She sighed. "I suppose I should have kept it, but I get all kinds of crazy mail. My policy is to pass everything on to Paul. I let him deal with it."

"And how did he deal with this letter?"

"He just said he'd take care of it. That was all I heard." She tossed a ball ahead, and A.M. raced after it. "But you can ask him. Like I said, he'll be coming by tomorrow for the show taping."

We had reached the practice courts. Jasmine set her gym bag onto a bench, and A.M. dropped the drool-covered ball at her feet.

I had just sat down to watch Jasmine hit with Tanner Axel when my beeper went off. I checked its brief message. Illuminated on the face were the words COME TO OFFICE. Winnifred, my secretary, was under strict orders not to call me when I was with a client unless it was an emergency. I gathered up A.M. and headed back to the main building, wondering what kind of emergency this could be. Of course, with Winnifred, the term "emergency" had a lot of flex to it.

Since my former assistant and friend, Tony, was killed in an explosion in the driveway right outside the Springs offices two years ago, it had been impossible for me to replace him. Tony was not in any way replaceable, in fact, and I couldn't imagine anybody else sitting at his desk outside my office. Bill had tactfully submitted résumés to me, but I had shied away from hiring anyone. Still, business needed to be conducted and I did require some support, so I had been filling in with a series of temps. The latest of these was Mrs. Winnifred Millstone. Winnifred was not an obvious choice, at least at first glance. She was eighty-two years old, a former executive secretary for the CEO of the Pilster Company, who'd been pensioned out. Her stamina, however, often seemed to exceed mine, and in the two months she'd been working for me, she'd taken over my office with a vengeance. The files had never been neater or the drawers cleaner. She typed like a pink-haired devil on speed. Hot tea, complete with silver strainers, was always available. Although she preferred a manual typewriter and rotary phone, she'd taken computer courses to remain current, and she was quite competent, as long as the computer monitor magnified the words to about one inch high. Winnifred had taken me under her wing from her first day on the job—a habit she claimed I should not take personally; it was simply ingrained from her twenty years as secretary to Mr. Pilster, a newspaper magnate. When I insisted she not baby me, she answered, "You're quite right, dear. Here's your tea and honey." Eventually, I gave up.

Winnifred was the kind of woman to whom an emergency might constitute, say, an impending nuclear attack; then again, it might be a call from the vet regarding making an appointment to have A.M.'s teeth cleaned. She was waiting at her desk, her pinky-apricot hair lacquered perfectly into place, her neckline draped in scarves, waving a page of paper in her hand. Winnifred was very fussy about her appearance. Her philosophy was basic: Dress in polka dots and wear a million scarves. Scarves in various shades complementing her spotted outfit of the day always were draped around her neck, tied onto the handle of her purse, and knotted around her shoulders. If the U.S. Signal Corps ever ran out of silk for flags, all they needed to do was call Winnifred.

"Do you know an Anna Martinez?" She squinted up at me from behind rhinestone-studded bifocals that were so thick they magnified her eyes into watery blue puddles.

"Anna Martinez?" The name didn't sound immediately familiar. The letter read:

Dear Jordan Myles:

I am writing you as well as anyone who might have any further information about the death of my daughter, Celine York. It has come to my attention that you were a network commentator during the tennis match at Madison Square Garden when Celine was taken ill and subsequently died. You may not realize that her death was the direct or indirect result of an evil conspiracy involving drugs. I am hoping that perhaps you noticed some details, personages, or incidents that might lead to the capture and conviction of the conspirators. Any information that leads to such conviction will result in a $10,000 reward, paid personally by myself.

Please contact me at the address on this letter at any time. Feel free to call collect. God thanks you for helping the soul of my Celine.

Sincerely,
Anna Martinez

I stared at the letter. In her grief, the poor mother was obviously contacting as many people as possible, desperately trying to make sense of the tragedy. "Is this what the emergency was?" I asked.

"That, and she's called here five times today, poor thing. She says she wants you to do an on-air piece about the conspiracy to kill her daughter. She claims she's also been in touch with the network and the press."

"The police?"

"She didn't mention them, but I'm sure they were on her list." Winnifred lifted a penciled eyebrow. "Everybody else was." She handed me the second page of the fax, which was a handwritten list of about twenty or thirty names, including tournament sponsors, players—including Jasmine and Seranata—umpires, Garden officials, the medical team, Garden concessionaries, the WTF, and the DEA. A very comprehensive listing of names indeed.

"Well, I'm just one name out of thirty or so. I think Jasmine got a letter like this too, which she passed on to her agent. I'll have to ask him more when he comes tomorrow for the taping. It's really not an emergency." I folded the fax and tucked it into the gym bag that I used as a briefcase.

"Well, dear, I didn't want to beep you off the court." I

hate being called dear and have tried to correct Winnifred. Unsuccessfully. "But this woman sounded real coco-loco, if you know what I mean."

"Her former boyfriend says she's really been knocked flat by her daughter's death. I'm sorry for her. I know how I still feel about Tony. It must be terrible. But there's really nothing I can do for her, Winnifred."

"So we don't want to call her or take her calls?"

"I'm not anxious to get involved. I think I'll show the letter to Gus and find out what he thinks the best way to handle something like this is. It's more in his arena." I grabbed a handful of granola—homemade, of course— from the bowl Winnifred kept on her desk and checked my watch. I still had plenty of time to get over to the practice courts and watch Jasmine in action.

"Be sure to eat lunch, dear," Winnifred called after me. "After breakfast, it's the most important meal of the day."

On the court, even with her wrist splinted, Jasmine was no less than thrilling to watch. Her grace and beauty were balletic in a way that hadn't surfaced in women's tennis since the legendary Suzanne Lenglen, who had mesmerized fans and transformed the game with her dancerlike play more than half a century ago. But it was Jasmine's intuitive take on the game that made her really unique. Chris had it, Tracy had it, Monica had it—the uncanny way of being exactly where a shot was hit. I'd had the challenge of facing this kind of talent myself when I played these women, and I could attest that it was an unnerving experience. This ability to hit shots at the right time and be in the right spot to return invariably causes the opponent to try to outguess such players, attempt to play above their level, and, ultimately, make errors.

If Jasmine was willing to work on her strength, her speed, and her game, she could progress not sporadically, as she had so far, but evenly upward into the top five. The potential was definitely there, and the star quality glittered. Those who had sniped that Jasmine had gotten ahead on her beauty were not, in my opinion, correct. She was, of course, very attractive. But she was not the first or the last female tennis player to be blessed with good looks. Jasmine Li had something more.

During a break, I asked Tanner what he thought. "She's everywhere, that's for sure," he said. "She's not that fast, but she makes up for it with her incredible sense of anticipation." He wiped his brow. Jasmine was keeping him running. "Charlie," he called to his assistant, who was watching from the sidelines, "can you take over?"

Charlie stepped forward, and he and Jasmine went back on the court.

It seemed to me that without having studied the game, Jasmine nonetheless managed to be a student of it. What was it, I wondered, that gave her that so-called sense of ESP? I had scrutinized dozens of tapes of her past matches, and what I was seeing on court reinforced what I had seen on the tapes. While most players manage to guess where the ball will be on a 50–50 success level, Jasmine's ratio was more like 90–10. Even when she seemed to be out of position, more often than not she found herself in the right place for the ball. Her speed needed work, though, as Tanner had pointed out. Her body was definitely out of balance.

"I think I'll suggest she get involved in different sports to force her body to work different ways—yoga, volleyball, kayaking, track. What do you think, Tanner?" I asked.

Tanner sat slumped beside me on the bench. His eyes were closed.

"Tanner?"

One of the top training pros in the business, Tanner Axel played all-out even in his practice matches. With his red hair and trademark red bandanna, he'd been a Davis Cup player who made it to the bottom of the top ten and then retired to coach others. Everyone on the tour loved him, because he had a terrific sense of humor and a subtle but strong way of working with his players. But today, Tanner seemed to be out of it.

"Tanner, are you all right?"

He opened his eyes a slit. "Of course I am. It seems to me *you're* the one who's never around here. I'm out here sweating my butt off every single day. It's no wonder I feel a little off sometimes."

I was stunned. Tanner was usually the sweetest of men. I'd never heard him talk like this.

He waved his hand disgustedly. "Forget it." He threw down his racket and walked off the court, glowering and rubbing his forehead.

Jasmine came over, concerned. "Maybe I pushed him too hard," she said jokingly.

"I think it was last night's tacos," Charlie confided.

I had to laugh. Tanner was usually as unstoppable as they come. Jasmine's game was something he could address in his sleep under normal circumstances. It would have taken some pretty raunchy guacamole to stop that man in his tracks. "He'll bounce back, don't worry," I said. "Okay, you finish up with Charlie. I'll see you after your nutrition workup."

She nodded and trotted back onto the court.

I had phone calls to catch up with, but on my way back

to the office I swung past the sports nutrition department. Sally Stone, our nutritionist, was meticulous about her work, and I knew she'd do a thorough job. Sally had been an exercise therapist with the women's tour, which is where I'd met her. After my accident, when I'd left the tour and gone to school, she'd coincidentally gone back to school also and gotten an advanced degree in sports nutrition. She reported directly to Gus, and together they made a formidable team. Any athlete who came through our doors found himself or herself virtually dissected atom by atom, until their physiological makeup was mapped and charted. The Springs philosophy is that in a world where athletes must perform on demand, mind and body must work in perfect synchronization. Improving human performance involves an interdisciplinary approach, and we deal with the human being as a whole. As a result, every mouthful of food, every sip of drink, every thought and every movement is broken down and analyzed and then adjusted, where necessary, to help the athlete reach peak performance. Jasmine would be extensively interviewed on her eating habits, and she would be given a special food diary in which she was expected to log every mouthful for the next three to seven days, at Sally's discretion. Only after that would an initial evaluation be made, which included menu planning for every situation. The follow-up program then traveled with the athlete, who was expected to fax pages of the food diary from all over the world.

As I entered Sally's office, I was amazed to find a large walruslike man with thinning hair and a white terry-cloth robe sitting across the desk from her.

"Hi, Jordan," said a familiar voice. "Surprise."

It was the last person on earth I ever expected to find

sitting in a nutritionist's office: Noel Fisher, a man who defies description. A specialist in pinpointing obscure information and/or individuals, he had worked for everybody from the FBI to the CIA and now had his own private security firm on the East Coast. A lumbering ox of a man, the Fish, as I like to call him, is professionally the best-connected human being I have ever encountered. There doesn't seem to be anyone he doesn't know, or at least can't get to. Personally, he's a total loner, his only close relationship being with his mother. The Fish is a slob, an enigma, a junk-food addict, and a male chauvinist, and although I couldn't imagine what he was doing here swathed in a terry-cloth robe, I was thrilled to see him. How else would you feel about somebody who has saved your life? It could be argued, as Gus has done, that the Fish was simply in the right place at the right time—theoretically bumbling onto me in a state of mortal peril—specifically, just as a lead pipe was about to connect with my head. But the Fish has more than a knack for showing up. He just doesn't discuss it. And as I recalled, he had never visited the Springs before.

I couldn't help but grin, then laugh hysterically, when I saw what the Fish held in his hands as I leaned over to kiss him on the cheek. It was a calorie chart. The Fish believes that people who count calories are in a class with those who think the earth is flat. "What in the world are you doing here?" I hiccuped, as soon as I could control myself. Sally just stared. She didn't get it.

The Fish slumped in his seat. The robe, combined with his droopy mustache, made him look like a fuzzy albino walrus. "Jordan, Jordan, I got troubles."

Quickly, I sat down. "What? Tell me."

"My cholesterol count." He looked at me mournfully. "It's closing in on four hundred."

"Good God!"

Sally grimaced.

"The docs at home, they said I had to do something right away. I was in the middle of an important case, I was about to expose this guy who was scamming insurance companies, but I had to drop out. It killed me, but they say this cholesterol thing could get me first." He sighed. "They wanted to send me to the Mayo Clinic for a complete rundown. A hospital! Medical jail! An active guy like me—I'd go nuts." The Fish threw his spongy hands into the air.

"Sure you would." I knew for a fact that the Fish moved only when necessary. His idea of brisk exercise was a repetitive activity involving moving french fries from hand to mouth.

"Well, I figured I'd better come here. You know my philosophy. Only deal when you know the people at the top. I thought, Who do I know at the top of a top medical facility? Ergo, here I am."

"Fish, I have to tell you. This isn't that kind of medical facility. It's not the Mayo Clinic. You sound like you need serious treatment. I'm really happy to see you, but maybe you should rethink this."

He lifted his chin. "I *have* thought about it. I'm here. I'm a paying customer."

Sally looked up helplessly from her desk. "He told admissions he was a close friend of yours. I was actually waiting for Jasmine, and he just sort of showed up."

"True, true, but I'd really rather have him get the right kind of care. The Springs is a sports facility."

The Fish threw open his arms. "Am I not a sport?

Besides, I've looked around this place. You guys are serious. This is no day at the spa."

"Just one minute." I motioned Sally out into the hall. "Sally, what's your opinion?" I asked.

"Frankly? With that cholesterol count, he should be dead."

"Can we help him?"

"Only as an interim step. I think he's in denial. He does need something more heavy-duty than we're able to offer, a serious health intervention. But maybe we can at least convince him to get that kind of help, to accept the situation. Acceptance of the facts—that should be our goal right now. We can't really solve the problem. He has to start doing that for himself."

"In that way, he's no different from our athletes, I suppose. If we do that much, it's a lot, considering who we're dealing with."

Sally frowned, unconvinced. "Well, he's your friend."

The Fish appeared in the doorway. "What's this whispering? I don't like conversations I can't hear."

With a little advance notice, he would have bugged the room. "The conversation is over," I announced. "We'll work with you. And when we've gone as far as we can, we'll refer you to the right people and still keep an eye on your case. How's that sound? I'd never refuse you, you know that."

He gave me a sly grin. "Well, dropping your name did help me get a very nice little villa. I'm the closest in. I don't have to walk very far."

I put my arm around him. "Maybe we can have dinner tonight. I'm really glad to see you."

He looked chagrined. "I don't think I'm allowed to eat anything ever again. Especially dinner."

"Well, we'll eat low fat."

"That's not eating. That's like eating corrugated cardboard. Can't we order in pizza? We can make it single cheese, not double like I usually have. Thin crust. It's even vegetarian."

"I'm afraid it's like this: If you're on the program here, you're on the program. No exceptions, even for good friends. Especially for good friends. Sally's going to give you a plan, and you'll start keeping a food journal and writing down every mouthful, and later you'll review it with her."

"Sounds like kindergarten," the Fish muttered.

"Our athletes do the exact same thing. And no cheating or leaving things off—you only cheat yourself. I'll have the kitchen prepare something that Sally says is on your diet plan and deliver it to my house tonight. I'll have my secretary leave directions to my house with the receptionist, and you can pick them up on your way out. I have a pre-production meeting at six, so—seven o'clock, okay?"

"Is there a KFC on the way? Get your secretary to mark it on her map."

"Stop it. I'll see you later. Don't disappear on me like you did in Paris."

I checked my watch. Jasmine would be showing up at Sally's office within a half hour. The cable crew was due to arrive early today, a day before we would actually tape the show, so they could scout the grounds for the best locations to shoot the interview with Jasmine and get set up. Tonight was a run-through of the show, including a review of the questions the writers had prepared for me to ask. We had not showed Jasmine the questions in advance because it was better if her answers were fresh and spontaneous.

Gus intercepted me as I left the nutrition center. "Your video crew is here. They're already disrupting everything, barging around, acting like they own the place, asking for this and that, taking up the staff's time—just like I said they would. I told them if they scratched the paint or wrecked the carpet laying down cable or moving heavy equipment through the premises, they'd be held accountable. And they'd better watch it; people don't expect to find that kind of stuff around here. Somebody could even trip and fall."

"Is that what you came to tell me?"

"No. I know you don't control that. I wanted to give you my Duration mock-up package. It's one-of-a-kind, and I wouldn't want anybody but you handling it. It's too valuable."

"I don't understand, Gus. What would I do with a package mock-up? I can look at it and give you my opinion, but I'm not very artistic."

"I thought you might have thought it over and decided to use it on your show."

"Gus, this is ridiculous. Duration isn't even on the market yet. And I told you I don't pitch products on the show."

"I know that. I don't want you to pitch it. I thought you could just have it sitting there, or incorporate it into Jasmine's regimen—you know, products that aren't available to the general public yet but which players can access. It would start to build familiarity."

I was not in the mood to argue with Gus. "Okay, I'll look at the packaging. Maybe I'll bring it up at our pre-pro meeting tonight. But if it doesn't work with the show format, I'm not going to push it."

He nodded and handed me a plastic bag. "Fair enough."

I looked down at the bag in my hand. Well, I'd keep my word. If there was a place for it in the segment, fine. If not, I wasn't going to force it. I hate those shows where so-called professionals in a field get on and pitch products at you. To me, they just seem like one long infomercial. That wasn't what I wanted my show to be. Gus had been spending too much time with his new buddy Trent. He was starting to think like a promoter. I stuffed the plastic bag into my gym bag. My fingers touched the fax from Anna Martinez. "You know, Gus, I have something to ask you. A professional question."

"About a client?"

"No. In fact, I don't even know this person." I handed him the fax. "It was sent by the mother of the little girl who died in the stands at the Saturnia. I understand she's contacting everybody who had anything to do with the tournament or the media coverage because she's convinced about the conspiracy thing. I wondered what you thought about this from a psychological point of view. After all, depression is one of your specialties." In fact, it had been Gus's handling of my own depression after my accident that gave me the motivation to continue with my life.

Gus nodded slowly as he read the fax. "This is very sad. Yes. The woman is delusional, no question."

"Should I notify the authorities or anything?"

"No, she's hardly dangerous. In my opinion, she's just looking for an avenue to vent her frustration and anger at not being able to do anything to change what happened, being unable to save her daughter. This is like a cleansing phase. Making these contacts may even help her get through it. The mere fact that there is someone on the other end—you—to send this to makes her feel she is *doing* something, gives her a semblance of control. People often act out like this when an uncontrollable tragedy strikes them. They grasp at straws. May I keep this? I'd like to think about it further."

"Sure. Keep it. Thanks for the POV. See you later."

I stopped back at my office and made a few notes to go over with Jasmine. We would work out a rehab program that would include squeezing a dead ball or Silly Putty and working with a resistance apparatus. I dictated my notes and then packed up for the pre-production meeting.

The production team was gathered at Harrison Barber's hotel suite. He and the crew were staying up the road, in Palm Springs proper, since every room and villa at the Springs was filled with clients. "Actually, we had one villa reserved, but they bumped us at the last minute for some VIP," grumbled Harrison. I cringed silently, knowing the "VIP" was undoubtedly none other than the Fish, who had dropped my name to grease his way into prime accommodations.

While some producers I've worked with have been superficial or even less than knowledgeable, Harrison knew his job inside out, and everybody else's as well, and everyone who worked with him respected him for it. I know I did. He took his job very seriously. As director of production for the East Coast, he liked to handle the details personally rather than delegate them. Last summer, when we were together doing the Wimbledon coverage in England, I cracked a tooth half an hour before I had to be live on the air. Harrison managed to locate a dentist and get him to come to our production complex on the Wimbledon grounds and put in a temporary on the spot. Another time, at the French Open, he found a bomb threat written on a Post-it stuck on the back of his chair. Rather than freak out—or use it for news value—like some people would have done, he quietly notified just one person, the head of security, so there would be no general panic, and the situation was subtly handled. Harrison was very small and emaciated, almost sickly looking, with milky skin that seemed to never have seen the light of day and transparent blond hair so thin you could see through to his scalp. A Southerner, he spoke with the strong accent of his Carolina coast home. His decisiveness and strength of character, however, belied his appearance and social approach. It had been Harrison who had believed in the *Woman/Sport* concept from the beginning, personally shepherding the pilot through the treacherous political waters of the network. There was more than one programming executive who felt that a show built around me, a relative novice, was a suicidal concept, but in the end Harrison's name and reputation were such that his affiliation with the project bestowed instant quality. The fact that he had been willing to take a risk with me had earned him my eternal respect and gratitude.

"You know, Harrison," I said, "this show could put us over the top. I've just spent a few days with Jasmine, and there's a lot more to her than the superficial beauty story. I think the viewers will be fascinated with her. Her romance with Malik is really just the icing on the cake."

"I'm sure you're right." He smiled, his vowels sounding like he had a mouthful of molasses. "I've always thought you had an instinct for this. Watch out, Diane Sawyer."

"Oh, come on. We all know you took a big chance on me. Why'd you do it?"

"Well, Jordan, let's just say you never tried to turn me into a concierge—say, asking me to make restaurant reservations for your distant cousins and whatnot. You'd be amazed what some prima donnas I've worked with seem to think of as my job description. I knew you'd let me do my job and you'd do yours. Which is what's happening, and we're doing great."

The team started assembling in the suite, many of them glassy-eyed from having flown in from the East Coast: Amy, the assistant producer; Carl, the cameraman; Roger, his assistant; Victor, the wardrobe guy; Shauna, who would be my assistant; Ellie, the production assistant; and finally Jeremy, the director, with Ed, the assistant director. We all said our hellos.

"Hail, hail, the gang's all here," said Harrison. "Everybody sit. We've got a lot to cover in one hour."

People scattered across couches, chairs, and the floor.

Amy passed out copies of the production books, which included the show rundown, production staff names and phone numbers, a map of the Springs grounds and buildings, and a list of contact names at the Springs. We went through everything, point by point. Each segment of the show was broken down into its components, including commercial lead-ins and graphics. My script involved the questions I would be asking Jasmine. It was important that I end the section before each commercial with a particularly provocative question so the viewers would want to stay tuned. The issue of location was brought up, and Polaroids of the various choices were discussed.

"Our first choice, the front of the facility, is out," said Harrison.

"Why?" I wondered.

"Dr. Augustus Laidlaw left a voice mail that our vans and equipment would be too disruptive to clinic business. He suggested the practice tennis courts—marked with an X on your maps, everybody."

"Well, we do have fifteen practice courts," I said. "And she is a tennis player, after all."

"Everybody's seen the girl play tennis; the plantings in front are really pretty. I was just hoping for something a little different, that's all," said Harrison. "But onward and upward. Now, Jordan, how are you going to handle the romance angle?"

"I think I'll cover it in the context of two people with similar professional and personal goals, trying to achieve those goals as a team."

"Good. I like that," said Jeremy. "Personal and professional."

We went through the rest of the book and the meeting drew to a close. "One last thing," Harrison said. "I need to ask everyone in this room if they have received any contact or communication from a Ms. Anna Martinez?"

Almost every hand in the room went up. I had planned to bring it up to Harrison after everyone else had left, but it was obviously time to speak up. "I got a fax from her today, Harrison. I asked Dr. Laidlaw, who as you know is a noted clinical psychologist, to take a look at it. In his professional opinion, she's a woman who is clearly crying for help, venting her frustration at being unable to control her daughter's death by taking action in any way she can. He thinks it's harmless, a phase she'll pass through."

"I see," he said. "But as she says in this fax I received, she is also 'following up,' as she calls it, with anyone who has any relationship with you or with the network, in case there is, quote, a 'link,' unquote, in the conspiracy. I've sent a copy of my fax on to network security, and I would ask everyone else who received such a fax to do the same immediately."

The meeting ended on an unsettling note. Anna Martinez seemed to be spreading a very wide net. I suddenly found myself shifting from feeling sympathy for this woman to wondering if she could be trusted to confine her "venting" to paper. What other form might it take?

FOUR

"All due respect to Doc Laidlaw," said the Fish, as he scraped the last remnants of the low-fat sauceless sole dinner that had been prepared for us by the clinic kitchens and brought over to my house by Winnifred, "but I think this Martinez woman is potentially extremely dangerous. I would not write her off as some hysterical grieving mother. She's out for action. She wants somebody to pay. It's a revenge motive. I've seen it dozens of times." He picked the plate up off the table. "I feel like licking this. But there's nothing to lick. I'm still starving. They're going to starve me to death before my cholesterol goes down a quarter of a point." Sadly, he put the plate back down. "You know, that Winnifred, your secretary, is very loyal. She even ran out and bought me some Twinkies."

"Twinkies? You have a death wish? Fish, there's nothing to avenge. The child died of natural causes."

"The mother doesn't care. Her kid is dead. That's her reality. Like I said, somebody's got to pay; that's how she sees it." He craned his neck in the direction of the kitchen. "Got any Häagen-Dazs in that freezer?"

"No, fresh out. But I'm not directly involved, so what

can I do? I'm one of who knows how many people that got a similar fax."

"You're prominent. You're in the media. You've gotta consider that. Most of those other people, they're behind the scenes. What about the two women who played the match on court during the seizure?"

"Jasmine got a letter too. I don't know about Seranata, but I would guess she did. I don't think there's been any coordinating effort to find out who got sent what. Most people just feel sorry for the woman and write it off. The network producer is contacting network security, though."

The Fish snorted. "Gee, network security. What are they? A bunch of guys who arrest you for trying to turn the dial on your TV? Some yo-yos in the lobby who scrutinize your building pass before they let you go to the elevator? Give me a break."

This was one area in which the Fish had a legitimate right to scoff. Although at first glance it was hard to believe, he had actually worked for the CIA and in the Office of Special Investigations at the Pentagon and, in fact, still carried his Pentagon pass and worked on an as-needed basis, as he called it, for the Defense Department. He claimed to have worked on the infamous Black Programs, the highest-security projects, which were so secret even the President sometimes didn't know about them. "Black Programs are programs that don't exist," he had told me. "They take an open mind and a closed mouth." The Fish had both.

"Maybe I better do some checking," he said. "This thing could be nothing, but then again it's better to be on the conservative side when you're dealing with the lunatic fringe. That's my policy. I don't want to see you get sucked into something, you know? You have a predisposition for that sort of thing."

"But Hank was doing the commentary from the floor, not me."

"Hank what's-his-name is just a talking head. You're the marquee name, the former tennis champion. Her kid died at a tennis tournament. There's dots there she could connect."

"Wait a minute here. Are you saying I'm in danger? That any of us are?"

The Fish stretched in his seat. "I'm not saying that. She may never act, and then again she might target you or somebody else. What I'm saying is, I can see more than one scenario here. Dr. Gus reads too many clinical books. This is the real world. People go nuts, they do God knows what. You can't close off any possibilities. Of course, there *is* one thing. She was a mother."

I stared at the Fish. Of course. "They're the worst. Ever hear of the American black bear? Threaten the mother's cubs and she turns you into human cole slaw. Mother elephants will charge if they even catch the scent of danger to their young. My own mother, who is so meek she almost fades into the upholstery, once threw a baby-sitter down a flight of stairs when she found out the woman spanked me. Or so she says. Actually, she probably minimized it."

I don't know why I hadn't thought along these lines before. Mothers who perceive that harm has been done to their children are not going to sit home and do nothing. It's animal nature, human nature, to fight back.

"You got it," said the Fish, blotting his mouth with the napkin. "The problem is, nobody's putting themselves in the shoes of the criminal."

"The woman is not a criminal."

"Okay. Put yourself in the shoes of the whatever. Just do that, then add a few drugs to distort your judgment." He pointed at A.M., who sat hopefully under the table. "Okay, so you're not the maternal type. What if someone kidnapped and tortured your dog?"

"I'd kill them."

"I rest my case."

The next morning, I was forced to put my concerns aside to concentrate on taping my show. Things got off to an early start at 8 A.M., when we all convened at the practice courts. The crew had already been there for an hour and a half, setting up. A large electronics truck and three RVs were pulled up along the access road behind the clay courts, thick cables ran across the ground like giant spaghetti everywhere you looked, and people rushed around carrying equipment and clipboards. A few chairs were set up around the monitor for the director to watch the takes and playbacks, but since shooting had not yet begun, most people were gathered around the food table, which was heaped with doughnuts, fruit, coffee cakes, bagels, cream cheese, yogurt, and jams, and chafing trays of bacon, scrambled eggs, and pancakes. On this shoot, as most others, the food was not health- or diet-oriented. We worked with union crews; their contracts provided for hot meals on location, and most of the camera and sound operators, engineers, and grips ignored the yogurt and loaded up on the doughnuts.

"Can I get you anything, Jordan?" asked Shauna, my assistant.

"Maybe a little fruit, thanks. Where's Jasmine?" I wondered.

"Wardrobe and makeup. You should probably go there now too. I'll bring your fruit."

I crossed the courts and went up the steps to the RV, which was serving as a dressing room. Jasmine was already in the makeup chair, draped in a smock, in front of a large mirror rimmed with theatrical lights. Stanley sat serenely on the counter. I said hi to Jasmine and the freelance makeup artist, who was dabbing powder on her cheeks.

"Jooor-dan! Hello, sweetie!" Katie waved a powder puff at me. She worked on all the major movie and TV sets, and she kept a well-known collection of what she called "celebrity powder puffs." After a makeup session with a star or celebrity, she kept the puff and mounted it in a little Plexiglas frame, with the person's name inked in beneath. The collection made up a fascinating display along an entire wall of her studio in Los Angeles.

"All done," said Katie, whipping off Jasmine's smock with a flourish. "Off to wardrobe."

Jasmine smiled and got up. "This is going to be a lot of fun, Jordan."

Katie motioned toward the back of the van. "Your turn, Jordan."

I put down my gym bag. I was still carrying Gus's prototype for Duration, although I had decided not to use it. I dropped into the chair, and tried to run mentally through my interview while Katie brushed out my hair, threw in a few hot rollers, and tended the eye shadow, lip liner, and mascara. She was dabbing at my lips with a small brush when the van door burst open and Paul Kessler stomped up the steps, followed by a slim, shapely blonde in a skintight thigh-high skirt and low-cut body-hugging tank top, all in matching lime green.

"This is Tiffany," he said.

"Hi." She smiled sweetly.

"Jordan! We have to discuss the questions," he announced. His companion busied herself at the mirror, fluffing her hair.

"Uh-uh," I mumbled. It was hard to talk with a brush on my lips.

"What do you mean, 'Uh-uh'? Is that supposed to mean no?"

"Uh-huh."

"For God's sake, Jordan, I have to see the questions, on behalf of my client. I can't let her get ambushed here."

I motioned Katie back from the makeup chair. "Who do you think is interviewing her, Woodward and Bernstein? She's not going to get ambushed. We've talked, and she feels very good about the way things are going. Why don't you go get a bagel or something?"

"I'm going to watch the monitor, and if I hear one thing I shouldn't, I'm going to yell 'Cut!' "

"So now you're the director? Come on, Paul, relax." I should have told Jasmine he couldn't come. Now, not only was he here but he had Tiffany stapled to his arm. Trouble was inevitable.

After makeup and wardrobe, we blocked out the interview on the set. Jasmine was a natural. She even managed to ignore Paul's wild and extremely distracting hand motions, which included, when she talked about Malik, a wild slashing motion across his throat.

"I really can't allow this," he said. "Malik is my client too, and I'm not sure this is what he would want. Concentrate on Stanley. Everybody loves penguins."

In the middle of this, my pager went off. I grabbed my cell phone. "What is it, Winnifred?"

"A very tall black man is here to see you, dear. He is most definitely not on the calendar. He's on his way out there now. As soon as I said you were taping at the tennis courts, he took off."

I looked up, and there he was: Malik. Six feet six and dressed in black jeans and a black T-shirt.

Before he could get too close, before even Jasmine could see him, Paul immediately raced to his side. I saw them whispering furiously, Malik's huge form bending over Paul like a shade tree. Then, just as quickly, he disappeared and Paul was back on the set, looking like a Cheshire cat.

"What is it?" I whispered to him.

"Malik does things his own way," he said enigmatically. "What can I say?"

"Is he planning on watching the interview?"

"No."

The director called us back for the next shot. I was supposed to ask Jasmine about her future plans.

"Rolling!" yelled the assistant director.

Suddenly Malik appeared behind Jasmine and put his hands over her eyes. His hands were so massive, they covered most of her delicate face.

"Malik!" she squealed, collapsing into laughter. He removed his hands and opened one of them to reveal a glittering diamond ring.

"Jasmine, I am asking you now, in front of all these people as my witnesses, to be my wife. Will you marry me?"

She froze, stunned. Then she seemed to realize the cameras were still rolling and collected herself. "I would be proud to be your wife." She smiled as he slipped the ring on the fourth finger of her left hand.

Jeremy, the director, motioned frantically to the cameraman to zoom in on the ring.

And then they kissed. It was the most perfect ending for any interview, or any moment in life, ever. After about five minutes of this embrace, Jeremy finally ventured, "Well, I guess, cut!"

Everyone laughed, cheered, and applauded. Tiffany jumped up and down, screaming. Then I noticed Gus, standing at the edge of the crowd. He was frowning. I rushed to him. "Isn't this great?" I prodded.

"I think it's the worst. It's begging for publicity, like a dog for a bone. What kind of egomaniac would propose in the middle of an interview? Tell me they weren't using you."

"Gus! Come on!"

"You don't see it, do you? Let's strip away the hearts and flowers here, Jordan. You completely lost control of this situation. You let someone who had nothing to do with the show—your show—take over. And instead of serious interview footage that would show your skills and give you some credibility in sports medicine, look what you've got—*Entertainment Tonight.*"

My cheeks burned. "Is that so bad? This isn't *Face the Nation* we're taping here."

"True, I suppose it depends on who you are." He walked slowly over to Malik and Jasmine, forced a smile, and joined the crowd to congratulate them.

Ginny Jennings, who had also appeared on the scene, along with what seemed like half the staff of the Springs, now that word was spreading, saw me standing there, watching Gus.

"A fight?"

I shook my head and sank onto a folding stool. "I wish

it had been. That I can at least understand. He just doesn't seem to go along with anything I do anymore, Gin." I watched Gus amble across the path to return to his office. "If I do something, I'm wrong. If I don't do something, I'm still wrong. I can't win these days. Do you think it was a mistake to let the show evolve like this?"

"Absolutely not." She squeezed my arm supportively. "This will be wonderful. Don't let him be a downer. He may be a brilliant doctor, but he's still a man who can't take competition."

"Me? Competition?" Gus was world class in his field. The fact that he might regard me in any competitive light seemed impossible. I filed this thought away until I could consider it reasonably. But right now I had a show to finish.

That night, we had a post-production party that turned into an engagement celebration. Winnifred, a true romantic, coordinated the whole thing. She booked a local Mexican restaurant, complete with strolling mariachis, and left messages for everybody who had been involved with the taping to come. She had a balloon company deliver dozens of white helium balloons, and she hung corny white-paper wedding bells from the ceiling. A slightly lopsided carrot cake, decorated with cactus flowers, had been homemade and brought in by Winnifred as her personal engagement gift.

Across the room, I noticed the Fish talking conspiratorially with Winnifred, and a Tupperware changed hands between them. I waved in their direction and crossed over to them.

"What's going on?" I asked.

"Fred here is a jewel of a girl," the Fish said enthusiastically.

"And what did she give you?" The package was suspiciously aromatic.

The Fish looked sheepish. "A Philly cheese steak. I was homesick."

"But you're not from Philly."

"My stomach is, periodically."

"Who told Winnifred she could butt in? You're on a strict diet—monitored intake, for God's sake! Didn't she know that?"

"Don't blame Fred. I told her this was on my diet." He sniffed the cheese steak longingly, passing the wrapped sandwich under his nose as if it were a fine cigar.

"It's your funeral," I said resignedly.

Jasmine and Malik, serenely happy, circulated among the group, accepting congratulations and hugs. Maxine Kellerman was there, chatting with Paul at a small table, and even Gus seemed to have put his foul mood behind him and relaxed enough to have a few margaritas. When he motioned me over, I had mellowed enough myself to listen.

"I apologize, Jordan," he said. "There's a lot of pressure right now. I didn't mean to take things out on you. I'm proud of what you're doing. This will be a real coup. It could move your show way up in the ratings."

"Well, I'm glad you see there are two sides to this."

"Did you figure out a way to work in my product?"

I sighed. "Actually, no. It didn't feel right."

He smiled. "Maybe next time."

I looked at Jasmine and Malik as they whispered together. She was tall herself, but he was so big that the top of her head barely reached his shoulder. Standing there together, they were a beautiful couple—a textbook example of physical perfection with an almost palpable aura of exotic excitement.

"Jordan, come over here!" Jasmine called out, waving, her wrist still splinted.

I grabbed Gus's hand and pulled him with me across the room, then introduced him to Malik.

"Dr. Laidlaw," Malik said, "I've read your book."

"Oh, really?" said Gus. "Which one?"

Malik smiled. "I look forward to coming to the clinic myself. From what Jasmine tells me, I could learn a lot here." I wondered if he'd really read Gus's book or if he was just humoring him, but before I could find out, a crowd of well-wishers closed around Malik and he drifted away.

"Look at them," I said to Gus. "The couple of the year. Paul must be licking his chops. The corporate sponsors are going to be beating down his door with a battering ram."

Indeed, Paul was beaming like the father of the bride, circling the room with an always-filled glass of champagne. He ambled over to me. "Well, this wasn't how I'd have planned it, but young people are impulsive these days. You're going to have one helluva show."

Bill made a late appearance, looking somber, and motioned me to his side. "Tanner's in the hospital. We've had a bit of an emergency, I'm afraid. I've just come from the ER."

"Oh, no! He was looking sick on the practice courts yesterday. What happened?"

Bill walked me over to the edge of the crowd, where we could talk more quietly. "He was rushed to the emergency room. He had a severe headache, and then he started vomiting uncontrollably. It could be food poisoning. Then again, the doctor in the emergency room said it could be something more serious. They're running tests."

"That's terrible, just terrible." The party atmosphere deflated around me like a pricked birthday balloon.

"That's not the end of it, I'm afraid," Bill continued, and the grim expression on his face reinforced the concern in his tone. "The Schidor brothers also became sick very suddenly." Dieter and Klaus Schidor, identical twins and perennial German bachelors in their early thirties, had been fixtures on the circuit for years and were major headliners in Europe. Known as the "playboy players," they partied hard but were nonetheless very driven to succeed, or at least to maintain the platform that allowed them to remain on the world circuit. Although both twins were barely good enough to stay in the top two hundred, and they usually never made it beyond the opening rounds of the major events, they were determined to keep a toehold in the rankings. Their winnings were negligible, but they were from a wealthy family and had the luxury of buttressing themselves with the best coaches and training that money could buy. They had installed courts of every surface at their side-by-side mansions in Boca Raton, and they periodically checked into the Springs to notch up their games.

"What were the symptoms?" I asked.

"Muscle ache, both of them. Severe nausea. Threw up so much, they got themselves dehydrated. They're on an IV drip to replace the electrolytes. We were joking that the emergency room should give us a group rate."

"Charlie said Tanner ate at a Mexican restaurant last night. Did Dieter and Klaus eat there too?"

"You know them. Identical in looks, but that's it. Dieter, Mr. Discipline, hasn't had a single mouthful off the premises. Our kitchens have prepared every bite he ate since he got here. Klaus orders in every meal, usually from KFC or Domino's Pizza."

A devastating thought occurred to me. "Oh, God, you don't suppose it was some of our food that went bad? Something they picked up in the dining room? Maybe there's an epidemic starting, or something in the water or the air filtration. You know, like Legionnaires' disease."

"Well, all we have are three sick men. That's hardly an epidemic. Be careful what you say, Jordan. With those network people here, things could get blown out of proportion. There could be a snowball effect. I'm going to personally make sure that Tanner and the Schidors get the best care possible. And, meanwhile, just so you know, I have quietly, very quietly, asked that the kitchen examine all the food and cooking surfaces and procedures." He turned away, the impeccable professional mask he wore so well back in place. "Paul!" he called out. "Congratulations to your clients. Now tell me, do you get a packaging fee for this relationship?"

I was in no mood to rejoin the celebration, so I headed for the door. On my way, I saw the Fish eating a large piece of cake.

I reached for the plate, but he skillfully evaded me. When the situation calls for it, the Fish can move like a greased eel.

"That's the trouble with you, Jordan," he said, his mouth full. "You can never mind your own business."

"What are you doing here?" I scolded.

"I smelled cake."

Then I noticed Winnifred making her way through the

crowd toward the Fish, carrying the contraband Philly cheese steak. I quickly intercepted her.

"Winnifred, these things are not on Mr. Fisher's diet."

"The poor man was starving. He said so himself. I thought you'd want him to eat a morsel or two."

"This is not a morsel. This is arterial suicide." I spun on the Fish. "You are manipulating my secretary to clog your arteries. I won't be a part of this." I gave him a withering look and left.

At home I lit some relaxation candles, took a long soak in the tub, and went to sleep. Somewhere in the middle of the night, the phone jolted me awake.

"He's dead," a whispery voice hissed. "Who will be next? Will it be *you*?" The phone clicked.

That woke me up—with a jolt. I sat up in bed. Who was dead? Who had called? I almost thought it was a dream. The illuminated clock by my bed said 3 A.M. The dog still lay sleeping beside me. My eyes flew to the control panel of the security system. A red light glowed—it was on and functional. For about fifteen minutes, I tossed and turned. Although I had an unlisted phone number, it wasn't unheard of to get crank calls, a problem faced by many people who have a high-profile career. Uneasily, I forced myself to go back to sleep.

When morning finally came, even before it was light, the phone rang again. In a restless half-sleep this time, I hesitated but answered it.

"I'm sorry to wake you up with bad news," Bill apologized. "Tanner had a heart attack last night. He didn't make it."

"He *died*?" I gasped.

"I'm afraid so."

"What about Dieter and Klaus?"

"They seem to be recovering, fortunately."

"When did you find out?"

"The hospital called me around four A.M., an hour ago, but I didn't want to wake you that early. I'm calling Gus and Charlie next."

"Poor Tanner," I said. "I don't know what to say." But I was thinking about my other phone call, at 3 A.M. Someone else had known Tanner was dead; they knew it before Bill, and they wanted me to know it too.

The question was who—and why?

FIVE

"Security," said Bill, as the partners convened in his office later that morning. An early round of frantic phone calls, trips to the hospital in Palm Springs, and hushed conversations had followed the horrible news in the night. Tanner's ex-wife and son had been notified and were en route from their home in Washington. The Schidors were still ill and under observation but were not deemed to be in any danger. At this point, they were still in the hospital because of what had happened to Tanner.

"We need to beef up security immediately," Bill said. "I'm not saying there was any foul play here, and I don't want to overreact, but three seemingly healthy men got sick, one of them died, and for the time being we can't discount anything."

"Bill, I got a very strange call last night," I began, and proceeded to tell him and Gus about it. "The thing is, three A.M. was before they called you. Who could have known about it?"

"I have no idea," Bill said. "Tanner died at two-thirty this morning. Whoever it was, they got very fast information."

"Who else was at the hospital?"

"As far as I know, nobody. I had stopped by earlier, as

you know, but the doctors didn't feel he was in immediate danger, so I left. Would you say the caller's tone of voice was threatening?"

"It was a whisper. I couldn't even tell if it was a man or a woman. The word that comes to mind is 'creepy.'"

"Maybe you shouldn't stay home alone," said Bill. "Ever since the Monica Seles incident, no one takes these things lightly."

"She can stay with me," Gus said.

I was amazed to hear him say that, because Gus has always fiercely resisted any suggestions of domesticity, even the most short-term sort. Although he certainly could afford to live however he wanted, his apartment is early bachelor pad, chosen for its proximity to the clinic rather than any aesthetic reason. A futon serves as a bed. A stair climber dominates the living room. Computer equipment, books, and files overrun the study. Only the kitchen is well furnished; it could have serviced a four-star restaurant.

If anyone tried to straighten the premises, or even move a pile of papers to put down a glass, Gus declared he could no longer find anything and his work had suffered an irreparable setback. As a result, we spent most of our time together at my house. I could only think that the thought of my staying with Gus must bother him as much as it did me, leading me to conclude that he must be seriously concerned for my safety.

"Thanks, Gus. I appreciate your concern, but I have a state-of-the-art security system," I said. "An ex-president lives in my complex. If it's safe enough for him, that's good enough for me. If I get another bizzarro call, I'll rethink this, but for now I'll stay put."

"We're going to try to keep this situation very low key," said Bill. "We don't want anyone to overreact. For now, it's business as usual—and we've never been busier. It would be nice to keep it that way."

There was a discussion about Tanner's funeral, which would undoubtedly be in Chicago, where he'd been born and gone to school. All three of us planned to go, once the date was set. Then I had to meet Jasmine at her villa. It was agreed that I would tell her what had happened.

As it turned out, however, she already knew.

"I got an anonymous call this morning, before it was even light out, from someone who told me Tanner had died."

She shuddered. There were dark circles under her eyes the color of bruised fruit.

"The phone rang. I probably shouldn't have answered it at that hour—phones that ring in the middle of the night are never good news. Anyhow, I was terribly sad, of course, but when I tried to ask about Tanner, this person hung up. And the voice said something else. It said I should watch my step—like a warning!" Jasmine wrung her hands nervously. "I woke up Malik; he just left to fly back east an hour ago. And the two of us sat up the rest of the night, talking. He calmed me down, and then Paul came over. But I'm still pretty tense."

"Believe me, Jasmine, I know exactly what you mean." *All too well,* I thought silently. "It's terrible news, and it comes at such a bad time for you. You should be enjoying your engagement." Her new diamond ring sparkled on her left hand. She should have been able to enjoy her first day as a prospective bride.

"You know, I'm very superstitious," she said. "This is a bad omen. I said so to Malik."

"Don't talk like that. This is all part of life. People die. Life goes on. You and Malik—you're what the future's about."

Paul Kessler emerged at the top of the stairs with Jasmine's suitcases. "You're all set," he announced. "Hi, Jordan. What bum luck for Tanner. He was a great guy."

"Yes, he was. You're leaving, Jasmine?"

"I'm too uptight to stay," she apologized. "But we had a good week, and I have my exercises now, and I'll follow them. I'll wear my splint. The interview will be great, I'm sure, but I've got to keep my mental state positive, and this is too distracting. I'm sure everybody here is very shook up."

Paul trotted down the carpeted stairs, a batch of tennis rackets in plastic bags under his arm. "We have some critical meetings that just came up. Counterpoint Athletic Shoes has called; they've set up a meeting as soon as possible at their corporate headquarters in Denver. They want to design a his-and-hers line endorsed by Jasmine and Malik," he said.

That was fast. It wasn't even lunchtime yet in Denver. Paul must have spent his night working the phone, announcing the engagement to his nearest and dearest sponsors.

"Malik will be checking in here at the clinic first thing next week. I'm assuming there's a successor in place for Tanner."

I winced at the poor taste and timing of this remark. "Take care of yourself, Jasmine," I said. "Enjoy your happiness. Your wrist should be fine if you follow the regimen and strengthen those muscles."

She stood up and gave me a hug. "Thanks for being so understanding," she whispered.

There was a knock at the door, and Kessler answered it. It was the Fish, dressed in chinos and a sport coat.

"Come in, Mr. Fisher," said Paul. "Here's a fax confirming that your plane ticket will be held at the ticket counter tomorrow." He handed him an envelope.

I looked curiously at the Fish, who gave me a shrug.

"What can I say? I'm checking out tomorrow afternoon. I was going to see you before I left."

"And what about your cholesterol?"

"What about my *stomach*? I was starving. At any rate, it's a moot point."

"I've just retained Mr. Fisher's services," announced Paul. "He will be head of security for our agency, and his first assignment will be to act as Jasmine's bodyguard until these hysterical letters and strange calls stop. I can't have her feeling nervous. It would hinder her concentration and focus on her game. In fact, Counterpoint will probably insist on twenty-four-hour coverage if we go with them—to protect their investment." He smiled, his smooth beardless cheeks like a fuzzless peach. "Mr. Fisher will be part of the package."

"Of course." The ink was obviously already dry on the deal.

"Send us a rough cut of the show when you've edited the tape," he added, sweeping through the living room, picking up errant tennis jackets and equipment.

"You know that's not what we do," I said.

"Well, you can make an exception. I'd like to have a tape to send a clip to Oprah and Letterman."

"I thought our interview was exclusive."

"For now, certainly. But once news of the engagement gets out, it's going to be like a tidal wave." He turned to Jasmine. "Let's go, Jas."

The Fish sauntered over to me.

"Can I at least contact a referral doctor so you can keep on your program?" I asked. "You need to do that. You can't just peacefully coexist with a cholesterol count like yours. It worries me."

"Sure. I'll let you know where I am. They're putting me into a corporate apartment in Boca. Now listen." He took me aside. "That mother. Remember what I said about her. I'll check into her from my end. Kessler kept the fax she sent Jasmine."

"I have a feeling she called me last night. And maybe Jasmine too. But I can't prove it. And how would she have known about Tanner?"

"You always ask questions I can't answer." He grinned. "But knowing you, you'll figure it out for yourself. Let me know when you do."

Since my schedule had suddenly cleared, I decided to drive to LA and spend the next day in the editing studio. I left word of my plans with Winnifred and the Fish, hopped in my truck, a beat-up blue Ford pickup, and took off, with A.M. in the passenger seat. Well before noon I was winding my way along Sunset, past the funky restaurants and stores to the studio in West Hollywood.

"Jordan, I am shocked," said Harrison, as I walked into the pitch-black editing room. My face looked back at me from six TV monitors. "I thought you'd be working with Jasmine."

"She left."

"What?" asked Ellie. "She didn't ask you to go with her to pick out a china pattern? I'd be hurt if I were you."

The production team sat facing a bank of video monitors, a broad bank of controls, and a computer keyboard, which was manned by a long-haired young black man barely out of his teens. His fingers flew over the keyboard as he programmed the edits into the Avid system. He was assisted by a blond woman who appeared to be in her late teens. The two of them worked seamlessly, rarely stopping to talk, crafting the tape we shot Thursday into a coherent whole.

"We've picked our select takes, the ones we can use for the finished segment," said Jeremy. "There's nothing to see yet. Maybe in an hour."

A.M. sniffed around the floor, hoping for some remnants from the breakfast snacks. I realized I'd left her water dish in the car. "Ellie, please watch A.M. I have to make a quick trip to the parking lot," I said.

I dashed out of the room, closing the heavy door behind me, ran through the lobby past the receptionist, and went blinking into the bright sunlight of the parking lot. I opened the car door, climbed inside, took out A.M.'s dish, and was about to get out when a black Porsche pulled up beside me. At first I thought it was someone looking for a parking place, but the driver, a woman with sunglasses and a head scarf, stared at me until I began to feel uneasy.

I decided to speak to her directly. "Can I help you?" I asked, lowering my window.

"You must listen," she said. "You must listen to me."

A chill pricked my spine. "What?"

"More people will die," she said. "You must stop this."

"Anna Martinez? Are you Anna?" The sunglasses and scarf hid too much for me to be certain.

"No. But you must listen. You must stop them. Before you die yourself." The Porsche leaped forward and squealed out of the parking lot.

I jammed my key into the ignition, threw the car into reverse, and maneuvered the truck out from between the rows of cars and over to the curb, where I caught sight of the Porsche, weaving through traffic, heading toward Sunset. Pounding the gas pedal, I shot into the street, hoping to catch up and force a confrontation or at least get the police on my cell phone.

The Porsche swung right at Sunset. I was too far behind, and there was too much traffic to catch up before she reached the Hollywood Bowl and slipped onto the expressway, leaving me with the license number I had jotted down as my only hope for tracing the driver.

I started to call the police but stopped short and dialed the Springs instead. If anyone could check a license number without fanfare or red tape, it was the Fish.

"Hellooo!" Winnifred answered my office line. She had trouble hearing and frequently yelled into the phone.

"Winnifred, it's me. Don't shout. I hear you fine."

"Hello, dear."

"Winnifred, I need you to locate Noel Fisher, wherever he is in the complex, and patch me through."

"Hold on, dear. By the way, your mother called. Perhaps you'd like to call her back first?"

"No, I wouldn't. I need Mr. Fisher right this minute."

"Certainly, dear."

A few seconds later she came back on the line. "I located Mr. Fisher for you. Apparently he is in the midst of a massage. Can I give you the extension number?" Winnifred never patched anybody through, because she only used a rotary phone. It was part of the reality of working with her that you just had to accept. I hung up and dialed the massage room.

"Yeah," grumbled the Fish.

"Sorry to interrupt, but I need an immediate trace on a license plate. Can you help? I don't have time to go through channels, and I thought—"

"How immediate? I'm on vacation for the next three hours."

"Now?" I gave him the plate number.

He sighed heavily. "If I find anything out, I'll get back to you."

Slowly, I drove back to the editing studio, the woman's words echoing in my head: *More people will die.* Suddenly the streets seemed ominous. I knew someone was watching me, unafraid of approaching me, and I couldn't judge whether the woman's words were a threat, a warning, or both.

Before we'd even gotten to editing the last of the Li-Malik segment, the Fish was on the phone to me in the studio. "I traced the car to Jake's Luxury Car Rental on La Cienega."

"Who rented it?"

"Nobody. The car never left the lot all day."

"Except it did. I saw it."

"Well, the manager checked. There's no record of a rental."

"So somebody didn't rent the car. They just took it."

"It's a start."

"Thanks, deserter. I respect your choices, but personally I don't see how you can work for Pinocchio— excuse me, Paul—Kessler."

"Hey, a gig's a gig. Business was slow. Besides, the man promises to feed me very well."

"I suppose we all have our priorities. Keep in touch— and thanks."

At the editing board, Jeremy was giving final instructions to the tape editor. "Anybody want to go for Thai food on Melrose?" asked Ellie.

"Thanks. Good job, everybody," I said. "I think I'll pass on Melrose." Actually, there was someplace else I wanted to go—the car rental on La Cienega.

It took less than thirty minutes to get there. The parking lot was full of Mercedes Benzes, Lincolns, BMWs, and, in the front corner, a black Porsche. I pulled in and cruised slowly past it. The license plate was the one I'd noted earlier. Immediately, I parked and went inside the rental office. Two people sat behind desks, one with a customer, the other intently reading the *Hollywood Reporter.*

"May I ask a question?" I asked the clerk who was buried in the *Hollywood Reporter.*

He glanced up, than back to the magazine. "Sure. Can I help you?"

"How would I rent that black Porsche in your lot?"

"Show me your license and a credit card, and it's yours."

"When was the last time you rented that car?"

He looked annoyed. "I assure you the car is very clean."

"I have a phobia. I absolutely have to know if it coincides with a certain astrological situation."

This struck a chord. The clerk put down the magazine and checked the computer. "It went out last week, but it came back three days ago and hasn't gone out since."

"Who rented it?"

"It was a long-term lease. That's confidential information."

"Was it Anna Martinez?"

"No."

"Where do you keep the keys?"

"In a locked cabinet, under the main desk."

There was a loud knocking on the window. "Adam, somebody left a wallet in the Silver Shadow!" one of the attendants in the parking lot shouted through the window. Adam leaped from his seat and dashed outside. I drifted over so I could see the computer screen, where the file for the Porsche remained on-line. The Porsche had been leased until last week, when it had been returned. The name of the person who had leased it was Arthur Lutz.

Artie Lutz.

"Thanks for everything!" I yelled over my shoulder as I ran out of the car rental. Rummaging through my backpack, I located Artie's card stuffed in a pocket of my wallet. His address was on Doheny, not far away. As I headed down San Vicente, I dialed Artie's number and connected with his voice mail.

"Artie, this is Jordan Myles. I need to speak with you right away. Please call me as soon as you get this message."

I hit redial at least three more times as I drove but only reached Artie's voice mail again. I swung onto Doheny and within ten minutes I was in front of Artie's high-rise. So was an entire complement of emergency vehicles—a fire engine, two police cars, and an ambulance—lights flashing. A uniformed police officer tried to wave me on, and I opened the window and leaned out of the truck.

"I've got to see someone inside that building. It's an emergency," I said.

"So is this. Keep moving."

I drove around the corner, parked, and ran back to

Artie's building just in time to see a stretcher coming out the door, a white-coated attendant trotting along on either side. A sheet was pulled over the face of the victim, who was strapped to the stretcher, the body size indicated only by a muffled shape. By this time, a small crowd had gathered in front of the building.

"Poor soul," said one woman sympathetically. "He seemed so sad recently. I saw him in the laundry room just last week."

I approached her. "What happened?"

She frowned sadly. "Suicide. He shot himself."

"Who, do you know?"

She nodded. "Mr. Lutz. Ten A."

"I don't think you should be driving back to Palm Springs by yourself, given the circumstances."

It was seven-thirty, and I had called Gus from the studio when A.M. and I were on our way out. The show had turned out wonderfully, with a romantic atmosphere that could never have been scripted. In fact, it was almost disconcerting to watch the innocence on the footage, knowing as we did now the tragic events that were about to occur.

"I don't think you should be driving that truck, period," Gus stated. "Artie Lutz may or may not have killed himself. And we don't know who that crazy woman was. She could be dangerous." Unspoken was the memory of Tony, killed in my car in an explosion meant for me. However, there had been a murder involved then. This time no one could say for sure what we were dealing with.

"Maybe I'll rent a car and drive back tomorrow," I said. "I can always stay with Ellie in Santa Monica. But how would I get the truck back to the Springs?"

"Ellie lives in Santa Monica? That's perfect. Have her drop you at the corporate terminal at the Santa Monica airport. I'll get Trent to send the BioTech chopper. They have a Bell Jet Ranger. Then tomorrow I'll send a couple of the interns down to pick up your truck and drive it back."

"Are you sure BioTech will have a helicopter just sitting there available?"

"They have two, actually. If there's a problem, I'll beep your pager."

"What about the Schidors?"

"Released from the hospital."

"Well, at least that's good news."

Ninety minutes later I found myself on the tarmac, ducking into the BioTech helicopter. Gus was waiting inside.

"You really didn't have to come over here," I said, clutching A.M. close on my lap in her gym bag. I petted her reassuringly. A.M. hates to fly. She has never understood the principles of aerodynamics.

"I know, but I wanted to," he said, as we took off, raising his voice to be heard over the blades as the engine started. "We're a team, you and me." He held my hand as the helicopter lifted off and the lights below us dissolved into a carpet of glitter far below.

"It was nice but unnecessary of Trent to send this chopper," I said. "Please thank him for me."

"I will," Gus said. "There are certain advantages to working with these big companies. In our world, we have to do everything ourselves. It's a one-on-one self-contained effort. They invented the term 'personal best' for us. But in the corporate world, the muscle of the whole machine goes to work for you. It's incremental power."

I couldn't imagine Gus as a corporate man, and I said so.

"You're right," he said. "But there are advantages to being *partners* with corporate people. I retain my integrity; they maintain theirs. So you see, Jordan, you really don't lose anything when you affiliate with a corporate sponsor."

"Is that a hint?"

"Well, I think you've just looked at the downside of endorsement. There are a lot of positives. Look at the resources I've accessed. It's not just the chopper. I can fly in the BioTech jet."

"I feel like I've got enough resources for what I want to do," I said.

"God, you're so prickly when it comes to business," Gus said.

"Drop it," I said. "The helicopter ride is nice. Let's leave it at that."

"They still want you as a spokesperson," Gus said.

I sighed. "Not interested."

Gus stared down at the view. "I'm making a wish," he said. "I wish we could stop living such separate lives and join forces for a change. Time flies along and we live our parallel lives and go home alone at the end of the day. More often than not, in separate time zones. I don't want to dwell on this, but I could really see us working together on a joint project."

"The *right* project," I said. In the darkness of the sky above Los Angeles, I wondered what life would be like as part of a couple, sharing a goal. Ever since we met, I have always relied on Gus to direct and advise me. It seemed like a natural progression that we would share our lives. Maybe my divorce made me wary, cloaking me in an emotional armor that I have trouble removing. Whatever it was, I couldn't play the scene as it should have been scripted. I put my hand on his shoulder. That was as far as I was able to go, for now.

At six o'clock the next morning, my doorbell rang. I froze, and Gus answered it. Then he dropped back onto the pillows and handed me the intercom receiver. It was Ginny, with a big smile in her voice.

"Did you get my message?" she said. "I'm going for a little hike. Want to come?"

"I didn't get the message, but sure. Give me five minutes." I rolled out of bed, threw on my tights, boots, thermal jacket, and cap, and met her outside. The desert is always cold in the morning.

"You need some fresh air," she said, as we took a Springs Jeep past the golf course and headed for the mountains. The Springs had marked off a trail, which we call the Lanyard Loop, that was just challenging enough to make a nice hike. For clients, there were printed maps and directions clearly posted along the path on wooden markers, but I'd traced this route so often I knew it by heart. The track was fairly rugged, but there were places to stop where you could sit on a rock, and you ended up at a picturesque overlook of the valley. For Ginny, of course, this kind of trail was a walk in the park.

"I'm going to be flying to San Francisco tomorrow to

film Billie Jean King," I said. "Sitting on a plane eating airplane food. This is the best antidote."

Ginny drove off the asphalt, and we bumped along in the dirt until we reached the starting point for the trail. "You know," she said, "I got a call from that guy Trent, who is working with Gus—the person from BioTech?"

"I met him," I said.

"They asked if I was interested in entering the Hawaii Ironman this year, sponsored by BioTech. They'd kick in equipment, a van, a backup team, clothes and supplies, and a training allowance."

"Of course their logo would be on everything."

"No doubt. And I would be photographed for a test commercial drinking a new product of theirs that supposedly builds endurance. There was also a nice fee."

"Is the product a system kind of thing called Duration?"

"I think so. But I'm not sure if I'll do it. I'm training, but they weren't clear on the specifics. If the test spot bombs, I don't get anything but the up-front money. That's all I know."

We reached the first marker, about fifteen minutes into the hike, which had a Day-Glo orange strip of fabric tied on it and pointed the direction of path and the mileage, and stretched a bit before we continued. The grade was not that steep, so we had no trouble talking as we kept up a brisk pace. Ginny carried a walking stick.

"They're really spreading a lot of money around for this product," I said. "When I was playing tennis, it was a different story, at least for me. I only got one endorsement in my entire career. And now Gus and this Trent guy want me to pitch this Duration thing, too—I think just because I'm on TV. To tell you the truth, that galls me. When I was accomplishing things in sports, when I won a Grand Slam, nobody was interested. Now that I'm on TV, with my show and doing commentary, that's viewed as some sort of accomplishment that's going to make people listen to me. It's so convoluted. They've got everything backward."

"Are you going to do it?"

"I don't think so. But I'll listen to them, for Gus's sake."

The path suddenly turned much steeper.

"So how are the twins?" asked Ginny.

"They left the hospital as soon as they both could walk and went back to Germany."

"What did the tests show?"

"Severe dehydration. They'll be fine."

"Is that normal?"

"Not normal, not abnormal. It happens, but rarely in double doses with twins. I don't know, Ginny. It wasn't that hot. They weren't that overextended. We never push our clients to that point. It doesn't add up. Besides, what they ate was completely different."

"And Tanner?"

"Heart attack. He didn't have a chance, poor guy. And he seemed so healthy. There are too many people getting sick, dying, and now Artie killing himself . . . it's like a plague, a terrible plague."

"Artie suffered from clinical depression. Didn't you yourself say he was on medication? Maybe he stopped taking it."

"If only I'd gone to his apartment an hour sooner. And who was the woman in the Porsche he'd rented the week before he died?"

"You're stressing out. Forget about taking on the problems of the world. This is supposed to be a relaxing walk. Enjoy the scenery."

I tried, but it was a challenge. I kept thinking about the woman in the Porsche. Who would be next? And why?

SIX

"Paul Kessler, aka Pinocchio," growled Harrison Barber. We had just wrapped up the San Francisco pre-production meeting for the next segment of *Woman/Sport* by going over the schedule and the details of the set. "I'm just throwing that name out for some feedback."

He might as well have thrown a bloody steak to a shark. Everyone in the room, from the assistants to Billie Jean King, who was to be my guest on the segment we were going to film the next day, had an opinion about Kessler.

"He represents some of the old-guard top players and some hot newer ones, like Jasmine Li and Malik," said the production assistant, sticking to the facts.

"He uses his big-name clients and they don't even know it," said someone else.

Billie Jean was more succinct. "He's a jerk, but somehow he always comes up smelling like a rose."

While many people are merely adept at lying, Kessler was a master. His face had a sweet, choirboy innocence that gave him the appearance of being incapable of doing anything more brutal than asking politely for cookies and a glass of milk. However, his full potential as a maestro of **untruth** was never completely realized because those who have known Paul for a long time know he is incapable of telling the truth and is pathologically driven to manipulate; in other words, they're on to him.

"They say he uses his players to get leverage—for instance, to force other players to play exhibitions. Certain opinions he bluntly states to be those of his players turn out to be coming from him, not them," said Harrison. "Why do people continue to buy into the guy?"

"He has leverage," I said. "To ignore or challenge Paul is to lose access to his stable of players, so people put up with him."

When Paul Kessler announced that, since their engagement, he was now representing Malik as well as Jasmine, few eyebrows were raised. I had checked out Malik's record. After two years of playing pro tennis, his accomplishments were uneven but his PR was incredible. He had won twenty thousand dollars here and there at satellite tournaments in Mexico and had started moving up to the lesser tournaments and qualifying for the Grand Slams. He managed to get as far as breaking into the top one-fifty, and he played qualifying events and got wild cards because of who he was. At the Lipton in Miami, Malik had appeared to much press fanfare, only to withdraw at the last minute due to an unspecified injury. That had become his pattern: a fair showing at one tournament, followed by withdrawal from the next. I wasn't sure what Paul could gain by representing someone with such a spotty record, beyond hype value of Malik and Jasmine as a couple—but then, that meant a lot to Paul.

"The word is, Malik got cut from the NBA," said Harrison. "He didn't want to play in Europe. I guess

Kessler convinced him he was promotable for a big sponsorship deal if he went multisport—maybe even *more* promotable—and landed on the idea of pulling him out of the big tournaments at the last minute to give it some press value."

"Well, it beats losing," I said. I picked A.M. and her pillow off my lap and settled her on the floor. She always came to pre-production meetings, which was natural since she was featured on every show. The viewers loved her; they sent her fan mail. I'd even received an offer from one fan who wanted to set up a website for her.

"The man's got to make a showing if he wants to keep his sponsors."

The fact was, Kessler was indeed intent on his newest client's making a showing—he had already checked Malik in at the Springs; he was waiting there now to work with me, and I was flying back to Palm Springs tomorrow as soon as the taping was over—but I couldn't reveal that to Harrison. I was always extremely careful to keep my clients' actions confidential and separate from my broadcast work. It was sometimes a difficult and fine line. This was clearly a case where it might net a few ratings points for our show if I told Harrison what I knew— but it would undermine the integrity of the Springs.

Harrison squinted at me. "You telling me everything you know, Jordan?"

"I'm telling you everything I'm going to tell you, Harrison." Every client deserves to be treated with integrity and confidentiality; Malik was no exception. And now, with two unexplained deaths, all of us associated with the clinic were being more conservative and cautious than ever.

"You know, you're going to have to decide which side you're on, kiddo," Harrison reprimanded me.

"I didn't know there were sides," I said.

"There are always sides. You were a player; you should know that."

My show is noncontroversial and has nothing to do with investigative tell-all journalism. *Woman/Sport* is about having fun with fitness and athletics; we go behind the scenes to show what motivates top women players in all kinds of sports. I didn't feel guilty that I wasn't sharing what I knew with Harrison.

After a fourteen-hour day of taping and a bumpy flight home, I arrived back at the Springs ready to sleep for the entire next day, but instead I had to meet with Paul Kessler and Malik. I went straight from the airport with my suitcase, dragging it behind me on wheels, like a stewardess, A.M. tucked into a carry-on gym bag.

The initial meeting with Malik was in Bill Stokes's office, and Bill had set out bottles of mineral water, fresh-squeezed vegetable and fruit juices from the clinic kitchen, a tofu spread, baskets of flatbread, and a platter of sliced vegetables. A small fire crackled in the adobe fireplace, a jazz CD was playing on the stereo system, and Bill, Paul, and Malik were sitting on couches and comfortable chairs as if this were a party.

Seeing him again made it clear to me why they called Malik "the Bat." He was six feet six, which is not remarkable for pro basketball but is a towering height on the tennis court, where his long arms and huge hands stretched to a wingspan of seven feet; with a racket in them, it was nine feet. Off the court, he dressed almost exclusively in black and had created a fashion stir by wearing black in tournament play wherever he could manage it. His hair was closely shaved; his eyes, inky in deep-set sockets, peered intently over the bridge of a hooked nose. When he rose to meet me, it felt like a dark stealthcraft was hovering over the room. Then he smiled. The smile was that of a brilliant twenty-four-year-old.

"Jordan, nice to see you again," he said, engulfing my hand. "Jasmine has told me a lot about you and your work here."

"We had a pretty good session last week," I said.

"Her wrist is improved already. I only hope you can do as much for me."

Paul Kessler spun around from where he'd been standing in front of the fire. He was wearing an immaculately tailored jacket, as usual, and a purposefully unshaved stubble that he cultivated to add a look of age and experience. Of course, age and experience had little to do with Paul's success, one way or another. It was his tactics and manipulations that bolstered his career. "Jordan," he said, his smile revealing perfectly capped teeth, like Chiclets. "Sit down, make yourself comfortable."

I glanced at Bill Stokes, who indicated a seat at the round glass table, and set down my backpack. "I'm glad to see you again, Malik, but I'm not clear on why you're here and what we'll be working on together. Do you have an injury?"

"Absolutely not," Paul answered, jumping in before Malik had a chance to answer. "Look at him! The man's a tank! A perfect physical specimen! We have two issues here, Jordan." He poured a cup of herbal tea from a glass pot that was on the table and offered it to me. "Issue number one, the only issue as I see it, is his serve."

"Do you agree?" I asked Malik. I didn't really understand this, since he was already known to have a powerhouse serve.

But he nodded. "Yeah, I have to work on my serve." His voice was soft, so low I had to strain to hear him. "I'm already serving one hundred and forty miles an hour. I got a second serve that's one-ten. But I know I can do better. I know I can be the first hundred-and-fifty-mile-an-hour server." He stretched out his arm, flexing and unflexing his hand. "See, I grew up pitching; that's what I did as a kid. So I've got the arm movement; my arm can really hurl the ball for my serve and overhead. I just need to take my serve to the next level."

Paul nodded enthusiastically. "That's it! The first hundred-fifty-mile-an-hour serve. Nobody can do it but Malik. The first guy who does it, the sponsors will carry him around in a sedan chair. And if he can serve like that, he's gonna blow the other players away. I keep telling him, all he needs is to fine-tune his strength work."

"What kind of program are you following now?" Bill asked.

"I spend twenty minutes a day in the weightless chamber," Malik said. "We'll be able to go over everything in detail. It's all here."

He reached into his bag, pulled out a pile of notebooks and file folders, and dropped them on the table.

"I keep a record of everything, so we can look it over and make adjustments. I got in here what I eat, the supplements I take, how much I sleep, the stretches I do, and my complete training program, of course: my log from the gym, aerobic and anaerobic, number of reps, amount of weight, number of strokes on each machine. Everything."

I was amazed. "Malik, you've got a lot of details accumulated here, a lot of data, and a lot of experience—but to what end? It sounds like you need a goal, something to focus on beyond that serve. A serve, even a hundred-fifty-mile-an-hour serve, isn't everything."

"Oh, we know that," agreed Paul, again speaking for his client. "But it's a hell of a way to start." He grinned ferally.

As I left Bill's office, I saw an eerie, flickering light coming from Gus's office across the hall. Walking over to the doorway, I looked in to find Gus still there, projecting slides onto a screen behind his desk.

"Working late?" I asked.

He looked up and flicked on the desk lamp. "Jordan, there you are. I'd heard you were coming back tonight. You're just in time to look at these test shots."

"Test?"

"For Duration."

"Oh, of course."

"We're moving along nicely," Gus said. "The guys at BioTech have made up some prototype ad layouts. What do you think of the logo? I like the shape, and the double oval logo is unique—it carries an echo of the infinity symbol. It's scientific but approachable." He dimmed the light, and a picture of the Duration bottle, on the baseline of a tennis court, appeared on the wall.

"It looks great. But I thought you were still working on the formula."

"I am, but we're very close. In fact, I was going to talk to you again. About being one of the spokespeople." He clicked to a different slide, a close-up of the label.

"We've discussed this enough. I already have sponsors on my TV show, and the network doesn't like to stir them up."

I could sense his frown, even in the dark. "Do you have a specific clause in your contract that keeps you from endorsing products?"

"Not specifically. But I have to be careful about it. I've sort of decided not to get into that area while I'm involved with the show. It would seem like selling out."

"Selling out? *Selling out?* What do you mean by that?" The projector clicked to a blank slide, projecting a white shape onto the wall.

"I don't mean anything about you, Gus. You're developing a product, and that's your business. I want to keep *my* business separate, that's all."

"I can't believe this." Gus stared at me in the dark.

"Why? I'm just not into commercial products."

"This is not merely a commercial product, Jordan. We're not talking about a new flavor of Kool-Aid. This is a major breakthrough, a sports drink and a vitamin system that help give players much greater endurance. You get a long match, a situation like Sampras at the Open, and Duration is going to address a real need in the marketplace. It's a perfect product for your show. I can understand why you didn't want to be part of the development process—that's a tedious amount of work. But a product endorsement is nothing. All you have to do is incorporate the Duration system into your training program and stand up in front of the camera holding the product."

"We don't push products on our show, Gus. You know that."

He turned on the light and tossed a handful of slides onto the table. "Great. This is just great." His face was sharp, his heavy eyebrows swooping downward over his wire-rimmed glasses. "I thought we were a team. I thought I heard you say, once upon a time, 'Gus, I can never repay you for helping me find who I really am and what I want to do.' Of course, that was *then*, when you were lying in a hospital bed like a bunch of broken pick-up sticks, and I was there to do anything I goddamn well could to help you. Where are you now, after I've put two years and my entire bank account into research and development and am trying to do something positive for athletes? What do you think I'm doing here? Can't you be supportive?"

"Gus," I pleaded, wondering why he always refused to hear me on this subject. "Try to understand. I *am* being supportive. I think it's great—for you. Just not for me. Yes, we're a team—but we're not twins, joined at the hip."

Gus turned off the projector, stuffed the slides into his backpack, and stalked toward the door.

I followed him out. "Please, Gus, let's not argue about this." Suddenly I was exhausted, certainly too tired to fight about Gus's business ventures.

"There are lots of other athletes I can get," he said angrily. "I thought I was doing you a favor, giving you the opportunity to get more exposure in the commercial environment."

"Can we talk about it later?" I asked, as he locked the door behind us. "I've been traveling all day, and I'd love to get some real food. Are you hungry?"

He glared at me. "No." He locked the office door,

jammed the keys into his pocket, and stalked off down the hall.

The next morning, Malik went through the routine physical exam and psychological profiling. By eleven o'clock, I was at the court with him, watching him hit with Charlie, who had been Tanner's assistant. Nobody had the heart yet to begin looking for a name candidate who could replace Tanner. We went through the usual drills: stroke repetition, hitting five hundred serves, a thousand forehand volleys, five hundred returns of serves. Malik was amazing. His first serve clocked at a hundred and ten miles an hour, and we got it on video to enlarge, enhance, and break it down later, when we would also overlay images of optimal shots over Malik's. He had left and right overheads, like Luke Jensen, and what looked like a thirty-eight-foot vertical jump—impossible to lob over him. His movement and balance reminded me of Edberg—catlike quickness at the net plus that incredible extra height.

I commented that while Malik had been a right-handed basketball player, he was a left-handed tennis player.

"I started out lefty," he said, "but my basketball coaches always corrected me and made me play right-handed."

"That would explain why your left arm seems to be somewhat weaker than the right," I said. "We can work on it with strength exercises."

Later in the day, Malik and Charlie got in some match play, and as the game progressed I saw Malik's focus drop off. He started clowning around, making jokes. He seemed to need outside stimulus to keep his attention level up. Had the same thing happened, I wondered, in the French Open, where Malik was badly beaten by a small, fast rabbit of a player who stood twenty feet behind the baseline for the return and actually managed to stop his serve? Or was he overprogrammed to the point where everything canceled itself out and he was simply going through the physical motions? This was what I suspected.

Back in the office, I rechecked Malik's record. I found a lot of matches where he was up—say, 6–0, 3–0—and then suddenly the match turned and he lost. I called Gus, who was doing the psychological profile, and we talked.

"It looks like he can't keep focused," I said. "What do you think?"

"Well, we're still running tests," Gus said, "although it looks like he's used to the quick pace of basketball and he's having trouble making the adjustment. His mind wanders. He seems to prefer fast action and the chance to take out physical aggression on his opponent."

"But he seems so soft-spoken and laid-back," I said.

"*Seems* is the operative word here. Looking over his tests, I'd say he's twelve on an aggressiveness scale of one to ten. He overcompensates socially, which is why he acts quiet. Let's put it this way. You don't want to end up on the bad side of this guy. He'd probably wipe the floor with anybody who crossed him."

"Thanks."

I hung up and called in Winnifred.

"I want you to call Noel Fisher," I said. "He checked in with Kessler and Malik."

Winnifred raised an eyebrow behind the frames of her rhinestone glasses. She never said anything, but I could tell she wasn't sure what to make of the Fish. She was meticulous; she must have hated that each time he stopped by the office, he would set a bag of take-out food or chips on her desk, leaving a telltale grease spot just where she had clipped her coupons. Of course, the Fish had never saved Winnifred's life. There are trade-offs.

Winnifred trotted back to her desk. I could hear her dial her rotary phone. A few quiet moments then, "Hello! Mr. Fisher, please! I have Ms. Myles on the line!" I cringed. Winnifred never spoke into the phone in less than foghorn tones. Nonetheless, she got results.

Thirty minutes later, the Fish had the goods.

"This Malik guy was a bad, bad boy," he said.

"What do you mean?" I asked.

"It's not on his record, because he was a juvenile and they wipe that, but I have a friend; we were in the CIA together . . . anyhow, before Malik was sixteen he'd been in jail three times. Robbery once, then he beat a guy with a lead pipe or something."

"But he hasn't been in trouble since he was a kid?"

"Nah, but you don't change the spots on an apple."

"Leopard."

"Whatever." The Fish ambled toward the door. "See ya, Jordan. Don't say you weren't warned. And if Kessler asks, we never had this conversation. Because so far he hasn't asked about Malik. I guess he doesn't want to look a gift horse in the throat."

"Mouth." I thought about this for a while. Clearly, Gus was right; Malik was dangerously aggressive underneath his calm surface. He probably figured he could beat the ball into submission by hitting it harder than anybody else. He'd have to learn to *control* opponents, not over-power them. It would not be an easy lesson.

* * *

The next morning, Malik, Paul, and I met just after sunrise to run together in the mountains, a little early morning warm-up. Paul had suited up and started the run with us, but he was not in shape for the altitude, and within fifteen minutes he was so far behind he was out of sight, which was exactly how I'd planned it.

Early mornings are beautiful in the desert. Every rock and mountain seems etched into the sky, which makes for a beautiful run. The path looped around the Springs grounds, past the golf course, and up the mountainside. Usually, I don't like to talk, but since Kessler seemed stapled to Malik's side, I seized the rare opportunity of his absence to level with him.

"You've got a great serve," I said. "You may make one-fifty. But it's not about a serve, Malik."

He frowned but said nothing.

"It's about having a match mentality, about not just going through the physical motions. You have to be able to interpret the ebb and flow of a match—when to turn it on, when to rise to the occasion. It goes beyond playing as hard as you can or hitting the ball a hundred and fifty—even two hundred miles an hour if that were possible."

Malik stared straight ahead and kept running as we left the golf course and headed toward the rougher terrain of the desert as it intersected the mountains.

"You know, Malik," I said as we ran, "when you're at the top of your sport, it's harder to see an improvement because improvements come in small increments. It's not like when you're just learning something and you see big results right away. I'm sure that when you first took up tennis it was a new sport for you, and you made big improvements fast. Now that you've made progress in the sport, the improvements seem to be coming slower, and you may feel a bit frustrated."

"Yeah, you're right," he said. "I don't see why I can't be better."

"It's going to take patience on your part. And some new learning. I've been studying tapes of your matches. You're great on the offensive, you dominate when you serve, but if somebody ever manages to attack you, you're vulnerable. You have no defense. It's your fatal flaw."

"My fatal flaw is not having that hundred-fifty-mile-an-hour serve. See, I know I can do that. I have to level with you. You're a player yourself. I can fool some of them, but not you. The rest of this strategy stuff—well, I'm not sure I can deliver."

"We can develop your game so you have more arrows in your quiver."

"Such as?"

"A bunt return. Hit a bunt return, close in on the net, force your opponent to lob, then hit the overhead of the century."

Malik finally smiled. "I like that. Especially the part about the overhead of the century."

"We'll practice chip-and-charge play—it's the opposite of, say, how an Agassi plays. We're going to bunt the ball and send it deep to the middle of the court. Therefore, the return won't have a lot of angle, and you'll only have to step to get to it."

"Sounds good to me."

Looking at Malik, with his clearly intense desire to

succeed at this sport, and knowing the discipline it had taken him to get to this point, it was hard to believe that this was once the tough kid the Fish described. I was almost tempted to ask him about his past, but I decided against it. The child was not necessarily the man.

At the turnaround point halfway up the mountain, we stopped, drank our water, and waited for Paul. Far down below, we could see the clinic complex, spread out along the floor of the valley—the whitewashed buildings, the fifteen tennis courts, the eighteen-hole golf course, and the 500,000-gallon super pool, all surrounded by date palms and indigenous desert shrubbery.

"How'd you like Jasmine?" he asked.

"She's fantastic," I said.

He beamed with pride. "Yeah, she is. She's the girl who turned me around. If it weren't for her, I'd be off the deep end by now."

"Well, congratulations."

He looked at his watch. "I was supposed to call her in half an hour." He pulled a tiny cell phone from his pocket.

I laughed. "Don't count on getting reception up here."

"Well, I gotta make this call. I don't want to wait all day for Paul. How do I get down?"

I pointed to the Springs complex. "You see where you're going. The path is marked. Follow the signs." I pointed to one, which had our logo painted on it. There were markers every hundred yards or so. Nobody had ever gotten lost on this path; you could see the complex from every point.

"I'm going on ahead, okay?"

"Fine. See you back at the ranch." I dreaded running

back with Paul, but Malik clearly wanted to sprint off and mull over our conversation.

Ten minutes later, Paul collapsed onto a rock beside me, dripping sweat. "Where's Malik?" he gasped.

"Didn't you see him? He went down ahead. He wanted to call Jasmine."

"I must have missed him," Paul said, breathing hard.

"How? He ran back the way we came. There's only one path up and down."

Paul mopped his face. "Well, to tell you the truth, I wasn't always on the path. I sort of stepped off at one point."

"Paul, it's not very safe to do that if you don't know your way around these hills. The footing isn't always that secure. That's why we mark the trail."

"Well, I felt sick. Didn't want to throw up on the path. Altitude sickness, that's what it is."

"It's not Mount Everest. You're probably dehydrated." I handed him my spare water bottle. "Let's get you home—slow and easy."

It had taken about forty minutes to get to the turn-around point with Malik. Going back with Paul, it took closer to an hour as he picked his way downhill. The worst part was being trapped with him, not unlike the agony of being strapped in an airplane seat for a cross-country flight next to someone whom you otherwise would avoid like the plague.

"So what do you think of my client so far?" he asked between labored breaths.

"Malik can be a phenomenal player. But he needs to develop his whole game."

"Fine. But the serve first, then the game. I got some

sponsors lined up—they're gonna come out with a racket called the Bat. And a sportswear line all in black. Footwear, that's definitely in the picture. And this drink your friend Gus is working on—Duration. Then there's the mass market for packaged goods: cereals, candy, over-the-counter drugs, personal care, like razors. . . . Malik is an ideal spokesman for just about any product you can mention."

"You've got all those sponsorship deals lined up?"

Paul stopped and rested for a minute, his chest heaving. "Malik doesn't like me discussing the specifics of his business."

In other words, he didn't have the deals in hand. Most likely, the sponsors were looking for the record-breaking serve Paul had promised them. It dawned on me that Paul probably didn't care at all about where his client stood in the top hundred, as long as he had that one-fifty serve. That *promotable* one-fifty serve.

Paul clutched his forehead. "I've been having these headaches. Is it possible I'm having warning signs of a stroke?"

I felt for his pulse: racing, but not off the charts. "Possible but not likely. We'll be down in half an hour. I'll have you checked out. When was your last physical?"

"Never. I'm too busy. God, it's hot. I'm not used to this heat. Heatstroke. That's what I have." He gulped more water.

"We'll take it very slow the rest of the way."

After we made our way down the hill and across the highway, Paul flagged the first golf cart in sight and commandeered it for a ride back to the clinic. I tried to get him to stop by the medical office, but he waved me off

A trip that I had made hundreds of times, savoring the view and the clean, clear air above Indian Wells, was unbearably nightmarish. Although I wanted to bolt down the hill, my descent was labored and excruciating. The sun, especially sweltering, beat down relentlessly. My ankle throbbed, and a quick look revealed that it had already swollen to half again its size. I knew it couldn't bear any weight, but I also knew that every second counted if Malik was to be saved. As I had so many times on court, and when I fell so much more precipitously in my near-fatal mountain climb, I focused on each slice of a moment and did my best to block the pain. It seemed like hours before I found myself back at my dirt bike, which I rode to the edge of the highway. A truck approached and I frantically flagged it down.

The driver squinted at me as if I were delusional, which is how I must have looked, but I managed to get him to pull over and let me use his CB to call the paramedics to bring helicopter support and alert the Springs of the situation. I told them I would wait at the side of the road to lead the rescuers to Malik.

"I'll stay with you," said the trucker, a young man with red hair and a beard. "Are you sure we can't just go up there right now and get the guy ourselves? I could help you carry him."

I shook my head. "I have medical training," I explained. "You can't move a person in that state without keeping him flat and stable. He may have broken his neck or his back. Or he may be bleeding internally. It's riskier to move him the wrong way than to leave him where he is. The helicopter will have the right equipment, and they'll be able to get to him faster than we could climb back up."

Sure enough, within minutes I heard the whine of sirens and the whir of an approaching helicopter overhead. The police cars and ambulance, lights flashing, formed a roadblock, and the helicopter set down on the highway. I thanked the trucker and hobbled into the chopper to direct the search. Flying overhead, we located Malik in less than five minutes, a dark shape that from above looked almost like a stain that had seeped into the russet earth and rocks. Nature was already at work, reclaiming him, pulling him back, as she does us all, if given the chance. Finding a landing spot was difficult, but the pilot was able to use the flat lookout point where Paul and I had stopped to rest. From there it was a scramble back down the hill for the EMS team, retracing the path that had led me to Malik. I limped along behind them as best as I could under the circumstances, my ankle now swollen to the point where I had to unlace my shoe.

When I reached Malik, the team had already begun their work. An IV was started and Malik was being moved onto the stretcher they had carried down the hill. It was an efficient, impersonal process, one of medical routine and rote. But to me it signified one thing: Malik was still alive.

"Did you see what happened?" a young woman asked as she strapped him onto the stretcher.

"No, I got here afterward. He was just lying here, pupils fixed, like you see him now. What do you think of the piece of wood that went through him?"

"I don't really know, but it looks bad. We're going to leave it in. They'll handle it at the hospital. If we removed it, he could lose even more blood."

"We have records of his blood type at Desert Springs."

She nodded. "That will help. The pilot will radio your medical office. Listen, the patient's gonna take up most of the room in the chopper. Can you get down from here on your own?"

"Sure." I watched as she and her associate carefully turned Malik just enough to move him onto the stretcher. As they strapped him in, the woman kept pressure around the wound to try and stop the bleeding. As they hoisted the stretcher, I helped them steady it and carry it back up the mountain to where the helicopter waited. Once the stretcher was loaded, the helicopter door slammed shut; I ducked as the engine started again and they took off in a whir of dust and whipping wind.

I watched the helicopter rise, then get smaller in the distance, as it headed for the hospital in Palm Springs. Only then did I permit myself to feel the pain in my ankle and realize I could have used a ride myself. Slipping, sliding, and picking, I somehow made my way down for the third time today. By the time I reached the bottom, my shins and palms were skinned and I couldn't put an ounce of weight on my leg, but otherwise I was in pretty good shape. My bike was still there, and so were the police and the redheaded trucker. I answered the police officers' questions and told them what I knew, which was minimal. Then I sagged to the ground, unable to stand for one more second. The trucker ambled over.

"I figured you wouldn't get far," he said, pointing to my bulging ankle. "Me, I got no medical training, but I got eyes. Get into the truck. I'm taking you to the emergency room for an X ray." He loaded me up with my bike, turned the truck around, and headed back up the highway toward Palm Springs.

* * *

I was in the hospital, lying on one of the examining tables behind a curtain and nursing a cold pack on my bandaged ankle, when the green fabric suddenly whipped aside and the Fish burst in. "I'll be damned if you won't do anything to get behind the scenes," he said.

I managed a groan.

"Well, I checked with the doc. Nothing's broken. Let's get you up and out of here."

I sat up. "What about Malik?"

The Fish's mouth tightened. "He didn't make it, Jordan. He died on the way, in the helicopter."

My face flushed with a hot sting, as if I'd been struck. "It's my fault. I let him veer off the path. I thought Paul needed more guidance, since he was having trouble. Then I left Malik when I first found him. Maybe if I'd carried him down—"

"You know you couldn't have done that, even without the ankle. You did exactly the right thing."

"Why did he die?"

"The autopsy will confirm things, but it looks like he lost a lot of blood."

I wrapped my head in my hands, as if I could blot this nightmare out. "This is unreal," I said. It seemed like illness and death were striking all around me, wherever I went: first the child in the stands at Madison Square Garden, then the twins and Tanner, and now this.

"There's a meeting at the clinic first thing in the morning," said the Fish. "We have to go out the back way. The place is already crawling with media types."

Numbly, I nodded, got up, and went through the motions of checking myself out. The doctor gave me a few brief instructions, which boiled down to keeping weight off my leg for the next twenty-four hours, and handed me a pair of crutches, and I left with the Fish, my ankle throbbing.

"I still can't believe it," I mumbled as we got into the Fish's car, a greasy-smelling rental Hyundai with a nest of old Big Mac wrappers wadded up in the backseat.

"On the outside, where I come from, everybody's saying that something's up. World-class athletes don't just fall off mountains," said the Fish. "They're saying the place is jinxed somehow."

"Oh, athletes don't fall, do they?" I said angrily. "What about me? I not only fell off a mountain, I practically swan-dived. Or do they think it's a syndrome? Jordan Myles Mountain Madness—stick with her and you too can fall off a cliff!"

We drove through the string of desert towns that ends at Indian Wells and turned into the gated entrance of my complex. I needed a few minutes to get my thoughts and myself together. The Fish assured me that he would delay the emergency meeting while I took a shower and cleaned up.

I had about twenty phone messages when I checked my voice mail—the network, my mother, Gus, Bill, the Fish, various tour members, and the press; Paul, screaming that I owed him answers; and, of course, Jasmine. Hers was the only call I returned.

Her mother answered. "She's not here," she said. "She left for Palm Springs as soon as she heard. What on earth happened out there?"

"He fell, Mrs. Li. That's all I know right now. It was an accident. He was alone on a mountain trail, and he must have lost his footing. It wasn't a difficult path, but . . ."

"Jasmine will be wanting to know," she said haltingly. Other than his immediate family, Jasmine was the person who deserved answers. The problem was, I had none to give her.

That, I vowed, would change. Because there is a reason for everything.

SEVEN

When I arrived at the meeting the next morning—on my crutches—the entire group was in chaos. Bill was attempting to keep order without success. A contingent I recognized as members of our PR firm sat grimly in a cluster, notebooks and pads in their laps. Two uniformed police officers were in a huddle with the Fish. A couple of men in suits whom I didn't know were deep in conversation at the table. Ginny was there, because of her background in climbing and familiarity with the local terrain.

"Now that Jordan is here we can get to work," announced Bill, summoning up the innate authority that had once helped make him an Olympic hero. "Jordan, would you please recap the events that led to this tragic situation."

I told the story, leaving out no details. "So you see," I said, "nobody saw what happened to Malik—at least Paul and I didn't. He was at another point on the path, out of our range of vision."

"That path is deceptive," said Ginny. "Especially if you decide to leave the marked trail, as Malik apparently did."

"He was probably trying to get down faster, in order to

119

call Jasmine," I said. "He was really anxious about
making that call."

"The fact is," said Bill, "we have to get through this
string of tragedies. Everything is accidental, but the
Springs is involved. And our staff." He looked at me.
"We have to protect our image and reinforce to the outside world that we are not implicated or negligent." He
turned to me. "To that point, Jordan, I would like to ask
that you intercede with your network and make sure that
the *Woman/Sport* segment that featured Jasmine Li and
Malik not be run."

"Bill, I can't control that. If they want to run it, they
own the footage."

"But it's your show. That's why we agreed you could
tape it here, on the grounds."

"I'm the personality who is the star, but I don't actually own it. The fact is, if sponsors buy time for that
segment—and I'm sure they will—it will run."

"I'd like you to see that it doesn't. Or, at the very
minimum, that Malik's footage is edited out. It will only
reinforce that this tragedy happened here. We don't need
that right now."

"I'll see what I can do, Bill, but it's unlikely that they
will do anything other than run the whole interview,
including the Malik footage. It's a tragedy, but viewers
will be curious about what happened. Networks depend
on that curiosity."

"As a partner, your first loyalty is with us," Bill stated,
with a finality that ended the issue, as far as he was concerned. On the other hand, I already knew that interview
was going to be featured by the network, and there was
nothing I could do about it.

"If the press asks any of you anything, the official

response is No comment," Bill stated. He went on to review the plans for those of us who would be flying to Chicago after the meeting to attend Tanner's funeral, but I only partially listened. I knew I could not comply with Bill's request. The network and the producers, of course, would have a totally opposite perspective.

"Bill," I said, taking him aside after the meeting, "I understand where you're coming from, but I think we also need to dig much deeper into what happened to Malik. This isn't about a TV show—mine or anybody else's. It's about what's going on here. We can't just sit back and accept events at face value."

"But it was an accident, wasn't it? We've gone over his record here—Max and Sally and I and, of course, the authorities. The worst thing Malik was doing was taking vitamin and mineral supplements. He was very healthy. And you saw the accident."

"I wasn't there when he actually fell, but there are some things I found out about his background that we should discuss. Nor can we overlook these ominous plot warnings that are coming in by fax. And how about this strange woman who approached me—and Artie's suicide? There's a so-called rational explanation for all these accidents and incidents if you take them one at a time. But the number of them makes me very uncomfortable."

"Jordan, let me clarify. I am only interested in how these tragedies impact on the Desert Springs Sports Science Clinic. Don't try to make this into something more than it is. We have enough to handle right here—among other things, there are still arrangements to be made for Malik. You have a tendency to overinvolve yourself in situations you can't control, and sometimes they back-fire. This time, for your own sake, I hope you'll stay close to the relevant issue. Now, we have a plane to catch. Are you packed?"

I am always packed. I keep a packed extra suitcase and have a coat on a hook in my closet at all times, just to ease the pressure. The clothes may be wrinkled when I get wherever I'm going, but at least they're there, and if I can't pick them up, somebody can always FedEx them to me.

On the way to the airport, I swung by the house, left a message for Winnifred to please take care of A.M., dragged out my suitcase and coat, and resolved to sleep the entire four hours on the plane. As for Gus's comments, I had no intention of taking them seriously. Ever since my accident, Gus has tended to continue his function as my caretaker, even when it is unnecessary and unwanted. We slipped into roles that were hard to change. I knew I had to reestablish the boundaries, but there was never time for relationships. There was always a plane to catch, a client to see, a show to tape.

I've always enjoyed going to Chicago, except, of course, in the depths of its sub-zero winters, when the wind slices across Lake Michigan and blasts your skin one step from frostbite. The weather had not reached that point yet, but it was getting ugly; the skies were gray and the lake leaden when I looked out the window of my room in the Drake Hotel the next morning. Funeral weather. I put on my black pantsuit and sweater and had my hand on the doorknob when I saw a message envelope that had been slipped under the door. On my way to the elevator I ripped it open. It was from Harrison Barber. The network was making a programming change; they were running the show with my Jasmine Li–Malik interview tonight at seven o'clock eastern standard time.

There was nothing I could do to prevent this. And when I saw Tanner's distraught family, I didn't care. Funerals have a way of putting things into perspective. All of us from the Springs who had worked with Tanner walked through the motions of the day, first at the funeral home and then at the cemetery. Tanner had not been a religious person, so there was no church service, just the memorial, at which Bill stood up and spoke about Tanner's indomitable drive and compassion, about how he had influenced so many people in his life. Afterward, our group went to dinner at a downtown sports bar. I had steamed vegetables and a baked potato, which was fine, since I didn't feel like eating at all. Just as they brought our order, my show came on the big-screen TV that dominated the bar. I heard the music of the opening montage and saw my face, intercut with Jasmine and Malik.

Bill and Gus saw it too.

"I thought we discussed this," Bill said quietly, putting down his fork as he stared at the screen.

"And I said there was nothing I could do."

"God, there's the front of the main gate," Bill said. "And our name. Right there."

Gus stared at his plate. A muscle twitched in his jaw.

"Everyone was happy about using the Springs as a location when I first got this show," I said hotly. I felt frustrated and angry, unable to do the right thing. "The problem is not that we taped the show there, it's that we have these accidents going on there that we can't control. What's happening isn't anyone's fault, so please stop trying to assign blame."

"It's been a rough day for all of us," Gus said gently. "Let's have our dinner and make it an early evening. It's not good to mix funerals with business discussions."

As usual on a business trip, Gus and I made a point of not staying in the same room, and I went to bed alone. That night, I had a frighteningly vivid dream. Malik and Jasmine were getting married. She was in a white lace gown with a train, he all in black. I held her bouquet during the ceremony and as they sealed their marriage with a kiss. When their kiss ended, they separated—and the front of Jasmine's gown was soaked with blood, which had also seeped halfway up her veil, and the fingers of her white gloves were also tipped in blood.

The horror of the dream startled me awake, and I realized that the phone was ringing. It was morning.

"Congratulations!" shouted Harrison Barber from New York. "We won the time slot. A forty share! Out of the park! Phenomenal. Do you know how many millions of people watched that show?"

Millions! I didn't know how to feel about this. "Harrison, I'm happy for the show, but right now I'm still in a very down mood from the funeral I attended yesterday."

"Well, this should help."

"Harrison, the point of the show was the romance between them. Now Malik is dead. Those people out there who tuned in are ghouls."

"It's news. And we got it. The word is they're gonna put in an order for six more shows. This is very, very big."

I hung up, resigned to the fact that some of the best news I'd ever had was also some of the worst news I'd ever had. Maybe Gus was right, and it was time to decide who I really wanted to be.

On the plane back to Palm Springs, I sat with Gus. "Bill's going to ask you to stop using the Springs for your show," he said. "He may even ask you to give it up."

"Well, I have a right to do the show. I may not give the answer he expects."

"You know, I have a thought," Gus said. "There is a way you can keep your show and also the integrity of your career. All you have to do is change the format a bit, so that you deal with harder-hitting issues, like sports medicine—which is, after all, your specialty—instead of romances and fluff pieces."

"Harder hitting?"

Gus nodded enthusiastically. It was clear he'd given this some thought. "Less of this up-close-and-personal stuff and more pieces with meat."

"Gus, the sponsors love up-close-and-personal stuff. They're not into the hard core of sports medicine. It's not mass market."

"Just hear me out. You wouldn't have a problem with sponsors for the show I have in mind. BioTech would sponsor it. You'd talk about some of their products as part of the deal. And you could have a talk show–type format, with current and former athletes discussing their health issues as relates to sports."

"This sounds like an infomercial. Like those things has-been actresses do for makeup companies. Exactly what products would I talk about, as part of this potential deal?"

"The good ones."

"Like, for instance, the Duration system?"

"Why not?"

"I can't believe you think *Woman/Sport* is too commercial, but you'd want me to get involved in something where I'd talk about particular products on the air."

"It's informative. Lots of doctors use this format, in fact."

"I'd feel like a shill. And totally uncreative."

Gus's face darkened. "There you go, being negative about a simple suggestion. It's only to help you that I thought of this, Jordan, because you seem so hell-bent on being on TV. I'm straining to find a way to make it professionally palatable. Sometimes I think you resist just in order to resist." He snapped open a magazine and stared at it.

"I'm sorry, Gus. I don't mean to be negative. But an infomercial is something entirely different. My show got fantastic ratings last night. I agree it wasn't a typical situation, but the point is, why would I change formats?"

His eyes didn't leave the magazine. "It may not be your decision."

As in so many other things, it turned out that Gus was right. The next day, I was back in my office at the Springs when I got a call from my agent, Holly Lister. "I have good news and bad news," she said.

"This is becoming a pattern. Okay, what?"

"The network has decided that *Woman/Sport* has real potential."

"Don't tell me. That's got to be the good news."

"Right. But not for us. They're moving the time slot into something better and—well, they're not renewing your contract as host."

"What! Why not?" I couldn't believe it. "The show was a big hit—"

"Right. And to make it a bigger hit still, they're going to bring in a name actress." She named a former soap star who'd had a number of prime-time series.

"That woman is an actress, not a sports personality. What does she know about women's sports?"

"She gets good ratings with men. Better than you."

"But *Woman/Sport* is a woman's show."

"Not anymore. It's too big for that. They're changing the name to *Sports Profiles*. It'll be a magazine format show, profiling major athletes on the personal level."

"I can't listen to this."

"They're going to keep you as a tennis commentator, though. That still goes."

"Big of them."

"I'm sorry about this, Jordan, but that's television. It's all about market share."

"I guess I delivered my one death, and they couldn't count on me for any more this season."

"They like your work, Jordan, they just think this actress will be better for all-around ratings."

"Fuck them!" I slammed down the phone.

"Dear!" Winnifred gasped from the next room. She appeared in the doorway, resplendent in lavender polka dots. "Such language!"

"Sorry, Winnifred. I got upset. Close the door. If I start screaming again, at least you won't hear it."

She drifted off. "No need, dear. I'll just turn off my hearing aid. It won't bother me at all. But it might bother your visitor."

"Visitor? Who?"

No response.

"Winnifred? Winnifred?"

Jasmine walked into the room. Her flowerlike face was

drawn and thin, her hair pulled back tightly in a bun. She wore no makeup, tight white jeans, and a fitted white jacket. "I'm sorry to show up like this," she whispered. "But I had to come. You saw him last."

Abruptly, she fell into a chair and began to sob.

I limped over and bent over her awkwardly, patting her shoulder. "I feel so sorry for you, so sad," I said. "There was nothing anyone could do."

Her tearstained face looked up at me. "I have to know—was he in pain?"

"No, I don't think so."

Jasmine wiped her eyes, and I could see that she still wore the diamond engagement ring. "You know, I didn't take that letter seriously. Nobody did. All I can think of now is that maybe we should have."

"I don't think this was part of a conspiracy, Jasmine. There's no proof of that."

"Well, the autopsy confirmed he died from that— thing—he fell on." She could barely get out the words. "But why did he fall? You were there." She repeated the words, as if they would prove something to her, or force me to remember something I had overlooked. "I got another fax," she said finally. "It was Malik's obituary, from the *LA Times*. With a typewritten note that said *Who will be next?* I feel like I'm being watched. Or targeted. I'm frightened, Jordan, but I'm also angry. Malik would not want me to give in to this stalker."

"Stalker?"

"What else can it be? I wonder if that person was on the mountain when you took the hike. Following you. Watching. Waiting to find someone alone."

I took Jasmine's hand and held it tightly. "Jasmine, you will be fine. You are strong. And you have Noel Fisher,

who is now in charge of security for Paul. Ask Paul to
assign him to you full-time while you get through this.
We can trace these letters and faxes and put an end to
them."

She managed a brittle laugh. "I've seen Mr. Fisher. He
is hardly a bodyguard."

"Trust me, he's better than a bodyguard. He saved my
life. I have no doubt he could save yours if, God forbid,
the necessity arose. I'll call him myself."

"I'm handling the service," she said. "Malik's family—
well, the lawyers got his mother to sign the documents so
I can take care of things on her behalf. That's all that matters. There's going to be a memorial in LA, where he
lived, but no funeral. He'll be cremated. That's what he
would have wanted. Fire and passion—that's what my
Malik was all about, like the elements. That's how it
should be." She didn't cry or stumble as she spoke but
seemed to gain strength from her words. Jasmine had to
have a remarkable ability to regenerate herself.

Talking to Jasmine had unnerved me but also spurred me
to action. I resolved to find out who was behind the
wheel of the black Porsche—before she could find me
again.

The first thing I did was call Gale Lieber and ask her to
meet me as soon as she could. Her husband told me she
was officiating at a charity tournament for handicapped
kids at the Hyatt, and I arranged to meet her between
matches.

The grounds were crowded, children and their parents
swarming under the blue-and-white striped awnings. As
always in this type of event, the kids were an inspiration.
Gale had been one of the founders of the tournament, and

as we talked we were constantly interrupted by people asking her for information or getting her approval on details. Several big-name movie stars had come out to support the charity, and there was a happy buzz in the air—a marked contrast to the grim atmosphere in which I'd spent the past days.

I didn't want to keep Gale from the kids, so I got right down to business. "What do you know about Anna Martinez, the mother of the little girl who died in New York?" I asked. "You told me you had dropped by to talk to Artie and saw the little girl in his hotel room."

"Poor Artie," said Gale. "I can't believe what happened. But then, in a way, I can." She squinted at me from beneath her blue visor.

"What do you mean?"

"He was just so wrapped up in that child. He'd never had a family, you know, and I really think the little girl was a big part of his attraction to the mother. He was beyond the babe stage; he was interested in settling down. At least that's what he hinted to me. I think he saw this as his future. When the child died, everything died for Artie. The relationship with the mother fell apart, from what I understand, and I don't think he had much to live for."

"Did you ever talk to Anna herself?"

"Once, when I was delivering the car keys. She was very particular about the kind of car Artie was getting. I mean, she didn't want to accept the tournament car, which was a Taurus or something. We had to get him a particular car."

"What kind of car?"

"I think it was a BMW sports car. Something very fancy. Everybody was really furious, because it came out of the tournament budget. But Artie controlled Seranata Aziz, and she was our headliner. You know how these things go—if he wasn't happy, she wasn't happy, and if she wasn't happy, maybe we would have a bigger problem of some sort. Under the best of circumstances, Aziz is not easy. The car was sort of an insurance policy against problems with her, so we went along with it."

"Was it Artie or Anna who wanted the car?"

Gale waved across the court at a teenager in a motorized wheelchair who was moving along purposefully, her racket slung sportily across the handles of the chair. "Hard to tell. But Artie himself was usually a cream puff, so if somebody was making demands, I would bet it wasn't him."

"What was Anna like?"

"She stayed in the background, pretty much. Not a very visible member of the Aziz entourage. She's attractive, not young—I'd say early forties, dark curly hair, nicely dressed. The type that fits in. The kid was the sparkler. She was really cute. Such a damned shame."

"Terrible. Too many bad things are happening to good people. Do you know where Anna is now?"

"Sure."

I jolted to attention. Somehow I'd assumed Anna Martinez would have melted into the shadows of her grief.

"She's working this tournament. Contacted me to volunteer about two weeks ago. I thought, with Artie's passing and all, and coming right on the heels of her daughter's death, she wouldn't be coming. But she insisted. Some people—being busy is their way of dealing with grief. She might be over there, at the press desk."

"Do you have a phone number and address for her?"

Gale nodded. "On the computer at home, if you need it."

"Thanks, Gale."

I made my way to the press desk and recognized Anna Martinez immediately as the woman who had been driving the Porsche. She wore a name tag and was handing out blue-covered press kits to a group of sponsors that included, to my astonishment, Trent Byers.

Trent noticed me immediately. "Jordan! Great to see you!"

I kept one eye on Anna, who appeared not to see me. "Hello, Trent. Is BioTech a sponsor here?"

"We made a donation, but next year we'll have a product to give them. I was just talking to Gus about a line extension for the kids' market. Maybe some far-out flavors in neon colors. The potential is definitely there, and we'll be doing research. For now, I'm just checking out the event. Will you join me in our box? And maybe lunch later?"

"I'm in kind of a rush. Thanks, but I don't think so."

"Well, there's our box." He gestured. "Drop by."

I moved past him to Anna, who was checking off something on a clipboard with a tournament pen that hung from her neck. At last, she looked at me. She had huge charcoal-brown eyes, a long pointed chin, and a wide mouth. She wore no makeup, and her dark hair was tied up in a bandanna.

"Anna Martinez?" I asked.

"Yes. May I help you?"

"I believe we met. In a parking lot."

Her stare revealed nothing. "I don't recall."

"First, let me tell you that I am very sorry about what happened to your daughter, and I wish I could have been of some assistance. I received your fax. However, I really couldn't add anything to the situation."

She nodded. "I understand. But you do not. We must talk, you and I."

"We can talk right now, or I can wait till your break."

"Now is fine. I'll just leave these press kits in a stack." She got up and we left the tennis area, passed the landscaped entrance to the hotel, and went into the hotel lobby, where there was an indoor atrium furnished with chairs and tables.

"Anna, I have to tell you," I began, "everyone is sympathetic to your tragic situation. But your letters and faxes are frightening people. And that scene in the parking lot, what was that all about?"

"Everyone *should* be frightened. Especially you."

"It's not right, Anna. Especially under the circumstances. Two people have died in the last week. Everyone is very edgy."

"Those were not accidents," she insisted. "I warned everyone."

"Artie committed suicide. Malik had a fall."

"It is all connected. I am sure of it. That's why I sent those letters and faxes. My poor little girl got in the way of the plot. They killed her."

"Anna," I said gently, "tell me why you think this."

"My daughter was in perfect health until she started being with Art. It's my fault, I brought her to him. And then she became interested in tennis, and then she was dead. Artie also. Tennis was his world, and now he is dead. And Malik. Football players are not dying. Soccer players are healthy. Only the tennis players and those around them are being struck down. It must be a plot."

The woman was irrational, but I hoped she might shed some light on Artie's suicide. "Why did Artie die?"

"The same forces made him take his own life. They as good as killed him."

"When did you speak to him last?"

"The day before he died. He was working on a product endorsement. It was evil. It promoted tennis. That's why he died."

"You mean the BioTech product? The man you were just talking to at the desk?"

"Yes. He is a very evil man." She leaned in closer to me. "I think he's in on the plot. So did Artie. He told me so."

"But Artie was working with him."

"Until he found out he was in on the plot. Then he wanted to quit."

"And what about the obituary Jasmine received? Didn't you realize how frightened and upset that would make her?"

Anna was resolute. "She needs to be frightened. Then she will pay attention."

"Mrs. Martinez, some people would call your actions harassment. Charges could be filed."

She crossed her arms defensively. "I am not hurting anyone. I am performing a public service. They should thank me. No one should have to lose a loved one—or a daughter. I only want to save lives."

"Mrs. Martinez," I said, trying to get her to grasp some level of reason, "I must ask you, have you seen a therapist, discussed your grief with a professional?"

"You are an arrogant woman. I had hoped you would help. That was why I came to you in the parking lot. But one look at you and I knew. I looked at you and I said to myself, 'Because she is on television, she assumes she is right.' I could see it on your face, and I see it again here, that you think I'm crazy. You diminish my daughter's death with such thoughts. You will see that it is I who is in the right. Your fame will be your downfall, Jordan Myles. Fame, youth, strength, talent, innocence—none of it matters to them." She turned and walked away from me. "I tried to help you, alert you, and the others. I hope it isn't too late for you," she hissed over her shoulder.

I got up. "Just a minute, Mrs. Martinez. I want to tell you that you can have your opinions, but you have got to stop spreading these faxes around. I don't want you around me or my car or my associates or my clients. You're frightening people, intruding on their lives, making them uncomfortable. If you persist, I will have to do something about it. And I will."

She looked at me pityingly. "You know nothing." Then she darted off across the lobby. The automatic glass doors opened and she kept going, shouldering her way past a bellman with a cart full of luggage and running across the driveway toward the tennis complex.

EIGHT

That evening, the Fish arrived back at the Springs to take charge of security arrangements for Malik's memorial and keep an eye on Jasmine. I went to his villa, where he had ordered in a complete steak dinner from one of the local restaurants, including a baked potato and side order of spinach for me.

"This is food," he said, slicing into the steak with relish. "So now I'm officially bicoastal. Paul Kessler got me a nice little apartment in Brentwood, not far from his office, and of course I'm keeping the place in Brooklyn." He dumped about a third of a bottle of ketchup over the steak and tasted it. "Better. You'll have to come and see the place. It's furnished. Didn't even have to buy a fork."

"I may visit sooner than you think," I said. "I really need to talk to Paul about Anna Martinez."

"The mother."

"She's really over the edge. I saw her today at a kids' benefit. She talked like a crazy woman about plots against the tennis community and how everybody had better watch out."

"What do we know about her?" The Fish took a butter pat and smeared it on top of the steak and ketchup. "It was dry," he explained.

136

"She was Artie Lutz's girlfriend; she traveled with him and the Aziz entourage; she was known to be demanding and seems to like fancy foreign sports cars. I really don't know how she supports herself now, or what she did before Artie. We need to find out. And I don't know anything about the little girl's father. That could figure in."

The Fish nodded as he chewed. "I already checked her out through my channels. She has no criminal record; she's just an average citizen. But then, I always say, that's the most dangerous kind. Criminals, you get a pattern of behavior. You can type them, sometimes even predict them. But ordinary Joes? It's a crap shoot. I'll take the criminal any day."

"I confronted her and it did no good. She only got worse."

The Fish laughed. "You could always have her on your show—interrogate her on the air."

"I could, except they canceled me off my own show."

"No! How could they do that?" The Fish's fork paused in midair.

"Too much negative press about the Schidor boys and Malik at the clinic, I guess. Or maybe they just wanted a ratings queen, somebody with a higher Q score—that's a personality awareness rating, to you. Guys like Bill Cosby have high Q scores. People like me barely register on the scale. So they're going to pay off my contract and keep me on commentary, and that's the end of my brilliant career as a show host."

"I guess it's a good thing you didn't quit your day job," the Fish noted philosophically.

"I guess I'll have a little free time," I said. "I was thinking, maybe I'll come into LA and we could do a little looking around about Anna Martinez. She's so unstable, she could go off at anybody anytime. And I'm at the top of her list, right up there with your new client."

The Fish sighed. "What do you mean 'we'? This kind of thing always gets you in the hospital. Or worse, me."

"We're not talking about solving a murder here," I pointed out. "We just need to find out where this woman is coming from. What if she pulls something during the memorial service?"

"Well," the Fish said finally, mopping his plate with a piece of garlic bread. "I got a sofa bed."

After dinner, the Fish dropped me off at my house. The lights were on; Gus had let himself in with his key.

"Did you feed A.M.?" I asked. A.M. stood on her hind legs for an ear scratch.

"Oops . . . sorry," Gus answered from the couch, where he was entrenched in a football game.

I went outside to the patio where I keep the dog food dishes and slid open the glass door. The food bowl was full. "What is it, girl, no appetite?" I bent over and shook the bowl, but then I noticed that the food pellets weren't the same size as those I kept in the house. A.M.'s dog chow was tiny pellets of lamb and rice. These were larger, much larger.

"Are you sure you didn't bring some new food for the dog?" I asked Gus.

He shook his head.

"This isn't her regular chow." I sniffed it, but it had no particular smell. Maybe Winnifred had stopped by with something new, which would be a mistake. A.M. has a very particular digestive system that does not respond well to changes in her routine. I called Winnifred at home.

"No, dear," she said. "I didn't take care of A.M. today. Remember, this is my manicure day, and then I had coupons to clip. It's food day in the newspaper."

"Oh, yes, right, Winnifred. Thanks anyhow."

I hung up. A.M. was dancing around at my feet, but I didn't want to put the dog dish down. Something didn't feel right. I shook the pellets into a Baggie and put the bowl into the dishwasher. I didn't want to be paranoid about this, but then again there seemed to be some justification for paranoia these days. It occurred to me that someone might have tampered with my dog's food. Maybe I was overreacting, but I felt I had to know. When it comes to A.M., I don't take chances.

"Gus," I said, "do you think the guys at the BioTech lab could run a check on dog food?"

"They'll think you're crazy," Gus grumbled. "What exactly are you doing, checking out the nutritional content of Kibbles 'n Bits?"

"I don't like the way this food mysteriously appeared on my patio. Can I FedEx this to somebody in R and D at BioTech?"

"Actually, I'll see Trent tomorrow at the ad agency presentation, and I was meaning to ask you if you'd come with me. We can give it to him then to pass on to the lab. The clinic's not too busy right now. About half of our clients have canceled, as you may have noticed. I thought you might be able to get away—it's better than sitting around here dwelling on Malik. Besides, it should be interesting. They've done some music tracks, and it's a creative meeting."

"This could work out. I was thinking of going into LA anyhow, to take care of some other things." I decided not to mention that I was going to drop in on Paul Kessler, and I certainly intended to avoid telling him that the Fish and I were going to do a little research on Anna Martinez. That would be like tossing gasoline onto a bonfire.

"The meeting's from one to three. I'd like to leave here no later than ten. Unless, of course, you're busy with your show."

"Fine." I figured I could ride in with Gus, attend the meeting with him, then swing by to pick up my truck—which was still at the Santa Monica airport. "And my show won't be a conflict anymore. I'm off it." I pulled back the fire screen and lit a gas log. I much prefer real wood fires, but I never have time to let them burn out before I have to leave and do something else, which in my mind would result in a flash fire.

"You're off the show? When did this happen?"

"As soon as it was a big hit in the ratings. I found out this morning. I guess they want it to be a bigger hit, so they're bringing in a bigger name."

Gus looked at me sympathetically. "I'm sorry to hear that, because I know it was important to you. But maybe there's a silver lining in this."

"Such as?"

He motioned for me to sit beside him on the couch. "This horrible string of deaths has made me rethink a lot of things. What about you?"

"I suppose I have. But what do you mean?"

"Our priorities have been pretty screwed up, when you think about it. Work, work, and more work."

"That's been your mantra, Gus."

"Well, I want to tell you it's a mistake. You have to think about your personal happiness—having a family, things you can't put off forever."

"But I don't think it would be fair to have a child and then spend all your time on your career. I know that's not what I would want to do. And between your work at the Springs and your private practice and your books, you don't have much room."

Gus took my hand. "You're right. That's the same conclusion I came to myself. What would you say if I told you I'm thinking about resigning from the Springs?"

I was stunned. "I wouldn't believe it. You and Bill were the two original founders. This place is your dream. Why would you walk away?"

"Some things are more important. That's why I'm devoting so much of my energy to the Duration line. Once it's established, it's turnkey. I'll get a royalty every year; all I'll have to do is sit back and collect a check. Then I can concentrate on the things that are really important—my research, my writing, and, I hope, when the time comes, my family." He had a sly smile on his face as he dropped the last words, and they hung in the air waiting for my response.

I swallowed hard. "Well, I hope you get what you want. You're right about one thing. What we've gone through recently only reminds me that there's just one life here for each of us, and we don't want to waste it, or any part of it. But Gus, without the clinic, are you sure you wouldn't be bored? I mean, this place has been such a big part of your life."

He waved a hand. "I've thought it through, actually. The great thing about getting into the world of product development is that once you have a successful product in the marketplace you can build on it. The first product is just the cornerstone of a successful franchise. And what we do now involves one hundred percent of our personal attention every day. There's no letup, no incremental reward. A licensing fee on a product—or, better still, a *line* of products—well, that's another story." He paused to drape the chenille throw from the back of the couch across my shoulders. "It's chilly in here."

"When I'm out, I keep the heat off. It takes a while to warm up."

"So tell me, are you warming to what I've been saying, Jordan? There's a real future for both of us, as a team."

"We've always been a team. That's why I came here, Gus, to be with you. This is *our* clinic." I could barely imagine that Gus would actually consider leaving this place, which had been so hard-won. But there had been a time when I thought his idea for this very clinic had been an unachievable fantasy. Gus is a dreamer, but he has an uncanny ability to make his dreams reality—and bring other people along with him. In many ways, I had hitch-hiked on his dreams to get where I was today. He had taken me, a physically broken ex–tennis player, and showed me how to reinvent my life, give it new meaning. I knew better than to question Gus's dreams. On the one hand, I should be more open to his new plans than I had been. If he was thinking of leaving the Springs, I knew it was time to listen much more seriously. On the other hand, I had my own career to think of. I'd fought so hard for it—first, to become a physical therapist and then to make some kind of mark in the media. I didn't see how I could do everything, at least not now, when I was par-ticularly vulnerable. I didn't want to make any decisions for the wrong reasons.

"Now that you see how strongly I feel about this,

Jordan, I hope you'll be part of it with me," Gus said. He rubbed my head gently, and I closed my eyes. "But I promise I won't pressure you. You'll have to make your own decision—which you always do anyhow."

"Thanks, Gus," I whispered.

We spent the night together.

McMurray and Krone, the advertising agency, was in Venice, about four blocks from the beach. From the front entrance it seemed more like an airplane hangar than a place of business. The building was a vast warehouse of galvanized steel. We walked through the front door and into a soaring three-story concrete atrium. A waterfall, flat and smooth as a thirty-foot wide satin ribbon, flowed noiselessly down one entire wall, making it seem like a living thing. The elevator door was covered in spray-painted graffiti, including the words STARK NAKED.

"It's supposedly a very trendy agency," Gus informed me. "We're lucky they took us on with a new product. It's risky for them. But they wanted to get into sports products. They have their eye on Nike."

A voice on the intercom directed us to the conference room on the third floor. It was more like a large loft, with bare wood floors, whitewashed walls, and exposed pipes. The electronics, however, were clearly state of the art. An oversized video screen was embedded in one wall, and there was an extensive control booth at one end of the room. A dazzling array of fruits, cheeses, and cut vegetables was laid out on a pine table. Gus and I were met immediately by Trent, who for today's meeting was creatively attired in jeans, a T-shirt, a sport coat, and ostrich cowboy boots.

Introductions were made and the meeting convened. Elvis Krone, the ad agency's head creative director, was a tall man with a platinum-blond buzz cut and an earring. Four of his staffers flanked him across the table from Trent, Gus, and me.

"I'm not going to go into an elaborate preamble," he said. "We prefer to let the work speak for itself. We've done a lot of work since the initial storyboards. We've made some changes. Unfortunately, we didn't have time to reedit the footage you're about to see to take out Malik's scenes. I'm sure you understand. Of course, when we find a new personality to replace him, we will shoot new footage.

"What we have here is what we call a rip-o-matic. We've ripped off existing footage from on-air commercials, matches, video, and other sources and pieced it together to a music track so you can get an idea of how the finished spot will flow. This is not the footage we'll be using—we'll ultimately be shooting much of it from scratch—although it would be great to have some of the actual match action scenes. Those can't be re-created. Remember, this is a new product launch. We have to come out with all guns blasting to be heard in the marketplace. We need to make a preemptive strike!" He signaled someone hidden behind the glass in the control booth. "Luther, hit it!"

The lights dimmed and an ominous music track came up. Then images of tennis players came on the video screen in a fast-paced montage cut to the music. There was a cutaway to Malik, kissing Jasmine in the marriage proposal, lifted from my show. There was footage of me at Wimbledon and at the U.S. Open. There were some shots of the Schidor brothers at the French. And there was a clip of Jasmine from the Australian, and a shot of Seranata, holding her trophy aloft. Intercut were shots of the product line, of Malik chugging the drink, and a chant of the product name, "Du-ra-tion!" At the end, there was a clip of me talking about the role of sports nutrition, also taken from my show, then back to the montage of various players until the picture froze on a shot of Malik, swooping at the camera like a bat, and the theme line *Go the Duration!* scrawled on in handwriting.

The lights came up.

"Of course, as I said, we'll be replacing that last shot and all the others of Malik," Elvis explained. "Not to be disrespectful, but as a matter of necessity, we are in the process of signing a suitable replacement. Paul Kessler is helping us find somebody, and we've also been in touch with the Global Sport Agency. Now, this is a work session, so—any questions?"

"I've got one," I said. "Why is there all that footage of me in your commercial?"

Elvis looked perplexed. "You're one of our key spokespeople."

"I am?" I shot a look at Gus. "I'm thinking about getting involved, Elvis, but I have not committed yet. This is great, but it's premature on my end."

"Gus?" said Trent quizzically.

"I thought it would be good for Jordan to see how she fit into the scheme of the commercial," Gus explained, looking straight at me. "As you can see, Jordan, you lend a lot of credibility, especially in the sports issues Q and A."

"Why couldn't *you* go on camera and talk about that,

Gus?" I questioned. "You're certainly as qualified as I am. More so."

"I don't have your high profile, Jordan."

"But you're a doctor."

"Too medical," Elvis cut in. "People don't want to take medicine. They want to have the energy and strength to 'Go the Duration.' For the infomercial, he'd be a great guest. And you two have marvelous chemistry."

It was getting confusing. "For the infomercial?" I asked. I turned back to Gus and leaned over. "I thought I said I didn't want to do an infomercial. And I don't recall agreeing to be in the commercial either," I whispered.

My obvious discomfort seemed to cast an air of hesitancy around the table.

"I'll tell you what. Elvis, let's immediately go back into the studio and replace the shots of Malik and give Jordan a copy of the tape so she can run this at home and think about it," Trent suggested. "Looking at that footage of the unfortunate guy is even upsetting *me*." He cleared his throat. "The work itself is great, very nice. But this was perhaps not the best timing, considering the circumstances."

Everyone filed out of the room, leaving Gus and me alone, still sitting at the conference table. Gus drummed his fingers on the steel tabletop. "So how did I end up in the cast for this thing?" I said.

"They explained it wasn't final, Jordan," Gus explained. "It was just to give you an idea of what it would be like."

"Well, I don't think I like it."

"You know, now that you don't have *Woman/Sport* anymore, you could use the visibility. The situation has changed for you. Have you thought about that?"

"I'm just not a pitchperson, Gus. It takes a certain type of person, and I don't see myself as that type."

"Can't you get beyond yourself here and look at it as building a business—together?"

"Was there some reason why it has to be me in that commercial? Jasmine and Malik I could understand, they were such a hot couple. And Seranata. She's a great champion. Where do I fit in? I just don't get the persistence here. There are lots of other more prominent personalities in tennis."

Gus stood up. "Well, maybe you're right. Without your show as a platform, you may have less appeal to consumers. They'd want to test that. And with Malik's death, things are in a state of flux. I'm sure we'll be rethinking the entire promotion strategy. Let's go. I'll drive you to your truck. We're just fifteen minutes from the Santa Monica airport."

"Can we do one thing first?" I asked.

"What?"

"I need to talk to Trent."

We went out into the hall.

"Trent," I said, "I'd like to apologize for not sounding more enthusiastic. This all came as quite a surprise, that's all. I have to give it some thought."

He smiled with understanding. "Of course. I should have walked you through all this beforehand. Maybe invited you to a couple of our focus groups. You'd be impressed to see how women age twenty to forty respond to you—you're a very popular personality. You're perceived as being much more of an authority figure and role model than most women in sports. They remember your comeback from that horrible accident and respect you for it. You'd be pleased."

"Well, that's very flattering. Trent, do you think you could do a favor for me, please? It's something important to me."

"Of course. The sky's the limit. We'll make it top priority. Dean!" He motioned to an assistant, who jumped to attention. "Listen to this. Whatever she wants, get it done."

I reached into my bag, pulled out the plastic bag of dog food, and handed it to Dean. "I need a scientific lab analysis of this as soon as possible."

Dean stared at the bag. "What is it?"

"Either Kibbles 'n Bits or Purina Dog Chow, I'm not sure."

Dean's eyelids half closed. I could tell he thought his career had sunk to a new low, but he pulled himself together. "I'll get right on it."

"Don't let anybody eat it."

"Somehow, I don't think that will be a problem."

I had left my truck in a parking lot across the street from a little café that bordered the runway called the Spitfire Grill, where I had arranged to meet the Fish. After Gus dropped me off, I sat at one of the tables in the little outdoor area, ordered an Evian, no ice, and watched the planes land and take off. (Not that I'm picky, but I don't see the point of drinking pure water when you have no idea where the ice comes from.) This was the runway used for private planes, corporate flights, and charters, and there were a number of Lears, G-2's, and even a news helicopter to see. The clientele was a mixture of airport types and screenwriters in jeans and the occasional executive in a suit and tie. I sipped my drink and tried to sort things out. Maybe Gus was right and I was resisting something that could be right for me, or at least not giving it a fair chance. On the other hand, maybe it was time for my life to take an entirely different course. Perhaps I should assume a less prominent profile and concentrate on my personal life rather than my career. Ever since I'd first picked up a tennis racket, my personal life had taken a backseat. Everything in me had always been directed toward, first, my tennis game and, later, my degrees, my work at the clinic, and, most recently, my media work. In the back of my mind, in spite of all our differences, I'd always thought that Gus and I would end up together because we were kindred spirits. Our life and work were so commingled they were one. We fought a lot, but so much of our conflict was over professional, not personal, issues. I wondered what would happen if we could relate just as two people, without all the other baggage. Or maybe we *were* all the other baggage.

I was on my second bottle of Evian when the Fish ambled over. He was wearing pants and a sport coat of two different blues and carrying a battered leather briefcase, which he heaved onto the table with a thud. "Sorry I'm late," he huffed, mopping his brow. "I'm still not used to the freeways. I meant to take the Santa Monica cutoff but I ended up on the ten, headed into Santa Monica. If there's that big a difference, they ought to mark it on the signs. Anyhow, I ended up at the ocean. Had to backtrack. But here I am. And I got some info on Anna Martinez."

"I can always count on you," I said, smiling because it was an understatement.

The Fish snapped open his briefcase and pulled out a yellow legal pad. "Here it is. Anna Martinez. Formerly Anna Lombardi until her marriage to Leo Martinez six years ago. He was in the army and died in a training accident in Texas. She had the kid and moved to LA. Got a job at Jake's Luxury Car Rental. There she meets Artie Lutz. I guess he was renting a car and she was the agent. They get friendly, and eventually she quits to travel with him on the tour. Takes the kid with them. Then the kid dies and they break up. End of story."

"She worked at the car rental place?"

"For close to a year."

"It seems she had a thing for nice cars, maybe that's why. Any strange behavior before this?"

"Funny you should ask. When her husband died, she sued the U.S. Army and actually got a settlement. She's a litigious type. At least it pays off for her."

"Well, that accounts for her attitude of somebody's-got-to-pay. But what about sending this string of letters and faxes and following me? That is very threatening behavior, as you pointed out."

"Can't say at the moment. But like I say, there's always a reason—we just don't know it yet."

The waitress delivered our check. The Fish paid and got the receipt and change. "I always deduct these things," he said and started to tuck it into his pocket. "Wait a minute." He looked at the receipt. "Check this."

I took the receipt and noticed something written on it:

Go to hangar #7. Urgent. T.

"T . . . Trent? Could it be Trent? What's he doing here? He's the guy from BioTech I just met with. He sent their plane for me when Malik died, but I didn't see him here today. He didn't mention coming here, and this is a pretty small place. It would be tough to miss him."

The Fish quizzed the waitress, who swore nobody had touched the check, but then she hadn't picked up the change right away and the cashier's counter was crowded—a lot of people this time of day, the start of Happy Hour. She couldn't say anything for sure. Anybody could have written this note.

"Well, just to be sure, where is hangar number seven?" I asked.

"Just a minute, I'll ask one of the pilots." She returned in a few minutes with directions. "Through that parking lot and take a left. It's toward the end of the runway, the southwest end."

"That could be where they keep the BioTech plane," I said. "I only saw it when I was ready to get on, never at the hangar."

We walked over to the hangar, which was one of many scattered across the area adjacent to the runway. Planes periodically roared by, taking off or landing, as we checked the hangar numbers.

We had almost reached the end of the runway when I saw it. "Here it is," I said. "Number seven. But it's closed and padlocked."

"I'll check the back," said the Fish.

"This doesn't seem right," I said. I stepped back to get a wider view of the hangar and suddenly the engine whine of a small jet taking off got closer and closer as it headed toward the end of the runway. Almost before I could take it in and process it as something that was happening, the plane veered sharply off the marked path of the runway and headed straight toward me. In less than an instant, I knew there was no place to run or dodge, no time to get out of the way. I threw myself on the ground and tried to fuse with the pavement, making my body as flat as possible as the jet's engines screamed over my head, the wind whipping my shirt and hair at what felt like hurricane force. It was like a nightmare beast unleashed, coming and coming—and then, in the flash of a moment before it seemed destined to slam into my body and on into the hangar itself, the jet lifted sharply and hurtled upward at almost a 90-degree angle, roaring over my head as I pressed my cheek into the rough concrete, covering my head and ears with my hands and arms. And then, just as quickly, it was gone, turning left in a shallow bank, cutting over the top of the Spitfire Grill, the noise evaporating, a cloak of the smell of jet fuel hanging in the air around me.

"Jordan, what was that?" The Fish came pounding from around the back of the hangar.

I lay on the ground for a few moments, my heart pounding. Then I sat up slowly. My face was scratched with gravel, and it stung when I touched it. My fingertips were wet with blood when I looked at them. I was going to have a nasty scab.

"What happened?" He squinted into the sky.

I wondered if my knees could take my weight, I was so unsteady. "I think he was aiming for me," I said shakily. "But if he hit me, he would have run dead on into the hangar and blown us all to smithereens, so he pulled up instead. Maybe I'm paranoid, but that's what it seemed like."

We walked slowly back through the parking lot. My ears were still ringing from the engine noise.

"You think that was your friend Trent?" said the Fish.

"I can't imagine it. If so, he never tried to fly the plane when I was on it. That note was just somebody's way of luring us over."

"How did anyone know you were here, and that you had met with Trent?"

"They would have had to be at the meeting and followed me. There's no other way."

"Was that the BioTech plane?"

"I don't really know. I didn't look that closely at the plane when I was on it. They looked similar, but to me a private jet's a private jet."

"Well, this is an airport," the Fish stated. "Let's see what the tower has to say."

We located the administration building and I ducked into a ladies' room to take care of my face. I splashed water onto my cheek and gingerly blotted it with a paper towel. The entire area between the top of my right cheekbone and my mouth looked like raw hamburger—a nasty abrasion, too big for a Band-Aid. I would have to pick up some ointment, gauze, and tape. But that could wait.

First I told my story to the airport manager, a middle-aged guy in a sport coat and tie who listened and then asked, "Were you on an active runway?"

"No, we were standing by hangar number seven."

"Did you get the tail number of the plane?"

The Fish and I looked at each other. I'd had my head buried face down, and he had been on the wrong side of the hangar. "No, we didn't," I admitted.

"It was a white jet with engines on the side and back, very sleek, with a T-tail," said the Fish.

"What was the takeoff time?"

"About five-fifteen," said the Fish.

"Let me check with the tower." He peered at my face. "You okay?"

"Fine. I'll take care of it shortly."

He disappeared. "Do you think he believed me?" I asked the Fish.

"He doesn't have to. The tower maintains a record of every plane that takes off."

Five minutes later, the manager reappeared. "There was a Cessna Citation, tail number N7864 Tango, that took off at that time," he said. "That plane would fit your description. It took off VFR at thirty-five hundred feet at full power. The pilot was taking off at a forty-five-degree angle over the golf course for noise abatement purposes and reported a temporary loss of power in one engine, which was probably why the plane seemed to be so low. It was unfortunate, but I wouldn't take it personally. And in future, I wouldn't be sightseeing so close to an active runway. That isn't the Santa Monica bike path out there. You know, a few years ago somebody got it in their head to have a hangar party, and, after a few beers and what-not, a guy had a fight with his girlfriend and stormed out onto the runway and was actually hit by a plane that was landing. Instant decapitation. I don't want to scare you, but these things happen when people get careless." I felt as if he were reprimanding a schoolchild for playing in the parking lot.

"I wasn't on an active runway. That plane tried to run me down, or at least tried to give me a good scare, which it accomplished."

He shrugged. "I'm sorry. My best advice is, stay off the runway."

"Is N7864 Tango the BioTech plane?"

"No, it was a leased plane, belonging to Executive

Charters. The tower didn't say who the lessee was, although there's a record if you really need to know."

"I do really need to know."

"Give me your card, and I'll look into the log and get back to you."

We exchanged cards, and as we walked back to the car I asked the Fish if he thought the pilot had tried to kill me.

"Nah. A jet plane is rarely anybody's choice of a murder weapon. One, it's too big to hide afterward and, two, it's impractical; how many people know how to use them? But what about this Trent guy whose initial was on the note?"

I pulled out my cell phone and Trent's business card and dialed his office. He answered on the second ring.

I tried to sound casual. "Hi, Trent. It's Jordan. I was just wondering if—you found out anything about the dog food yet."

"Not yet, Jordan. Traffic was bad. I just got back to the office about a half hour ago."

"Thanks, Trent. I—was just curious." I hung up. "Obviously, he wasn't at the controls of that plane or even on it. I know where his offices are. In rush-hour traffic, I don't think he could have gotten back there by now if he'd followed me to the Spitfire Grill."

"That leaves everybody else," said the Fish. "It should be easy enough to find out who the pilot was and who the plane belongs to. They keep records."

"What about Anna Martinez?"

"You think she can pilot a jet?"

"No. But we know she can write a note. Let's pick up my truck and pay her a visit. I got her address from Gale Lieber."

"What about your face?" said the Fish. "It looks like it smarts."

"We'll swing by a Seven-Eleven and pick up a little Bactine. I'll live."

NINE

According to Gale's records, Anna Martinez lived in a guest house in Westwood not far from UCLA. The main house belonged to a European soccer star who was rarely there but employed a fleet of housekeepers, gardeners, and maintenance workers to keep the house and grounds in shape. Such guest houses are coveted properties in the LA area, usually available only by word of mouth within certain circles. Rents are often ridiculously low, with the unwritten agreement that the renter will watch the owner's main property or pets or run small errands in return. The soccer star had been a friend of Artie's, and Artie had gotten the guest house for Anna.

The house was not gated, and the guest house was accessible by a bougainvillea-covered driveway alongside the main house. It had obviously been a garage at one time, but it was nevertheless charming, with pink stucco walls and a roof overgrown with flowered vines. It backed onto a large yard with an illuminated lap pool that shimmered in the night.

The lights were out except for one in a back room. The front door was standing open, and when I looked in as I knocked, I could see that the curtains had been taken down and moving boxes were piled everywhere.

"Anna?" I called. "Anna, it's Jordan Myles."

There was no answer. "What do you think?" I asked the Fish.

"I think she's moving."

"Well, that much is obvious."

"Maybe there's a forwarding address on one of those boxes. She might already be there."

From across the yard I heard a door slam. Anna ran out of the main house and across the lawn toward us, her hair flying. It was dark in the yard, but as she got closer I could see something glinting in her hand.

The Fish put his hand to his chest. Inside his jacket, I knew, was a gun in a shoulder holster.

"Anna!" I yelled. "Stop! It's Jordan. I don't mean to intrude, but I need to talk to you!"

She ran under a floodlight and I could see that the glinting object was a large pair of shears. I braced myself for the confrontation as she stopped a few feet away. "Why are you here?" was all she said. She wore a night-gown and looked very disheveled.

"This is Mr. Fisher," I said, indicating the Fish, whose hand was still on his shirt. "He works with me. A few hours ago, someone put me in a very dangerous situation, and since you had warned me that I was in danger, I thought you might help me find out why."

Anna made a brittle, hard sound. "Ha! If I knew, I would kill them myself, like they killed my child." She waved the shears, and for an instant I flinched. "Excuse me, I'm in the middle of packing. I just went to the house over there to get some scissors to cut the packing tape. I am forced to move. The lease was in Art's name, and the owner is reclaiming this guest house for his sister." Her voice dropped to a murmur. "Just as well. There are too many memories."

"Mrs. Martinez, I have to wonder, what exactly makes you think there is a plot at work?" the Fish asked.

Her eyes blazed from the shadows. "I knew it immediately. Nobody wanted me to ask any questions about my baby's death, and I am the mother. Everybody wanted me to take a pill and be quiet. My baby was a healthy girl. She never even had a cold. All she wanted was to be a tennis player, like Seranata. And she died for no reason, and suddenly they come up with this so-called heart problem? I say, what heart problem? Something killed her, and it was not her heart. And then all the others. The ones who got sick. The ones who died. And Art. Art killed himself because he couldn't live with knowing I had been right. Yes, I was right, and I am warning those of you who were there that night—you are being watched and you will be hunted." Her face crumpled. "Go, please. I have to finish my packing. The movers come tomorrow morning. I am putting everything in storage and moving to the Highland Apartment Hotel. You can call me there." She swept past us and slammed the door. Inside, some more lights went on, and a radio came on full blast.

The Fish motioned to the walkway and we left.

"You were right, she's crazy," he said. "I think she believes what she's saying, though. She never varies."

"You know, there may not be this nutty master plot, but she may very well be involved in whatever it is. Who's with Jasmine?"

"One of my best men. She'll be okay."

"Can you get somebody to track Anna for a while, at least a few days?"

"Sure."

"Tomorrow morning I think we should talk to Paul and see if he can give us some resources to look into all this. And I'll talk to Gus and Bill. In fact, I'll see if I can call them from the truck."

The Fish led the way to his place, and I followed in the truck. I called in for my messages and was surprised that Winnifred picked up the phone.

"It's almost six-thirty," I said. "Why are you working so late?"

"Dear, it's been a very busy evening," she said. "What with the news."

"News? What news?"

"Dr. Laidlaw's announcement that he's leaving the company."

"What?" I wondered if I'd heard correctly.

Winnie chattered on. "Of course I'm sure he told you. But everyone else is buzzing around in a tizzy!"

"When did he make the announcement?"

"Mr. Stokes called a meeting at five. He read a letter from Dr. Laidlaw, who wasn't there himself. Dear, I don't mean to criticize, but I think things would have gone much more smoothly if he'd served a little something to the group. I mean, it was after five. A little nip might have taken the edge off, don't you think?" Her voice seemed to be getting louder.

"I can hear you, Winnifred. You don't need to shout. I guess I need to get back to you."

"Is there anything you want me to do?"

"No. Not right now." I hung up, more stunned than I had been when the jet dive-bombed me. Gus was leaving. He'd hinted, but he hadn't told me. Nor had Bill. How long had they both known about this? Was Gus so certain of my disapproval that he had decided to leave me in the dark until after the fact? *Had* I become so disapproving? Driving along, following the Fish's taillights, I knew two things:

I had never felt less secure about my safety and my future.

I had never felt so alone.

TEN

"It's obvious," the Fish said, as I sat on his couch, staring unenthusiastically at three remaining slices of triple-cheese pizza he had ordered from Domino's, which had congealed into a vulcanized state. "Gus Laidlaw didn't want you there when they announced he was leaving. He knew you weren't going to be there; he arranged it that way. He wasn't there himself. Who knows why, and does it matter? The fact is, the guy's leaving. Deal from the top of that deck."

"I can't imagine the clinic without Gus. He's always been the backbone of the entire operation." I hoped I didn't sound morose.

"That's what they said about George Washington. But the country managed without him." The Fish reached for a piece of pizza and handed it to me. It was rock hard, like a corpse after rigor mortis had set in, and I recoiled. "Do you mind? I hate to waste food." He retracted the pizza and stuffed it into his mouth.

"Choose your poison. What happened to your organic diet?"

I looked around the room. It was a typical residential apartment hotel suite, the kind you rent by the week or

162

month: brown industrial carpet, beige walls, and a step-up dining area with a wooden railing that led to a small kitchenette. The living room featured a television in a simple pine cabinet and a gas-log fireplace with a glass screen. Behind the beige curtains were sliding glass doors that led to a balcony that was never used. It was a perfect environment for the Fish.

"He wanted me to join him in a new venture he's been working on, but I wasn't sure I wanted to get involved. Not that it wasn't a good idea. I just wasn't sure it was right for me. I guess he'd really made his decision. He was obviously farther along that continuum than I realized. Anyhow, maybe he didn't want me raining on his parade—probably figured I'd try to talk him out of it. He's actually a very nonconfrontational person. I'm sure that's why he wasn't at the announcement himself."

"Would you have tried to talk him out of it?"

"I don't think so. He'd hinted to me about it before, and I never put down the idea. What he does with his life is his decision. And there was a lot of money involved—major seven figures. Probably too much money to dilute his efforts and attention."

The Fish nodded as he chewed. "There's a certain logic to that. Maybe he was being generous, offering to cut you in."

"Oh, no question he was. The money in endorsements is huge."

"How much can these people make?"

"Well, it depends on your appeal and what you've done. On the high end, look at the golfer Tiger Woods—sixty million from Nike for endorsing their products, and he was barely in his twenties and had turned pro about thirty seconds before he made the deal. These days, anything less than five hundred thousand is considered paltry in the endorsement arena for a star. And then there's the perks. For instance, the sponsor can set you up in an office, give you a car, or let you fly on the corporate jet."

"Like the BioTech jet."

"Exactly. Some celebrity endorsers have arrangements where they never have to fly commercial for the term of their deal. The company just sends the jet."

"That didn't appeal to you?"

"Well, there were other issues involved."

"Such as?"

"They wanted me to endorse the product, but since this was a product that was Gus's invention, he stood to do much better than just an endorsement fee. He'd get a percentage of the profits and a piece of the business. So it was more meaningful to him. I was just going to be a pitchperson. On infomercials." I sighed. "I don't know. Maybe I'm a purist, but it seemed like selling out for me to endorse a product that way. I mean, what would my clients think? And, true, the money was nice, but I'm not starving. On the other hand, to Gus, it seemed like my TV show was the real sellout, a commercial prostitution." I laughed. "At least he can't criticize that anymore."

"He criticized you?"

"Well, he seemed very pressured by all this." I tried to explain. "It really upset him when I wouldn't agree to work with him, so I think he sort of retaliated by criticizing my show." I sighed. "Bottom line: The whole thing was petty, on both our parts."

"So what are you going to do?"

"I'm going to see what happens. I don't have to do anything. I have clients to worry about and a full schedule through the summer. Then I'll reassess the situation."

"Wait and see. That's usually a foolproof strategy." The Fish nodded, stretching out on the velour couch.

"I know it's a major benefit to be brought in on a situation like this—there are lots of athletes and personalities, particularly women, who would jump at it. He's offering me a big consideration. But then I do bring something to the party besides my relationship with Gus. I mean, I was a world-class tennis player and I'm also a physical therapist and a TV personality. I have a few credentials of my own. That all has to count for something." I feigned a confidence I didn't completely feel.

"Bingo," said the Fish.

"What?"

"You just said it."

"Said what?"

"Why he got petty. He couldn't replace you. In certain respects, you're sui generis. Did you ever think he *needs* you?"

I laughed. "Gus doesn't need anything or anybody."

"Maybe. But maybe he does. Or maybe he just doesn't want to do it without you, for whatever the reason. Maybe he likes company when he's making those millions. Somebody to shop with, perhaps?"

"Well, I'll find out soon enough."

The Fish struggled to his feet, wadded up the empty pizza box, and carried it into the kitchen. "I feel bad eating like this in front of you. My mother would be all over my manners. Are you sure you're not hungry?

Wait, I got a little something in the fridge I think you're gonna like." I heard rummaging and the sound of a refrigerator door opening and closing. Three minutes later, the Fish returned, carrying a single paper plate on which rested a head of lettuce. In his other hand, he held a bottle of Italian dressing and a plastic fork. "Dinner is served, madam," he announced, setting the lettuce in front of me as if it were a five-star meal. "You gotta eat. You'll get weak." He unfurled a roll of paper towels, ripped off a square, and spread it on my lap. "You know, I had a pet iguana once," he said. "It ate exactly this same dinner—a head of lettuce. A head of lettuce, and a light-bulb to keep warm, was all that thing needed. Has it occurred to you that your eating habits verge on the prehistoric?"

"Fine with me. I don't recall seeing any cave paintings of obese cavemen," I said. I was thinking about Anna, and the feeling I'd had that someone was in her house. It was just that—a feeling. "Fish, did you think Anna was alone when we were there?"

"I didn't see anyone else, if that's what you mean. Why?"

"I don't know. I just had a sense that somebody was there, watching. And at one point I thought I saw a curtain move, but maybe I didn't. It was night. . . ." As I was saying these words, I became more convinced that I *had* seen someone. My visual perception has always been acute; it's one of the reasons I was a good tennis player. I register small things, sometimes unconsciously, like little flashes of movement on the edges of my peripheral vision that could be a ball coming at me at eighty or ninety miles an hour—or a person dodging behind a curtain.

"If you thought you saw something, I'd bet my money something was there," said the Fish. "The question is, who or what? And why would they be slinking around?"

It was getting late, and I was exhausted. "As Scarlett O'Hara once said, 'I'll think about it tomorrow,' " I announced, with a yawn and a stretch.

The Fish pointed to the bedroom. "You sleep there. I had the housekeeping service put on fresh sheets. I'll take the sofa bed. Feel free to use the phone."

"I think I'll just try Gus." I dialed his number, but there was no answer, not even voice mail. I supposed he didn't want to be deluged with calls after the announcement. I hung up and tried my own messages. There was one from the airport safety manager at the Santa Monica airport. The plane that had tried to flatten me was indeed a charter, but there had been a report from the pilot that the plane had been forced to make an emergency maneuver to avoid running into a flock of birds it had encountered on takeoff. The pilot was fully justified in this and there would be no further action or citation. Did I have any questions?

I had plenty of questions, and beginning tomorrow I certainly planned to ask them.

Morning *chez* Fish involved the prerequisite stops for an Egg McMuffin and Dunkin' Donuts on our way to Paul's office. Paul worked in a modern building on El Camino, a tree-shaded street near Wilshire Boulevard and just down from the rococo iron gates of the Regent Beverly Wilshire Hotel. It was one of Beverly Hills's power blocks, with several major law firms and two or three of the mega-talent agencies located within a three-block radius, all within walking distance of Rodeo Drive. The cool marble structure was a tribute to Paul's success. The place looked like a modern-day fortress as interpreted by a mortuary architect. The building was a solid seamless slab of flawless flesh-colored marble. Windows were high and slitlike, as if the work going on inside were so highly confidential that potential visual access needed to be eliminated from the outset. It was rumored that Paul, nervous about the confidentiality of his conversations and deals, had installed a state-of-the-art scrambler system that blanketed the entire premises, including the garage, and made mobile phones go haywire for blocks in the vicinity.

A receptionist in a cordless headset called Paul's office, and his assistant, a young man who also wore a headset—this one unplugged and hanging around his neck like an electronic tie—escorted us back to the inner sanctum.

Paul's office was huge and uncluttered, except for a single calla lily in a vase. No papers marred the granite surface of his desk.

"So you've coopted my new chief of security," Paul scolded me. "What's the deal?" He motioned toward the couch, which faced a huge saltwater aquarium. A small gray shark circled slowly, zigzagging through the brightly colored coral. "That's Adolf," said Paul. "Isn't he something? He's got a great disposition. He killed everybody else in the tank—the angelfish, the little neons, the squid, even the eel."

"I thought the fish in these decorative aquariums were supposed to be tame and beautiful," I said.

"Beauty is in the eye of the beholder. I didn't put

any food in the tank for two weeks, just to see what would happen," Paul said gleefully. "It was a survival-of-the-fittest kind of thing. My buddy Adolf kicked butt in there. He must be a night feeder, because everything would be calm in the daytime, and you'd think, what the hell, nothing's happening; then we'd close the office and go home for the night, and the next morning there'd be one or two fewer fish, maybe a fin or a piece of shell floating here and there. I used to post the body count on our internal E-mail. Everybody got into it. It was raw nature. Killer instinct. Kind of like my business." He grinned. He had perfect teeth, the kind nobody is born with.

"Sort of like an aquatic Roman amphitheater on a very small scale," I said. "I just hate to lose."

"Exactly! The relationship between predator and victim has always fascinated me. As it must you, Jordan, having been a world-class competitor."

"I don't think of being competitive as being predatory," I said.

Paul poured three glasses of ice water. "I think the killer instinct exists in all of us, to varying degrees. Those of us who must win, who refuse to be bettered, like Adolf here or a champion athlete or a winning deal-maker in business, simply have evolved the instinct to a higher level, where it becomes, you might say, a talent." He handed me some water. "The line is very finely drawn, in any case."

"On the flip side," I said, "surely you must agree that when this instinct is warped or misdirected, those of us who are responsible members of the community must guard against it. Which is why I'd like to suggest that we band together to make sure the Anna Martinez situation is resolved."

He shrugged. "What can I do? She's not one of my clients. I can't control the woman."

"But I think you should start taking her seriously, Paul. She's frightening your clients, and she's so unstable she could fixate her desire for revenge on anyone at this point. The results could be tragic."

"I'd like to step up my security efforts around Jasmine until this crisis period with the memorial service for Malik is over," suggested the Fish. "I'm not sure there isn't another party involved here, stirring up this woman and using her to cause trouble."

"What would be the point of that?" Paul frowned.

"Just to take advantage of Anna Martinez's insecurities for personal benefit."

"Who stands to benefit from this sort of thing?" Paul said.

"For instance, somebody might want to frighten Jasmine so badly that she blew a match or pulled out entirely."

Paul raised his eyebrows. "You think that's what's going on?"

"I don't know. But if I look into it, maybe I can find out."

"What's your part in this, Jordan?"

"Well, the atmosphere out at the Sports Science Clinic is not very good right now. Malik's death still makes no sense. And then there's the Schidor twins, and Tanner. Now Gus has announced he's leaving."

"So I heard."

"News travels fast. We can't handle any more problems. And I'm personally involved here—tennis is my area, and that's where all these medical problems are arising. I have to review how we're handling our clients, what we're exposing them to, how we're protecting them. If Jasmine is at risk because of events that occurred on our watch, on our property, I'm personally responsible. I want to identify and remove that risk."

Paul leaned back in his huge leather chair. "Very idealistic words, but the fact is, you're a little late. Let me get right to it. My client, a world-class athlete in his prime, is dead after a simple walk my grandmother should be able to take without incident. You took him on that walk."

I said nothing. After all, he was right.

Paul continued. "Whatever security measures or concerns you or your organization should have registered, this should have been done before a single client crossed your threshold. Now you want me to dip into my corporate resources"—he nodded toward the Fish—"to bail you out." Paul sighed. "You're aware, of course, that Malik's estate is preparing a negligence lawsuit against the Desert Springs Sports Science Clinic?"

"No, I wasn't."

"Well, it's no secret. I'm sure that was one motivating factor in Gus Laidlaw's decision to step down. Bill Stokes is very smart. Stokes needed Gus off the masthead so there's somebody to go down who won't take the entire ship with him. This retirement thing is a little too convenient."

"I don't think that's the case at all," I said hotly.

Paul waved his hands dismissively. "Be that as it may, here's what I'm prepared to do. Fisher, you have my authorization to do whatever it takes to safeguard Jasmine, period. You have no authorization to expend resources on behalf of the Desert Springs Sports Science Clinic. They can hire their own security. It's that simple. It's not that I'm being a hard-ass here, Jordan. It's a simple business decision."

The Fish nodded laconically. I knew that as always he would do whatever he pleased. But I wondered what was behind Paul's insistent statement. He always had a reason for everything.

He reached out and patted my shoulder. "I know you guys are going through some tough times," he said magnanimously. "I sympathize. You know, with Gus leaving, maybe you might consider sharing some resources on a formalized basis." He stretched nonchalantly in his chair. "Some sort of partnership might make sense."

I glanced at the shark tank. When he said the word "partnership," I began to understand. You could never take Pinocchio at face value. Paul Kessler didn't really want to help the Springs in any way or be a partner with us. More likely, he wanted to force us into a situation where we would accept a takeover or a buyout—by him. At an advantageous price, of course.

"I'll think about it and bring it up with Bill." I smiled but, suspecting a hidden agenda, I had to wonder: Could he have played any part in these threats?

When we left Paul's office, I asked the Fish.

"Could be," he said. "I know he wants a full report on anything that goes on at the Springs, no matter how seemingly insignificant. Guys like him, they see information as power."

"He thinks the fact that Gus is leaving is a weak spot," I said. "And he's like that shark of his—attacking if he senses weakness."

The Fish nodded. "You seem to have your eyes open."

"It never occurred to me that somebody else might move in on the Springs. But Gus is bound to sell his shares. The board of directors will insist on it."

I wondered what valuation had been put on them, and if I could buy them myself. Bill was no doubt wondering the same thing. Maybe we could manage it jointly and succeed in keeping unwanted outsiders out of the business. Right now, what I wanted to do most was get back to the Springs and talk to Gus. But first, I wanted to stop by the Santa Monica airport and see what I could find out about the jet.

"I think I'll keep an eye on our friend Anna for a while," the Fish said. "Call me from Palm Springs and let me know what's up. The memorial for Malik is planned for next week in Santa Monica. You'll be there?"

"Of course."

We agreed to meet again afterward.

I drove directly to the administration building, parked in the lot, and went to the second floor, through the pilot's lounge and to the security office. It was closed and locked, but there was a man in the office next door.

"Can I help you?" he asked.

"As a matter of fact, I was hoping that someone could help me find out information about a plane that I encountered just off the runway last night."

"Come in," he said. He handed me a card and introduced himself as Carl Waters, Airside Operations. "I handle noise management," he said, settling in behind a standard-issue gray metal desk. Carl was middle-aged and gray-haired, with an easygoing manner.

I repeated my story to him. "Is there any way I can find out something about this plane?" I asked.

"Well, if there were violations, the FAA would have a record." He picked up a sheaf of papers from his desk. "Give me what you have," he said, and I repeated the time and the plane's tail number. He scrutinized his papers. "Interesting. I got a call on file that was made this morning by a neighborhood resident who complained that a jet went over his house last night real low and real loud at a time that correlates with your reported incident. If you'll give me a little time, I can go into my automated monitoring system and confirm the tail number, and then I can get the audio tapes from the control tower and see if something was out of the ordinary during takeoff."

"You have an audio tape of the takeoff?"

"Sure. Every takeoff is on audio tape. From the tail number, we'll be able to get the point of origination and then, if it's a local plane, I can call the fixed base operator, where the plane was serviced, and see who it belongs to and who the pilot was. If the plane violated noise regulations by being too low over homes, I'll have to write the owner a warning letter anyway."

"How long will that take?"

"If it turns out to be a local plane, about thirty minutes."

I hung out in the pilot's lounge for the next half hour, watching the planes land and take off. Finally Carl stuck his head out of his office door. "Ms. Myles? I've got something for you."

We reconvened at his desk.

"I played back the audio tapes and cross-checked the log, and it appears that this particular jet, Cessna Citation N7864 Tango, taking off on runway twenty-one at seven P.M., did not accelerate at the normal rate of climb. The pilot reported encountering a flock of birds and exercised his right to make a safety-related decision. If birds get sucked into a jet engine, they can cause a crash, you see. There is no cause here for a violation citation. I'm not really authorized to go into this any further. I'd have to contact the FAA and—"

"Wait a minute, Carl. You mean a plane can buzz a person, almost take your head off out there on the tarmac, and nobody can say anything about it?"

"If a pilot makes a safety-related judgment, it's out of my hands. Safety comes first. A pilot is allowed to negotiate a move to avoid something in the path of the plane."

"How do you know if this so-called flock of birds was real?"

"We don't. But why would somebody make it up?"

"Where did the plane originate?"

"Well, that I did find out. It's from here, from Jetstream Air, one of our major FBOs. That's Fixed Base Operator."

"And who was the pilot?"

"You'll have to ask them. They're across the airfield, by the executive terminal."

I thanked Carl and drove over to the north side of the airport, parked in front of the Museum of Flying, and went into the executive terminal, where I had boarded the BioTech helicopter with Gus. Jetstream had the first office as I went into the terminal building. A tall, slim, red-haired woman in a very short pleated skirt, fitted jacket, and high heels that made her appear even taller greeted me.

"Do you have an appointment?" she asked. Her makeup was perfect.

"I just want to ask a few questions about a particular jet that's in your fleet."

"I suggest you write a letter and include all the relevant information. Someone will get back to you."

"It's just a quick question—"

"We're very busy right now. You'll really have to make an appointment." She gave me a programmed smile.

"Sunday, telephone." Someone handed her the receiver, ending our conversation.

Sunday. The name jolted me. Wasn't Sunday the name of the pilot of the BioTech jet? It was such an unusual name, it had stuck with me when Gus mentioned it. I waited till she hung up.

"Are you Sunday?"

"Yes."

"Don't you pilot the BioTech jet?"

"BioTech leases one of our jets, and sometimes I pilot it, yes."

"Did you pilot the Citation last night when it took off at seven P.M.?"

"No, I wasn't working last night. One of our other pilots was on."

"Do you know his name?"

"I'm not sure who was working. Why do you ask?"

"Where can I reach the head of the company?"

"Mr. Altone is flying to France today on company business and won't be back for a week."

I handed her my card. "Please ask him to call me."

"Fine," she said. "But it's really best to put your questions in writing. Be specific—the more details, the better we can respond."

"Gee, I'm sorry, but I wasn't taking notes when the person I think was your pilot almost ground me into the pavement last night." I figured she'd remember to give him *that* message.

"What?"

"He'll know what I mean." I turned and pushed through the glass door and into the lobby of the executive terminal. Large, cushy leather chairs surrounded a low coffee table in a room that faced directly onto the runway. Sitting in one of them was Gus. He was wearing chinos and a white shirt, no tie, and his sport coat was draped over the back of the chair.

Sunday walked over to him and sat on the arm of the chair, and they talked for a few moments as I watched. Probably confirming his flight arrangements, I thought. At this point he was no doubt a regular passenger on the BioTech plane. He didn't have any luggage, so he was probably commuting in for the day to meet with the lab or discuss his new situation.

I tapped him on the shoulder "Gus, hi. Are you coming or going?"

He swiveled around, surprised. "Jordan! I guess I'm— making plans. BioTech has a very ambitious itinerary planned for me in the upcoming weeks. I was trying to see where they could squeeze me into the flight schedule." He stood up and nodded to Sunday. "This is Sunday Stanley, one of their pilots. Sunday, this is Jordan Myles, my partner."

"*Former* partner," I corrected.

"Sunday, question!" somebody yelled from the office.

"We've met. Excuse me." She smiled politely and slipped off.

"Looks like we have some things to discuss," I said. "Got a few minutes?"

"Sure," said Gus easily. "It looks like I've got a lifetime."

ELEVEN

"I wish I could have told you, Jordan," Gus said quietly. We'd circumvented the runways and reached the Spitfire Grill to talk things through. "I didn't mean to take you by surprise, but the truth is, I signed a confidentiality agreement and that's a legal document I couldn't break, not even for you. Bill and the board were afraid that, if word got out prematurely, there would be a bad impact on business and some investors might pull out. And with you so closely aligned with the media these days, it was a sensitive issue. Anyhow, I saw their point and agreed to handle it their way." He reached across the table and covered my hand with his. "I hope you'll understand."

"I know. It's business." Still, I also wished he had told me. It hurt to think that Bill and Gus, especially, could entertain the thought that I would use this story on TV. "What are your plans now?" I asked. "Will you stay in Palm Springs?"

"Of course, that's my home. I'll keep my place there— although I'll also need an apartment here in LA. I'll be commuting back and forth until the product launch."

"And then?"

"I guess it depends on how successful Duration is."

I toyed with my glass, scraping tracks in the condensation with my fingertip. "I'm glad you're doing what you want to do, but it's going to take some getting used to—the Springs without you." I sighed. "I don't know why I thought things would never change. I was lulled into feeling that we were all in a time capsule together, I guess."

"But Jordan, you broke out of the capsule first, with your TV work."

"But I'm still tethered to the Springs. It's my home base. Without it, I'm not sure I could do the other things I've gotten involved with. You have more guts than I, Gus. You've cut the cord. I couldn't do that. I wouldn't want to."

"It's a matter of priorities," Gus said. "I rethought what I wanted to do with my life."

"What about your stock in the Springs?" I asked. "There's been more than a little speculation about it, and I for one am extremely curious."

"I'll be selling my shares, it's true. I'd have too much money tied up there otherwise. In a new venture, anything can happen. I'll want to be liquid, just in case."

"I saw Paul Kessler today. I suspect he'd like to buy your shares and get a nice fat interest in the Springs."

Gus chuckled. "Oh, would he? That doesn't surprise me. Paul would control the universe if he could."

I was alarmed. "You're not going to sell to him, are you?"

"No, my shares are going where I can keep an eye on them."

"Meaning?"

"BioTech. The company has agreed to buy me out."

"What? And Bill agrees?"

"It's not up to him. I didn't have to ask his permission."

"Or mine, obviously."

"Be a grown-up, Jordan."

I leaned closer across the table, as if I could physically remove the distance between us.

Gus touched my cheek, where I had scraped it on the pavement. It was scabbed over now. "What happened to your face?"

"Close encounter of an unfriendly kind. Listen, I know this is business, but Gus, they're outsiders. Think about what you're doing to the integrity of the place."

"Don't think I haven't thought about it for months. Let's face it. The Springs is a very expensive facility to operate, and we're always teetering on the edge of solvency. A little bad PR is all it takes to send us into the red. Either that, or we're at the mercy of Bill's bankers. That is not my idea of integrity. A major shareholder with some available funds could be a very attractive addition."

"Paul Kessler may fight for this. He seemed pretty determined."

Gus's eyes narrowed. "There's no doubt going to be some restructuring involved. You'll have a say, Jordan. Use it."

"I don't like the idea of arguing for something I don't believe in." I felt vaguely trapped. None of the available choices seemed appealing.

"Well, the status quo is no longer feasible. You'll have to make another choice."

I wondered again if I could raise the money myself. "Just give me a little time," I said. "I'd like to explore some options."

"That's arrangeable," Gus said. "And meanwhile, maybe you could rethink the idea of joining me." He held

up a hand. "Now, don't jump to conclusions, I don't
mean leaving the Springs, just forming the alliance
we've been discussing on the Duration business. Let me
lay it on the line, Jordan. They are willing to pay you one
million dollars for your endorsement on an infomercial.
That kind of payout might be especially meaningful right
now."

"A million dollars?" I wondered how many of Gus's
shares I could acquire with that kind of windfall. Just as
quickly, I wondered why BioTech was willing to pay so
much. If they would put a million on the table at this
point, it was probably just the first bid. I could probably
bargain for much more, particularly if I brought in a
skillful lawyer or agent to negotiate. I had a recognizable
name, that much I knew, but this kind of money was
more than I'd ever been paid for an endorsement. When I
was on the Grand Slam circuit, I got an endorsement deal
from a sock manufacturer, but it wasn't even six figures.
It was hard to walk away from that kind of money.

"You've got to understand, Jordan, the game has
changed. It's not just about sports anymore. It's about
integrated marketing: sports and products and locations
and personalities and entertainment all blended together
to form a whole that's greater than any individual part.
That's why they're putting sports figures into movies and
putting movies in theme parks. That's why, say, Nike is
so much more than a pair of shoes. There's a synergy at
work. You want to be a part of that."

"I do?"

"Well, if you want to make any real money, that's
where it's at. And you're already halfway there, with
your show."

"My former show, you mean."

"Still, your name is out there."

I thought about it for a minute. I thought about my love of tennis—all sports, really—and my work. "What you're saying isn't that far-fetched, Gus, but I think it's a question of where to draw the line."

"Exactly my point," he retorted. "That line is getting blurred."

"A million dollars?" I asked again, trying out the feel of the words as I said it. "Really?"

"Really. Of course, it's your decision, but personally I see no reason why you shouldn't take it. I don't understand you, Jordan. You act as if somebody's trying to cheat you out of something, instead of looking at this from a simple business perspective. If you don't accept the offer, they're just going to go and approach Chrissie or somebody else. And rather soon, I'd imagine."

"A lot of fuss for a little drink," I said wryly. I couldn't help myself. As soon as I said it, I knew I'd made a mistake. Gus's face hardened, and the corners of his mouth tightened. I might as well have said he had a little—well, choose your part of the male anatomy.

"It's not some 'little drink,'" he said, measuring out each word as if with an eyedropper. "It's a major multimillion-dollar marketing program." He stared at me uncomprehendingly across the table. "You are so totally self-involved you have never once heard what I've said, Jordan. It's very sad that you've let yourself get to this point. You can't even see an opportunity when it grabs you by the shoulders and shakes you. And you can't support me or anyone but yourself. I suggest you step back and take a good look at yourself and what's happening to you."

He paid the bill in silence.

Finally I said, "You know, there are a lot of people getting sick for some reason, and some of our friends and clients have died. There is a dead child. There's a mother who's gone over the edge. There are rampant death threats. The Springs is in the middle of this madness. Sometimes there are more important things than money." I picked up my bag and hoisted it over my shoulder.

"And as usual, Jordan Myles, girl detective, is launching herself into the middle of something that should be a police matter," Gus said. He pocketed his change and looked past me somewhere. I stared at his long legs and his boots and remembered how well we used to get along.

"Moving right along, how well do you know Sunday Stanley, the pilot?" I asked.

Gus finally looked at me. "Not well. Just from the BioTech trips. Why?"

"You seemed to know her back there at the airport, that's all, and I'm trying to get some information about one of their pilots. Because somebody over there is completely irresponsible. This pilot, whoever it was, supposedly was dodging birds but in fact he—or she—almost took my head off last night."

"Were you on the runway?"

"Near the runway."

"Too near, I'd say. I'll ask Sunday about it the next time I see her, but when you're close to an active runway at night, you can't be surprised by these kinds of activities. This is exactly the sort of thing I'm talking about, Jordan."

"You're probably right. I think from now on I'll stay home and take up crocheting. Maybe in five years I'll have made an afghan."

A jet roared by, taking off into a foggy sky the color of dishwater.

"If it'll make you feel better about it, I'll ask Sunday to look into this thing personally. But what can you do, arrest a flock of seagulls?"

I had to laugh. "You never know. Some of them look pretty diabolical. Especially if you have a sandwich at the beach."

Gus grinned. "That's more like it. For a while, I was afraid you'd lost your sense of humor. Where's your truck?"

"Just down the street. I'm heading back to the Springs."

He nodded. "Then I'll see you at the memorial service. I have some business in LA today, and I'm not sure how long it'll take. Meanwhile, will you please think about what I've been saying? There's no reason why we can't be together in this. And just be together, period. Let's look at this as a new start." He pulled me close to him, and for a minute I really believed we could bring back every shred of what we'd had.

"I'll try," I whispered. "Maybe you're right."

I spent most of the drive home on the car phone. I kept hearing Gus's words over and over, and I couldn't stop thinking about the thought of a million-dollar endorsement. By the time I was twenty miles out of LA, I'd reached my accountant and asked him about the tax implications of that kind of money, and we'd gone over a plan for my purchase of Gus's shares in the Springs.

I walked into my house to find A.M. up on Winnifred's lap. She was painting the dog's toenails.

"Winnifred, what on earth are you doing?" I tossed my

bag down and rushed over to rescue my poor long-suffering dog.

"Shush, dear," Winnifred scolded. "She's such a beautiful little thing. She deserves to be prettied up a bit from time to time."

A.M. cocked her head and gave a little yelp. She made a move, as if to get up, but Winnifred instantly reached into a jar of dried liver snacks and dangled one under her nose. A.M. licked it up and settled contentedly back onto Winnifred's lap for her top coat.

Winnifred looked up at me from behind her rhinestone-rimmed glasses. "You told me to look after her."

"Yes, I did, that's true. Fine. She'll have pink nails. Just this once." I had more significant things to worry about than a canine pedicure.

"Not pink, dear. That's over. They're blue."

"Blue. I have a dog with blue toenails."

Winnifred grabbed a blue-tipped paw and waved it at me. "Aren't we beautiful? Just like Madonna."

I tried not to look too closely.

"Just one thing, dear."

"What's that, Winnifred?"

"I wondered if I might stay with you for a bit. Would it be a problem?"

"Well, no, but why would you want to do that?"

"I got a rather frightening phone call at the office, and I really don't want to be alone just now."

"Frightening?"

"Yes, dear. I didn't want to worry you, but someone was whispering into the phone that if I wasn't careful I might meet a very untidy demise." She bit her lip.

I rushed over and put my arm around her. "Winnifred, I am so sorry! I feel terrible! I'm sure that call was meant for me. This thing is way out of hand. Maybe you should take a few days off, till it all blows over. In fact, take a vacation. Go visit your sister in Toronto." After what happened to Tony, I had to keep Winnifred safe. I felt frantic. The poor woman was so sweet and helpless. She probably had no idea what danger she was in or how to protect herself.

Winnifred thrust her chin in the air and smoothed the polka-dot ribbon in her hair. "Well, they haven't seen the last of me!" she vowed passionately, her voice quavering. "I had the police put a tracer on all your phones, dear. If it happens again, we'll know for sure who's doing the calling. And I do carry a gun."

"What?" It was like imagining Bambi—or Bambi's grandmother—with an Uzi.

"A teensie-weensie little gun. Just in case. I keep it in my purse, right next to my lipstick."

"My God. A gun!" I couldn't imagine Winnifred carrying anything more threatening than a knitting needle.

"It's nothing, dear." She picked up her purse from the floor, opened it, and pulled out a small revolver. "A Smith & Wesson .38 snubnose. It holds five little teeny bullets. I used to carry it for my former employer. He was security-conscious."

"Just do me a favor, Winnifred. I'm happy to have you stay here. The sofa bed in the den is always made up and ready. But please leave your teensie-weensie little gun at home. And please consider taking a trip to your sister's. I'll buy your ticket."

She smiled beatifically. "Whatever you say, dear. But if these people who are making threats show their ugly selves in my vicinity, I will blow them away." She smoothed her skirt and folded her hands demurely.

"Let's leave that to the action movies. And I think I'd better hold on to that gun for you." Winnifred's vision was so bad, there was no way she could hit a target unless it was an inch from her face. More likely, she'd shoot me, or A.M.

She sighed and handed me the gun. I hated the feel of it in my hand. "Be careful, now," she said.

"I used to shoot targets, for sport. I'll be careful." I wrapped the pistol in a T-shirt and tucked it into my backpack. My main goal was to get it out of the house.

"Dear?"

"Yes, Winnifred."

"Eat. I picked up a little something for the refrigerator. It looked so bare in there."

"What did you get?"

"A cheesecake."

"Thanks. It sounds great, but I'm not hungry."

"Would you like to try some of this blue nail polish then? It's really quite attractive."

"I see. A.M. and I can have matching toes. Winnifred, let's just get your room ready."

After I'd settled Winnifred in, I went to my own room and called Bill. His wife answered.

"We have a few friends over for dinner," Evie said. "Can it wait?"

"I suppose so. Tell Bill I'll see him tomorrow." I hung up and caught up on some bills for a while. Then I took a bath, turned on the TV, and painted my toenails blue.

The next morning, I met Bill as we both pulled into the parking lot. He was carrying a copy of *The Wall Street Journal* under his arm.

"It's in the *Journal*," Bill said, by way of greeting.

"What's that?"

"The news of Gus's resignation."

"Well, that's good," I said pointedly, catching up with him. Bill walks faster than any human being I have ever known. "The papers knew it before I did, I guess."

He stopped. "Jordan, I know how close you are to Gus, but it was his personal decision, and we did have a confidentiality agreement. I'm not surprised you're not happy about the way this was handled—I expected you to be disturbed, in fact, and I understand—but this was the way it had to be."

"Fine, Bill. I accept that." We both nodded to the guard at the front door. "But what now?"

He headed toward his office. "Let's discuss this. Come in for a cup of tea. There's something I'd like to show you."

We went in. Bill took off his windbreaker, walked over to his bar, and turned on his electric kettle.

"Things have been happening so fast, Jordan, that it's not easy to keep you in the loop if you're not actually on the premises. But you're among the first to see this." He pointed to a sheet-covered form that took up most of the side table along the window wall. "Step over here."

We walked over and stood by the table, and he carefully pulled the sheet off to reveal a scale model of the Springs. Except it wasn't the Springs at all, it was a much larger place. "I don't understand," I said.

"It's a scale model for a proposed expansion. Here's our current property." He pointed to the buildings at the core of the model. "And here is a vision for the future. That's the hotel. The condominiums are just to the left of the tennis courts. The spa is just adjacent to the rock-climbing environment—"

"Wait a minute. When did anybody start talking about this kind of expansion?" I stared at the model. From what I could see, it made the Springs seem more like Disneyland than a serious sports medicine facility. "Where did this come from?"

"As I said, it's just a concept. Certainly nothing definite. But the objective is to increase business by broadening our base beyond professional athletes into the consumer sector. We could become much more profitable by doing that."

"I can see it now. Crowds of people in terry-cloth robes running around getting massages and taking water aerobics in the pool. I *hate* this."

"You might like the bottom line, however. This particular plan doesn't exclude our professional sports program, it just broadens and enhances it."

He sounded like Trent talking. Come to think of it, a lot of people these days seemed to sound like Trent talking.

"We're in a competitive arena, Jordan," said Bill, as he settled in on his couch, motioning me to sit next to him. "Right now, we have a very small slice of the pie. We already have most of the top athletes as clients, and there are only so many of them. That pool is not going to increase in the near future. So we need to get a bigger base. It's simple, and it makes sense to me. What's more, we won't lose anything. We can still keep our professional sports clientele. There's no reason why that should go away. Just think, Jordan, what a unique facility we'll have."

"It's just different, that's all," I said.

Bill's words did hold a certain inarguable logic, I had to admit. And it was true that sports medicine and training have branched out far beyond the confines of actual professional athletes. Even every-other-weekend runners have shoes that could take them to the Olympics these days, and beginning tennis players are ordering custom-made rackets. Then there are the wardrobes. It doesn't matter if you're a woman or a man, even if you can't lift a racket, swing a club, or shoot a hoop you can dress like a champion of any sport. All it takes to be an "athlete" is a credit card and a trip to the mall. And sports training and therapy are a natural extension of that. Already, sports clubs have climbing walls, ski simulators, fat-level analyzers, and some of the most sophisticated equipment available to people who move their bodies maybe once a week. Soon, I supposed, that same weekend athlete would be wanting to have his or her pupil dilation analyzed to help come one step closer to championship form. Bill was proposing that we meet such an athlete head on.

He handed me a thick notebook. "The entire proposed plan is outlined in here," he said. "Study it and we'll talk further. I'm anxious to have your input. We're not going to move ahead unless all the partners approve."

"Which brings me to my next point, Bill," I said. "What about Gus's shares? I understand he has to be bought out."

He nodded. "True. If any partner leaves the company, he or she must sell their shares."

"Can an outsider acquire them?" I asked nervously.

Bill laughed. "Oh, no danger of that. According to the way our charter is set up, as long as the Springs remains a privately held company, only company shareholders can buy stock from one another. And the other shareholders have a vote on the potential buyer."

"Good. That makes me feel much better."

"You don't have to worry about hostile takeovers, Jordan, if that's been on your mind."

Outside the picture window, I saw Jasmine walk by, wearing sunglasses, the collar of her windbreaker turned up, hands stuffed in the pockets of her black jeans.

"Jasmine's still here?" I asked.

"Yes," said Bill. "We'll all be going to LA together to Malik's memorial service tomorrow. It's going to be on the beach in Malibu, on the site where the wedding would have been held."

"It will be very emotional," I said. "Who is 'we'?"

"Well, Jasmine and her mother; Evie and I, of course; Ginny Jennings; and you're included in the invitation. BioTech is sending a plane for us. Gus arranged it. I told them you'd be there."

"Of course."

"We'll leave from the parking lot at eight-thirty tomorrow."

When I left Bill's office, I saw Jasmine far down the path, walking toward the pool. I broke into a run to catch up with her.

"How're you doing?" I asked when I was at her side. She looked drawn and thin, her cheekbones jutting sharply against the planes of her face.

"I'm hanging in there," she said, managing a faint smile. "I thought I'd take a swim. The water blocks things out."

I noticed she was wearing her diamond engagement ring.

"It's hard to believe that, instead of planning a wedding, I'm planning a funeral. The bride wore black. Is that how it goes?"

"Don't torture yourself," I said. "He would have hated that."

"I've made a decision," she said. "As soon as this is over, I'm going immediately back to tennis. I'm really going to play, this time, not just play at playing. I think that's what I was doing before. But this time, I'm going to win, for his sake. He gave it his all. I can do as much." Her voice was fierce, and she gripped my hand as she spoke. Her nails dug into my palms. "Will you help me?" she whispered. "Will you?" Behind the sunglasses, her eyes were masked.

"If I can," I said.

The next morning, I pressed a confirmation fax for a ticket to Toronto in Winnifred's hand, told her to leave A.M. with the housekeeper, and then met Bill and Jasmine and the others in the parking lot and drove to the Palm Springs airport. I was surprised to see Paul Kessler there, with the Fish; Kessler had put his arm around Jasmine and was talking quietly to her.

"We flew in at dawn," said the Fish. "He didn't want her to make the trip alone."

"She's hardly alone, as you can see," I said.

"Well, it's a gesture. Any word from the airport?"

"Officially, it's a flock of birds. That's as far as I seem to be getting."

The Fish scrutinized the jet as we walked to it. "Look familiar?"

"Well, *she* certainly does." At the foot of the stairway stood Sunday Stanley in a tailored black pantsuit, her red hair neatly pulled back off her face. She looked as if she had combed her eyelashes and was ready to attend a power lunch at the Four Seasons rather than fly a jet. She nodded at me as we boarded. Once on the plane, everyone was quiet, talking in hushed tones as they settled into their seats. I leaned back, strapped myself in, and closed my eyes.

Minutes later, it seemed, I felt a tap on my shoulder. Could I have fallen asleep so quickly that we had already landed and I hadn't been aware of the trip? I opened my eyes to see Sunday leaning over me.

"Ms. Myles, excuse me, we're deplaning."

"What?"

"I have to ask everyone to get off the plane."

I unclipped my seat belt and leaned forward. "Why? Is there a problem?" Looking around, I saw everyone filing out. Outside the window, the Fish and Paul Kessler were escorting Jasmine hurriedly down the tarmac.

"Probably not, but please get off the aircraft as quickly as possible."

"Are you going to tell me why?"

She frowned. "I'm not at liberty to discuss the situation, but I must insist you get off the plane with the others. Now." She whirled around and strode back to the cockpit.

I got up and followed everyone off the plane, then ran down the runway and caught up with the Fish, Paul, and Jasmine. Jasmine's eyes were swollen and red, and she seemed to be about to start crying again at any minute. Paul's arm was protectively around her waist, and her head was practically buried in his shoulder.

"What's going on?" I whispered to the Fish.

Behind his sunglasses, he was scanning the area. "Bomb threat," he said softly. "We don't want to panic anybody, so keep it quiet. Somebody called the Santa Monica airport."

"Did they trace the call?"

"Couldn't. It was too quick." He held the terminal door open for Jasmine and Paul.

"Good God. Now what? Do we wait while they search the plane?"

"Nope. They'll search it, all right, but not with us on it. Kessler chartered another plane. We'll be taking that in a few minutes. After they go through all the luggage with sniffer dogs and a fine-tooth comb, that is."

"All these bomb threats," I said angrily. "When do we stop taking them seriously?"

"Never," said the Fish. "The one you ignore is the one that gets you."

"Poor Jasmine. She's a wreck." I noticed that Paul had placed himself firmly next to her and was holding her hand and stroking it. Jasmine seemed numb. She sat stone still, staring straight ahead, her posture erect, her face a mask.

Security officers appeared and questioned each one of us. Did we pack every item ourselves? Had anyone approached us before we boarded the plane? Was there anyone we knew of who could have made this threat? What were our plans in LA? An officer went through my bag, item by item. Finally, after about an hour, we were allowed to board the new airplane, and the trip resumed uneventfully.

This time, however, I did not try to sleep. This time I felt nervous as we took off. I thought of Tony, of the explosion that had killed him. I thought of Malik.

On the ground in Santa Monica, a procession of limousines stood waiting to take us to Malibu, a trip of about thirty minutes up the Pacific Coast Highway at this time of day. It was a chilly spring day. Bright patches of flowers dotted the hillsides. The beaches were empty, but the ocean shimmered and I could see surfers in wet suits, a few surf casters, and flocks of seabirds skimming over the waves.

We reached Cliffside Drive, passed through a private gate, and got out at Paul Kessler's massive Spanish-style house. He led the way, escorting Jasmine down a path that led past the house and ended at a long flight of steps that dropped almost vertically down to the wide sandy beach. She had changed into a simple dress of black gauze and wore black sandals and a large black hat that had been on the seat next to her on the plane.

On the beach, about fifty people waited. I spotted a group from the Springs, including Ginny Jennings, and a few familiar faces from BioTech, led by Trent. A clutch of what I supposed to be friends and family of Malik's stood close by Jasmine, her mother, and Paul, many of them in tears. Gus came over to join me and took my hand. He pointed out a tall, regal black woman whose face seemed frozen. "That's Doris Evans, Malik's mother," he said.

The service was short: a reading by a minister, another by Jasmine, and a song by a guitarist. Paul Kessler spoke about Malik, of the promise of his short life and his love for Jasmine. Then Jasmine threw a bouquet of wild-flowers tied in black ribbon into the waves. We all stood on shore and watched the flowers drift farther and farther out to sea, until a large wave rolled in and they disappeared into the white foam at its crest. Just then, a pod of six dolphins appeared, their large dark bodies gracefully curving with the surf, fins breaking the surface. They swam parallel to the shore, about fifteen feet out, and we watched them until they disappeared up the coastline, toward Zuma Beach. Then everyone climbed the steep stairs and returned to Paul's house for a light lunch.

The house was incredible, a testament to Paul's monetary, if not spiritual, success. Although most of the homes along the Malibu coast nestle side by side on their multimillion-dollar lots, Paul's lot was wide, landscaped, and separated from his neighbors by a tennis court complex and, across the street, a stable and riding ring. Huge expanses of curved windows thirty feet high, trimmed with mahogany, framed magnificent ocean views and opened onto a flower-shaded deck. The furniture was a combination of modern classic and antique Indian, the curving lines of teak and mahogany and caned chairbacks giving the house a slightly exotic flair. Indian artwork lined the walls, and huge baskets of shells, driftwood, and beach stones sat on every tabletop. A raw bar had been set up along one side of the room, tended by servers in buttoned-up white shirts and black vests.

Paul appeared beside Gus and me. "Feel free to wander through the house," he said. "They wanted to do a spread in *Architectural Digest*, but as I told the editor who called, this isn't really up their alley. It's too small, for one. The main house is only eleven thousand square feet, good enough, but still on the modest side." He leaned close. "I'm not one to get carried away, but the fireplace in the guest room alone cost fifty grand—it's made of blue Brazilian marble. Even Barbra doesn't have that. All the window treatments are motorized, of course."

"Of course."

"And the 'hers' bathroom of the his-and-hers—you gotta open the cabinets and look in—they're lined in refinished salmon skin. The real thing. Of course, there is no 'her'—yet." He stared across the room at Jasmine and took a sip of wine.

"It's quite a place," I had to agree, noticing that he was looking at Jasmine as if she were a pastry in a bakery window. She was oblivious, holding her mother's hand and talking quietly. I had to wonder if it was a good idea for her to stay here in this house, but at least the Fish would be on hand.

"Well, gotta mingle," Paul said as he slithered off.

"Fifty thousand for the guest-room fireplace?" said Gus, clearly impressed. "Did he say salmon *skin*?"

The Fish came up to us, and we stood watching Paul tell another mourner about the motorized window treatments. "The guy's got a way about him," the Fish noted.

"He's like the roach," I noted. "One of those life forms whose survival skills would keep him alive even after a nuclear wipeout."

"At least we haven't had any trouble so far," said the Fish, scanning the crowd. "The airplane thing had me worried, but it turned out to be amateur hour."

"Things went smoothly, considering," Gus agreed. The Fish's gaze was now directed longingly at the mounds of stone crab claws, oysters, clams, and shrimp.

"I had fifteen men covering the area," he said. "They should have. The president of the United States should have my kind of advance work."

"I never saw them!"

"That's the whole point."

Trent motioned Gus to his side, and he excused himself. "Your friend Anna Martinez?" the Fish said.

"Yes?"

"She's moving to Florida. Got a job there with a sportswear company called Filament."

"Well, that's a relief. Maybe she's going to start a new life."

"It's a pretty good job," said the Fish. "Six figures. A *suspiciously* good job."

"Really? She deserves some luck, poor woman. But if she's in Florida, who made the threat at the airport?"

"The possibilities are endless."

I looked over at Jasmine. Paul Kessler had cut her out of the group and repositioned her on a sofa on a small balcony above the living room, where they sat talking. A knockout blond caterer in a black pantsuit carried a small tray of food and drinks up to them. "Oh, another small detail for you to consider. Someone threatened my secretary," I said.

"Oh, no. Fred? Somebody threatened Fred?" He chuckled. "God help them."

"I gave her a ticket to Toronto. It's making me crazy."

Gus came over and handed me a glass of mineral water, no ice, the way I like it, but before I could drink it, Paul leaned over the balcony and summoned me to join him and Jasmine.

"It was a lovely memorial, Jasmine," I said.

"It would have been a lovelier wedding," she said ruefully. "But I have to get past that now. Paul and I have been talking. I'm going to go back at Hilton Head in May."

"That sounds fine. You'll have a few months off, time to get your game together. It's not good to rush at it."

Paul rubbed Jasmine's shoulder. "She's doing great; she's a strong girl. She's a true champion."

"She's asked me to work with her."

Paul held up a hand. "In time, in time. But right now she needs a change. I can't have her go back to the

Springs, where—*it*—happened. Not yet. You understand. It would be too difficult for her. So for the time being, Jasmine will be moving in here with me."

"In here?"

"Well, why not? I have four tennis courts—two clay—a gym, all the facilities. Actually, she'll be taking over the main house. I'll be staying in the city. That way, we can make sure she's safe. Mr. Fisher just designed a totally new state-of-the-art security system. We'll put her coach here with her. It will be good for Jas to be at the beach." He patted her protectively.

"I'm going to concentrate on my game and block out everything else," said Jasmine. "That way, I can get through this."

"I understand," I said. And I did. That was how I felt when I got my degree, after my fall.

"I'm going to win at Hilton Head," she said firmly. "Paul is hiring me a new coach, and I'm going to do nothing but train on clay for the next three months. It'll take my mind off things. I'm going to win—for Malik."

It certainly wasn't impossible. "I hope you do," I said.

"And I've been talking with his mother. We're going to set up a fund in Malik's name. Something for young kids who are starting out. He would have liked that."

"Yes, he would have," I agreed, and we hugged.

"Paul's been so sweet," she said. "I don't know how I would have gotten through this without him. I'm just leaving everything about the business end in his hands, so I can concentrate on my game. Please, do you think you could come up and work with me—continue the program we started at the Springs, before all this happened?"

"I'm sure I can rearrange some things. Let me look into it."

I went back down and reclaimed my water glass.

"Jordan, I have something to tell you," Gus said. "Trent just told me. Remember the dog food sample you gave Dean?"

"Sure."

"Trent sent it to the lab. I have to admit, we didn't put any priority on it, because—well, it was just dog food and it seemed far-fetched. But apparently they called him yesterday after I saw you. That dog food was poisoned. If A.M. had eaten it, it would probably have killed her."

"God. You're serious?"

"Unfortunately, I am."

"Thank God Winnifred's out of there," I said.

I motioned the Fish over, to share Gus's news, but suddenly noticed that he didn't look well at all.

"Are you all right?" I asked.

"Sure I am. Why do you ask?" His tone was nonchalant, but his eyelids fluttered. Then he pitched forward onto me, pushing me over backward and pinning me to the floor.

I tried to move, but I was trapped under close to three hundred pounds of dead weight and could barely breathe. Someone rolled him away, off me, and I staggered to my knees. The Fish's face looked like wax, as if it had been embalmed, and he seemed to be gasping for breath. Gus leaped onto his inert form and ripped open his shirt, and I began CPR, tilting his chin back, clearing the airway, and placing my mouth over his as Gus pushed on his chest. I had no idea what was wrong, and at the moment it didn't matter; what counted was keeping the Fish alive until more definitive measures could be taken. Luckily, due to the state-of-the-art alarm system the Fish himself had designed, the paramedics arrived within minutes.

"Airway's still obstructed," one of them announced. They worked feverishly to stabilize him, inserting an IV and continuing CPR. I stayed beside the stretcher as they rushed the Fish through the house, toward the front door, where an ambulance stood waiting outside.

The group of mourners was deathly silent, except for Jasmine, who stood on the balcony and screamed, her cries echoing in my head as the ambulance hurtled toward LA and the nearest hospital.

TWELVE

I sat in cold dread on a hard plastic seat in the hall of the emergency room. Scenarios for what could have happened whirled through my imagination: poison, mysterious illness, more horrors in the seemingly endless litany of illnesses that were connected in some way to the Springs and the tennis world. The Fish was tough as shark hide—I'd seen him survive a brutal beating in Paris that would have killed most normal people. The question was, How many lives does one man have?

The double doors swung open and a doctor emerged and beckoned me over. "Allergic reaction," he pronounced.

"Allergic? To what?" I had no idea that the Fish had allergies, but then there were more things I *didn't* know about him than things that I did.

The doctor continued. "Judging from the iodine levels in his blood, Mr. Fisher must have eaten half the contents of the Pacific Ocean. He went into anaphylactic shock, angioedema—a major allergic response. The hives virtually closed off his airway from the inside. That's why he couldn't breathe. It was fortunate that the EMS crew got there so promptly, because CPR isn't much good in a case like this. You need to medicate, and fast. After he came out of it, Mr. Fisher did tell me he had seafood allergies. He just pushed his luck too far."

Anaphylactic shock is a serious and truly terrifying condition of uncontrolled internal and/or external swelling, but I sagged with relief just to hear a rational medical explanation. "How is he?" I asked.

"We had to inject him directly in the heart, but he responded. The swelling's subsiding. He's shaky, but we pulled him out of it. You can see him if you'd like." He led me back to the examining cubicle where the Fish lay behind a green curtain. "We're sending him home with a prednisone regimen, an EpiPen, and strict instructions to stay away from seafood." He looked sternly at the Fish. "You hear that?"

The Fish smiled weakly from his bed. "Death by raw bar," he managed to mumble thickly.

"What did you do to yourself?" I asked, shaking my head.

"I was trying to stick to my diet. Seafood is on my diet."

"How much seafood?"

"I don't know." His head lolled on the pillow. "I guess I had a few crab claws while the caterers were setting up. Just something to tide me over."

"Like how many crab claws?"

The Fish closed his eyes. "Maybe thirty. Plus a few shrimp as chasers."

"God, you almost killed yourself."

He licked his lips. "It was worth it. You never see stone crab like that on Long Island."

"Besides that, you scared the hell out of me and everybody else. Jasmine's probably under sedation."

The Fish struggled to sit up. "Oh, no, poor kid. That's terrible. I'll talk to her."

I put one hand on his chest and shoved him back down to the mattress. "Stay where you are. You've just had some powerful drugs. You may not be stable for a while."

He nodded meekly.

"They should chain you to the bed and keep you here for your own good, with monitored food intake. Maybe something they put through a blender that you eat with a tube in your throat, so they can see what's going in. But thanks to the miracles of modern medicine, they're releasing you. I'll get a taxi and take you back to your place."

The Fish tried to sit up again. "But Jasmine—"

"I'll leave word for her that you're okay and this is an allergy problem." I sat down on the edge of the bed. "You know, she's not wrong to be worried. Things are getting pretty dicey. Somebody got into my back patio area and put poisoned dog food out there. Trent had the food tested."

"How'd they get onto your patio in the first place?" asked the Fish, as he struggled to sit up.

"It's completely enclosed, and the entire community is gated and guarded. I don't know; it worries me a lot. That's why I asked Winnifred to leave. After what happened to Tony—"

"It's a classic pattern," said the Fish. "It's like concentric circles—they don't actually touch the center at first, they just get smaller and smaller as they approach it." He stared at me, bug-eyed. "God, I am so wired."

"It's the medications. They had to jump-start you. It'll wear off."

I looked at the Fish, who seemed about ready to jump out of his skin. His hair was sticking straight up, revealing the bald area beneath the comb-over; he looked like a walleyed pike with a Mohawk.

"What happens when these circles finally reach the center?"

"The thing is, we don't want things to get to that point. Preventive work is always much easier than cleanup."

"Well, at least we know who's behind your little side trip here," I said. "You."

The Fish hung his head humbly. "I've learned my lesson, I swear to God."

"Good."

"From now on, I'll stick to the four basic food groups—Domino's Pizza, Dunkin' Donuts, Mickey D's, and Taco Bell."

"When did the doctor say you could go back to work?"

"Tomorrow—no problem."

"Get dressed," I ordered him. "We're leaving."

As I sat in the hall and waited for the Fish, a Styrofoam cup of hot herbal tea materialized. Holding it was Gus.

"How is he?"

"Fine. It was an allergy. They're letting him out." I took the tea gratefully. My throat was parched from anxiety, and the hot cup felt good in my hand. "I'm going to take him home."

"Everyone is very concerned. Let me take you both to Fisher's place," Gus said. "We can get him safely home; then you and I can go on together. It's late. How are you getting back tonight?"

"I hadn't thought about that."

"I booked a room at the Bel Air. We'll have dinner there and spend the night."

The Fish emerged from his cubicle, his shirt open at the collar, his tie loosely draped around his neck. "Hi, doctor," he said. "Sorry I scared the troops."

Outside the hospital, a long black limousine was idling by the emergency room entrance. A uniformed driver sprang out and opened the door for us.

"Your car, Gus?"

"Trent told me to take it. He was going to order another one for him and his people."

"They do things in style."

"Well, it's a different world."

"Quite a change from the way I came in," cracked the Fish, noting the cut crystal decanters and color television built into a burled wood panel. "I must be moving up in the world."

We took the Fish to his building and then drove down Sunset, turned through the gates to the exclusive community of Bel Air, and wound along Stone Canyon Road to the Bel Air Hotel. The main building glowed a soft pearl pink in the shadows of the evening and the overgrown subtropical shrubbery. We checked in and were escorted to a small but exquisite pink villa with a living room with fireplace, bedroom with canopy bed, and sumptuous marble bath. The fire was already lit.

I took a long, lingering bubble bath and changed back into my black pantsuit, leaving off the jacket. Then we made our way to the dining room and had dinner outside, under a trellised canopy of vines and flowers, candles flickering on our table. Gus ordered a nice wine, and for the first time in months, in spite of everything, I felt relaxed.

"Did you know they're thinking of expanding the

Springs into a hotel and sports spa that's open to the general public?" I asked. "I saw the model. It's quite ambitious."

Gus nodded. "I know. It could be a big business, if it's done well."

"But everything would change, wouldn't it?" I said. "A spa may turn off the athletes who are now the mainstay of our business."

"You know, Jordan," Gus answered, as we started our salads, "when things change, it can be a great opportunity. You had an opportunity when you left tennis, although at the time you didn't see it that way. But it proved to be a fine thing for you, didn't it?"

"Yes, I admit it. By now, if I'd stayed in tennis, I'd have been a washed-up player looking for something to do."

"And now you have another chance to move on with your life."

"You mean the BioTech thing?"

Gus smiled. "No, I mean me. I was thinking, maybe we should talk about getting married."

My fork stopped halfway to my mouth, then dropped to my plate with a clatter. "Married?"

"Well, it's not unheard of. I was going to say this later, at some more appropriate time, but now I realize there *is* no appropriate time. Think of what a team we'd make, Jordan. We'd work together and live together, be real partners."

I stared at him. "Married," I said again, trying out the word.

"I know your last marriage didn't work, but you were so young. Now you know who you are and what you want, and so do I." He pushed a small envelope toward me. "I don't expect you to answer immediately. Think about it. And in the meantime, wear this."

I opened the envelope and took out a slim gold bracelet, studded with amethysts, my favorite stones. It glittered in the candlelight. Gus reached across the table and snapped it on my wrist. "Victorian," he said. "I thought it would be right for you. I've been carrying it around for weeks."

I stroked the bracelet. "It's perfect." I leaned across the table and kissed him. At that moment, marrying Gus seemed like the most natural thing in the world—but somehow I still wasn't ready to do it. "You know how much you mean to me, Gus," I said, "but can I have a little time to sort this out?"

"Of course you can. I expected that. You never do anything on the spur of the moment. If you'd said yes on the spot, I'd probably have keeled over myself, and you would have had to make another trip to the emergency room." He laughed, and so did I. "But you'll think about it?"

"I'm thinking, I'm thinking."

"Fine. To be continued."

I raised my wineglass. "To be continued." In a way, I wished I could have said yes right that minute, without reservations, made a commitment, rushed off to buy a white gown and veil. But the fact was that to commit to Gus was to commit to more than a man—it meant signing on for an entire lifestyle; he was that kind of person. Years ago, when I left tennis, I abruptly vacated the only life I had ever known. Facing a blank future, I was too numb to create a world of my own, so I wholeheartedly embraced the entire package Gus offered. It was the best time in our relationship, because there was no conflict. Everything was his way, and I cruised along, but at least the territory was familiar. His world was my dream too. Now, we'd grown in different directions, and that was no longer the case. His lifestyle was foreign to me, a kaleidoscope of products and corporations, limos and perks. I couldn't delude myself into thinking that this wouldn't be my world, too, if we were married. Once Duration had been launched and the initial push was over, things would probably calm down. Maybe then I'd get a more accurate reading on what a future with Gus might involve. Besides, I told myself, so many negative things were happening right now. I didn't want my personal life to get swept into this whirlpool of disasters. There were, it seemed, a lot of reasons to wait.

But there was no reason not to enjoy the evening for what it was. Gus and I finished the dinner, we finished the wine, and we talked till there was nothing more to say. Then we walked down a fragrant path back to the room, where logs crackled in the fireplace, the bed had been turned back to reveal smooth, expensive sheets, a three-tiered tray of tiny pastries and chocolates had been placed on the night table, and a bottle of chilled wine stood in a cooler. Somehow, in the midst of the shock and sadness of the day, we had a perfect night.

The next afternoon, I was the sole passenger on the BioTech plane for the return trip to Palm Springs. Sunday Stanley was the pilot. When I got on the plane, I had a few minutes to talk to her.

"What happened with the bomb threat?" I asked. "Did they ever learn who made it?"

"Not that I know of," she said. "If they ever find out, though, the person could be put in jail. You don't mess with aviation. They take a threat very seriously. Of course, it could just have been a nuisance call. We get those from time to time."

"Speaking of which, did anyone ever learn more about the pilot who tried to trim my hair the other day?" I asked.

"Not really. He's out of the country now, I understand. I'm sure it was just a maneuver he had to make. I wouldn't worry about it. Things happen at airports for reasons that involve the planes, not the people on the ground. We have more major issues to think about, like flying."

"So you don't fly full time for BioTech? You're with the charter company?"

"Well, actually, I personally fly for BioTech exclusively, but you have to have more than one pilot. There are turnaround times to consider, and geographic things. For instance, last week I had to fly this plane to Florida. It's a five-hour trip. I couldn't turn around and come back, then climb back into the cockpit immediately and fly again; it would be against regulations. So if they needed the plane after that, they would arrange for another pilot to take over and I would deadhead back to LA on another plane, with the charter company."

"I see. Do you do those cross-country trips often?"

"Well, Florida's a pretty frequent trip, and they have offices in some other cities on the East Coast, so, yes, fairly often. But I don't mind. I love to move around. I'd be bored out of my mind with a desk job."

"I know what you mean," I said.

Sunday adjourned to the cockpit for her preflight

checklist, and I settled into a wide burgundy leather seat to go over some reading about the new product that Gus had given me. As the plane took off, I looked out the window when we passed the hangar where I had stood near the runway. I could see how sharply the plane would have had to have veered to come so close to me.

I thumbed through the folder on my lap. In one of the pockets was a glossy brochure, with a picture of the Duration drink, power bar, and vitamin/mineral supplements on the cover. Inside, almost every page featured a testimonial from a famous athlete, including Malik. They would have to reprint the brochures, I thought. I closed the brochure and pulled out another sheet, which listed information about the BioTech Corporation, obviously to provide information to press or investors. The company was even bigger than I'd thought. There were ten subsidiaries, but the only name familiar to me was a clothing manufacturer. I was about to stick the sheet back in the folder when one name jumped out at me: Filament. The Filament Group, a sportswear manufacturer headquartered in Boca Raton, Florida. *Filament*. That was the name of the company Anna Martinez had gone to work for—in Florida. The Filament Group. I let the name sink in. Anna Martinez had gotten a job with a BioTech subsidiary. Apparently, even the Fish didn't realize that the Filament Group was part of BioTech. Or maybe it wasn't so much that Anna had gotten a job as that BioTech had *given* her a job. Could they have recruited her and moved her to Florida? But why would they do that?

When the plane landed after our short flight, I stuck my head in the cockpit. "It was a very nice flight."

"Thank you," said Sunday.

"Your trips to Florida that you mentioned—do you by any chance fly to Boca Raton?" I asked.

Sunday turned in her seat, still wearing her headphones. "That's one of our destinations."

"Who goes on these trips?"

"You know, Ms. Myles, I'm really not at liberty to discuss my employer's business. But I'm sure they'll be happy to answer your questions if you ask them personally. Now, if you'll excuse me, I have to file my flight plan." She turned back into the cockpit and busied herself with the instruments.

I went straight to the office. There, at her desk, peering intently at the one-inch-tall magnified blue type on her computer screen, sat Winnifred, with A.M. cozily ensconced on her lap. "Winnifred! You're supposed to be in Canada!"

A.M. leaped down to lick my ankles.

"Well, dear, we had work to do. The mail and the messages don't stop just because you're not here, you know. And that fax! There's a wicked invention, if there ever was one." She continued to scroll the screen.

"Winnifred, what am I going to do with you?" I pleaded. "Don't you realize you could be in danger? I couldn't bear to have anything happen to you." The memory of Tony made my chest physically ache. "Please, please, go to your sister's!"

Winnifred looked up from the screen, her eyes blazing behind the rhinestone frames. "Dear, I am an old lady. I have always lived my life exactly as I chose, and I do not intend to change now." She lifted her chin defiantly. "You will have to fire me if you want me to leave, and you know I have a terrible hearing problem and wouldn't be able to hear you if you did. Now that's final." She resumed poking at the keyboard.

I sighed and leaned over to give her a hug. "What am I going to do with you?" I said.

"Work. We're behind. Now get to your desk and man the stations!" She flicked me off with a wave of her hand.

I walked into my office. A small nosegay of fresh violets, my favorite flower, lay on top of my desk. I didn't have to ask who they were from: Gus had sent violets to me twice before—when I got out of the hospital and the day I started work as a partner at the Springs. I knew that fresh violets were almost impossible to obtain this time of year; Gus would have had to have them flown in from somewhere. I picked up the nosegay and stroked the small, velvety faces of the flowers. The purple shade matched the stones in my bracelet.

The first thing I wanted to do was learn more about the Filament Group. I put a call in to the Fish, then logged on to the Internet, starting with a keyword search on Filament. There were dozens of articles. I pulled up a piece from *Forbes* magazine that told how the company had originated the concept of professional women's sportswear designed by female designers—a "for women, by women" positioning that made them unique in the market. It was interesting but not revealing. I pulled up another piece, this one from a month-old issue of *The Wall Street Journal*. This one examined how Wall Street was following the Filament Group in the "wake of rumors that the privately held company would soon go public." I plowed through three or four more articles, until one came up from the *Miami Herald*. My eyes froze on the page when I saw Trent's name. Trent was quoted as saying that the BioTech family was "a dimensional-ized organization that was like the human body, an organism with a head, heart, and limbs"—typical Trent-speak—and the Filament Group was the "legs" of the company's future. I reread that one, trying to figure out what the link was between BioTech and the Filament Group, and what could make the Filament Group so critical to BioTech that they considered them their so-called legs. Of course, it could all be puffery and corpo-rate PR, but there was the matter of Anna Martinez and her six-figure job. As the Fish had predicted, the concen-tric circles were beginning to converge.

When the Fish answered his beeper page, I filled him in. "I really got an education today," I said. "What do you know about the Filament Group, and what does Anna Martinez have to do with it, and how did she get there?"

"This company has more arms than a mutated octopus," said the Fish. "I'll get into it. As for Anna Martinez, this does not seem like your everyday coincidence."

"Agreed."

"I'll get the personnel records. Let me get back to you. I'm not in the office."

"Where are you?"

"Still in Malibu. Kessler's got me attached to Jasmine. The woman combs her hair, it goes into my report."

"I know some scary things are going on, but don't you think that's overdoing it?"

"Probably, but you know Kessler. Besides, this isn't a bad vantage point. You see some interesting things."

"Such as?"

"Such as Kessler seems to be really going all out for

this girl. He's moved out of his own place, and there's like a permanent deal with the florist. He sends her flowers on a daily basis. Jewelry, too."

"Sounds personal to me," I said. Paul Kessler was known to hit on every woman on the tour. That he was trying to add Jasmine to his list surprised me only by the tasteless timing of his effort. "Is she practicing?"

"Yeah, it's intense. They brought in a new coach. And Billie Jean King is coming in for a week. I got the schedule. Jasmine's going down to Hilton Head a week early, to practice."

"Do you think the bomb threat was connected to Anna Martinez?"

"Well, she's in Florida."

"She could have called long distance. They never found anything on the plane or in anybody's luggage, did they?"

"No. It was just a scare. But to be safe, they're questioning the airport personnel."

"This whole thing is connected somehow, that's what I think. But how?"

"Well, you can think about it when you get here."

"What do you mean?"

"You'll be hearing from Kessler. Jasmine's asking for you to help her train."

At that minute, Winnifred came in and thrust a fax under my nose. It was from Paul, and, just as the Fish had said, he was asking me to come to Malibu to help Jasmine train for Hilton Head. "Yeah," I said. "Here it is. He sent a fax."

"You coming out?"

I didn't have to think about it. "I'll do it for two reasons," I said. "One, because I feel I owe it to Jas to help her get back on her feet. Two, because I owe it to Jas to pry Kessler off her. The scumbag."

The Fish snorted. "You could be his next target."

"Oh, please!" I hung up and handed the fax back to Winnifred. "Call Paul Kessler and tell him I'll drive up in two days. I don't feel like encountering any more airports just now."

Winnifred nodded and put a pile of mail on the table in front of me. Today, her polka-dot thematic was pink. She tapped the top piece of paper with a matching pink fingernail. "This one is from the network. They want you to do commentary at Hilton Head. Actually, your friend Harrison called while you were at the funeral, but I didn't think it seemly to put him through."

I suspected that the network was more than a little interested in my relationship with Jasmine at this point. The fact that Paul had her sequestered would only serve to make her a hotter media commodity. They probably hoped to use me to get an up-close-and-personal interview with her at Hilton Head. But two could play that game. I could use them, too. I knew if I stayed in the background and lost my visibility, I'd also lose my leverage. "Tell them I'll do it," I said.

I spent the next hour going over the notebook Bill had given me, which described the proposed Desert Springs Sports Science *Spa* and Sports Science Clinic. The front half of the book was an elaborate pictorial layout, with an artist's rendering of what the Springs would look like after the proposed expansion, right down to a three-page spread on the hotel, complete with room interiors and fabric swatches. The back half of the book was twenty pages of numbers, projected payout plans and five- and ten-year projections. I had to admit it was professionally put together. The numbers didn't mean anything to me, but I assumed they showed it was profitable, or they wouldn't have included them in the book. Looking at the plans, though, I couldn't see where I would fit in. There was a page called Professional Sports Program, but it seemed like more of a footnote to the expansive hotel and merchandising program. The book felt heavy in my hands, leaden. Maybe TV was the place for me now. Or maybe with Gus. I looked at the amethyst bracelet.

After work, I went for a bike ride with Ginny Jennings. We rode into the desert, which was monochromatically beautiful, somehow reflecting the sky in its cold dustiness.

"It's beautiful—but are you going to do it? Marry Gus?" she asked after I showed her the bracelet.

"I don't know," I admitted. "I don't want to hurtle off into marriage because nothing else is working out. That's a bad reason."

"Of course. But it's not as if you're rushing into this, Jordan. You two have been together off and on for years now, and each time things get close, one of you pulls out. It boils down to this: What are you really interested in doing with your life? What do you really want to do?"

"Work with tennis players."

"I don't hear the words 'family' or 'commitment' in there."

I sighed. "I guess tennis is still the bottom line for me. Helping people with their game, even interviewing them, the whole world I grew up in. That was my family; that was my life and the only world I've ever known. I can't imagine myself tied up in a marriage, either to a person or a product. Maybe I'm a selfish, small-picture person. But I have a feeling of family and commitment about the Springs. I've put my heart and soul into this place. I don't want to lose it now. I want to get Gus's shares and vote to keep it the way it is."

"I hear the shares are promised already."

"That's impossible. It's in the bylaws that only existing shareholders can purchase them."

"Well, I heard through the fund-raising grapevine—I talk to a lot of people in the financial community, you know, and they have a way of hearing things. It's like jungle drums out there. Supposedly an offer is out."

I braked my bike and skidded to a stop. "You're serious? Who's made this offer?"

Ginny circled back. "Somebody from BioTech. They're trying to work something out. That's the word."

"They won't do it," I said firmly. "The shares can't be acquired by outsiders."

"Bylaws have been known to change, if boards vote that way."

I felt angry and betrayed. "What is BioTech trying to do? This isn't their business."

"I'd say they're trying to make it their business," said Ginny. "Wouldn't you?"

"I've got to go back, right now. Sorry, Gin."

We rode back to the Springs and I went immediately to Bill's office without even changing my clothes. I was dripping with sweat and probably smelled less than pleasant, but I didn't care.

"He's in the middle of an interview with a European magazine," said Kim, his secretary, motioning toward the closed office door. "Do you want to come back?"

"I'll wait." I paced outside his secretary's doorway

until I saw the interviewer leave; then, without the nicety of asking Kim to announce me, I stormed past her desk and into his office.

"What's going on, Bill?" I demanded. "I understand there's a rumor that Gus's stock is being acquired by an outsider."

Bill lifted an eyebrow when he saw me, in bike shorts and still rumpled from my ride. "Jordan! I don't see why you're shouting. Please lower your voice and we'll have a logical discussion." Bill, as usual, was glassily calm, sitting with his hands in his lap, his face unreadable. He would have made an excellent poker player. "First of all, you're misinformed. An outsider is not acquiring any stock. I thought we discussed that earlier."

"Really?" I stood there, feeling slightly foolish. I pulled off my biking gloves and wadded them into my pocket.

"If you'll sit down, I'll go over everything with you."

I perched on the arm of a couch, forcing myself to not tap my foot impatiently.

"Now, here's the scenario. Did you read the material I gave you?"

"I did. I thought it was very—slick."

"Well, the benefits, in the mind of the board and my own as well, are obvious. BioTech is going to make a firm offer to become our partner, which would give us a major cash infusion—and we don't need to go over the benefits of that again. If this were to occur, Gus would, as part of our partnership company, still be part of the corporate family. In which case, of course, he wouldn't need to sell his stock. He would have the option to retain it."

"Or someone else could buy it from him," I noted. "Like Trent. Or one of those other sharks he works with."

"You mean our new partners."

"Call them what you will."

"You know, Jordan, you're such a purist. That's one of the things I admire about you. But it's to your benefit that this works out as well. BioTech is a blue chip company. They offer us incredible expansion possibilities. The value of all our stock will go up as a result of this expansion. In a few years, we'll be in a position to put together a major public offering. Do you have any idea how much money would be involved?"

"I suppose you're right in principle, Bill, but I can't help but wonder if things will stay the same," I said.

Bill smiled. "You're right. Things might not stay the same. But is that always bad?"

"I suppose the jury's going to be out on our situation for a while."

"What do you say we don't pre-guess the verdict? I know change is uncomfortable, Jordan. I can't say I'm not nervous myself. But one thing's sure: Nobody's railroading anything through here. The plan is to have an open forum and a vote of all the shareholders after Hilton Head. All the facts will be on the table, and we'll have had plenty of time to get to know all the players. You'll have your chance to have your say, I promise you. Until then, this is all very confidential and preliminary."

I nodded, but I was only partly relieved. I wasn't so naive as to think that the lure of big stock gains and commercialization wouldn't be a highly tempting proposition. What I'd seen of Trent and Company didn't make me feel much better about getting into bed with them, so to speak. I didn't think I was cut out to be a corporate type. And then there was the rash of threats, the deaths, the string of mishaps. It was as if someone had put a curse on us, and we couldn't escape it. Somehow, this merger opportunity seemed like another link in a chain of events that I wished had never happened.

THIRTEEN

I drove straight through to Malibu from Palm Springs without stopping in LA. I wanted to start working with Jasmine as soon as possible, as much for my own sake as for hers. The ocean air was always relaxing, and I hoped the intense work we were going to do would clear my head. There was just one distraction: Winnifred. Since she absolutely refused to be sent to visit her sister, and I didn't feel secure about leaving her at the Springs, the only solution I could think of was to take her along with me. In Malibu, the house was gated and guarded, and the Fish and I would be there to watch out for her. At least I wouldn't have to worry about her, and she could take care of A.M. while I worked with Jasmine. Paul told me it would be fine if I brought my secretary.

The three of us—Winnifred, A.M., and me—arrived at Paul's house and I announced us through the intercom. The gate swung open and a young blue-jeaned guard appeared and directed us to the coach house, where we left the car and our few bags. "I'm Jimmy," he introduced himself. "You'll have the observatory suite, Ms. Myles," he said, leading the way into the house.

"Observatory?"

He smiled over his shoulder. "Mr. Kessler is an amateur astronomer."

"Really?" The only stars I knew Paul to observe were those on the pages of the sports magazines and tabloids.

"Yes," Jimmy continued. "I'm an astronomy student myself, at Cal State. He has a professional-quality observatory, with a high-power telescope and lab—pretty impressive setup. We were able to see the last comet before anybody else on the coastline. There are also complete living facilities attached to the lab, including a kitchen and sauna. I'm sure you'll enjoy it."

I laughed. "I can barely pick out the Milky Way."

"Well, Mr. Kessler doesn't use the lab very often," Jimmy said. He opened the door with a key card and led us through the front of the house, which I remembered from the memorial service, to another door, which led to a separate wing overlooking the ocean. At the end of a hall, some skylit spiral stairs led up several flights. "That takes you to the lab," Jimmy said. "But unless you're planning to plot some constellations, you'll be in these three rooms. The sauna is adjacent to the bathroom. You'll find everything you need—robes, slippers, hair dryers—and the refrigerator is stocked. There's even dog food. I'll just put your bags in the bedroom."

"Thank you, Jimmy."

"Now isn't this sweet!" exclaimed Winnifred, gazing out the floor-to-ceiling windows to the ocean. She immediately plunked herself down on an overstuffed sofa and took out her embroidery, as A.M. sniffed the perimeter of the sisal rug. "I'll just make myself comfy," Winnifred said. "You go on with your work, dear."

"Jasmine is waiting for you at the tennis court," said Jimmy.

I followed him back through the main house, with its double-height ceilings, and out a side door. A series of decks overlooked the tennis courts, where Jasmine was working on her backhand with a hitting partner. She saw me and waved, then set down her racket and dashed up the steps to the deck.

"I'm so glad you're here, Jordan," she said. "I need to focus. Ever since the memorial, I can't concentrate at all." She sank dejectedly into a deck chair.

"How much tennis have you been playing?"

"Six hours a day. At least it keeps my mind off other things."

"Six hours? Jasmine, the first thing you're going to do is stop playing so much."

"Stop? But—"

"Remember what I told you at the Springs? You need to develop *all* your muscles, be more balanced with your strength. We're going to cross-train. This is the perfect place."

"Whatever you say. What do you have in mind?"

"Well, we're at the beach, so we'll run wind sprints on the sand. We'll take out the kayaks. We'll swim. I see Paul has a basketball hoop—we'll play a little serious one-on-one. And maybe we'll do some horseback riding. How's that sound for starters?"

"Fun." She smiled. "See? I knew it was a good idea to bring you here. Do you think I have a chance to win at Hilton Head?"

"No promises, Jasmine. We'll work hard. But in the end, the winning part is up to you—and the player you're up against. If I learned one thing in my years on the tour, it's never predict. It has been a very hard time for you

emotionally, I know that. But I can tell you this much—
some people say that winning in tennis is as much as
ninety percent mental. Without confidence, you can never
reach the performance level that your body is capable of.
I'll work with you on the physical aspects, but in the
end the mindset is yours. You have an outcome goal:
Win the tournament. But the truth is, no one can control
an outcome goal. What you *can* control is your own
performance—giving one hundred percent; looking and
feeling strong and confident, even when it gets tough out
there. That's realistic. It's achievable. And one can lead
to the other. Let's work together on that."

Jasmine nodded solemnly. "When do we start?"

"How about today? Go put on your running shoes."

I ran inside, found my way to the conservatory to
change and pulled on my shorts, T-shirt, and windbreaker, then looped my stopwatch on a cord around my
neck. The Fish was in our little sitting room, chatting
with Winnifred, when I came out of the bedroom.

"Fred here was telling me that you're engaged," said
the Fish.

"Fred is misinformed." I shot her a look.

"Well, dear, it *is* the next logical step. And you're not
getting any younger."

"Thank God."

"I have some word for you about the Filament Group,"
said the Fish.

"And Anna Martinez?"

"Right. Confidentially, of course. According to the
personnel files, she was highly recommended by Dr.
Laidlaw."

"What?"

"That's right. Dr. Gus himself pulled strings to get her

the job. She's working in public relations. Her background was barely sufficient, but she immediately became the prime candidate. And they paid for her move."

"There has to be a reason for this," I said.

"There's a reason for everything. We just don't know it yet."

"We will soon, you better believe that." I grabbed the phone and dialed Gus at the BioTech office. He was in a meeting. "Well, get him out. This is Jordan Myles, and it's very important," I found myself barking into the phone.

"Jordan." Gus was abrupt. "What's so urgent? Where are you?"

"I'm at Paul Kessler's in Malibu, with Jasmine."

"Maybe I can drive down and meet you for dinner at Granita."

"I'm not calling about dinner plans. I need to ask you—what's this about Anna Martinez?"

"It's no secret. I arranged to have Trent relocate her. She's in Florida."

"So I understand. But why?"

"She was driving you and everybody else crazy. It's psychological, Jordan. Rather than have her be a continual antagonist—a hysteric, in fact—my professional opinion was, Let's give the poor woman a new purpose in life. We can't make up for the loss of her daughter, God knows, but at least she can make a new start. I'm hoping the threats and the hysterics will stop now. It's time to turn the page."

"You never mentioned it, Gus."

"Why should I? You have enough on your mind. And she's adjusting well to her new job, they tell me. At least, I haven't heard otherwise."

"So now you're playing God? Did you by any chance stop by her place when she was moving?"

"Let's not start, Jordan. How about dinner at Granita?"

"Fine. But there's a lot unresolved here. I'm not sure it's so simple. The woman needed help, not career counseling. She's not a chess piece who can simply be repositioned."

"I'm the psychologist, if you recall."

"That you are." I still wondered if it had been Gus behind the curtains that night.

"I'll see you tonight. Granita, eight o'clock."

I hung up.

"So was I right?" asked the Fish, who'd been listening to my end of the conversation.

"You were right. And I hope Gus is too. I hope it was that simple—giving her a job and moving her out."

"Doesn't explain the bomb threat on the plane," said the Fish.

"Maybe she's part of an international network," volunteered Winnifred, clearly relishing the prospect.

"Maybe she can still use the phone," I said. "You watch too many thrillers on TV, Winnifred. But I still think that just relocating somebody isn't going to stop how they think, especially if they're irrational. Gus should know that. Like he reminded me, he *is* a psychologist. Now if you'll excuse me, I'm going to run on the beach with Jasmine."

The Fish stood up. "I'll go with you."

I stared at him. "Please. You'll just slow us down."

"I'm supposed to guard Jasmine and make sure nothing happens to her, remember?"

"If you try to keep up with us on the beach, you'll keel over and we'll be rushing you back to the hospital again.

Do us both a favor and watch from the window or the balcony, okay?"

The beach was almost deserted as Jasmine and I ran along the hard sand at the water's edge of Point Dume Beach, toward Zuma. We passed a lone emergency station, where a lifeguard in red shorts was washing down his yellow truck with a hose. The concessions and beach-front restaurant were closed and shuttered until summer, when they would once again be mobbed by sun seekers. High on the cliffs above us, houses stood side by side, multimillion-dollar sentinels of the view. Back at Paul's after our run, we broke for a pasta lunch, served on the deck. The slope was too steep and the beach too wide for us to carry the kayaks down to the water ourselves, so I asked Jimmy to load them into the van Paul had left for the house and bring them down to the shore.

"Have you ever done any kayaking?" I asked Jasmine.

"No, I haven't. It looks like fun. But won't the water be cold?"

"Mr. Kessler has wet suits in every size in the pool house for the use of his guests," said Jimmy. "That should help keep you dry and at least reasonably warm."

"In that case," I said, "the only tricky part is getting out past the breakers and then steering clear of the kelp beds. Just follow me. Oh, and don't stand up in the boat."

Soon we were stroking smoothly along the coastline, enjoying the view, the ocean, and the workout simultaneously. After two hours of kayaking we came in, changed and played some basketball, and then, as it was getting dark, we finally called it a day.

"That's going to be our routine," I said. "Weight training first thing, then tennis with your coach in the morning only. After lunch, we'll do other things, rotating hill climbing, kayaking, swimming, running, basketball, and whatever else I can throw into the mix. When we get closer to the tournament, we'll narrow it down to strictly tennis, but for now you need the variety and you need to strengthen your wrist in other ways than just by serving a tennis ball."

"I'm actually looking forward to this," said Jasmine, shaking out her hair. "I can't believe it. For a while I thought I would never be interested in anything again. Thanks."

"Don't thank me yet. We have a lot of hard work ahead of us."

That night, I met Gus at Granita, which is located in a shopping mall but still manages to be one of Malibu's most celebrity-oriented restaurants. It's low key but so-phisticated, which attracts a lot of the stars in the area, particularly during the summer season. Since it was a weeknight and not summer, however, there was a sparse crowd when I arrived.

Gus met me at the table, leaned in for a quick kiss, and ordered a bottle of wine.

"So I guess we're going to be partners again," I said. "Bill told me about the BioTech offer."

"The board still has to vote," said Gus.

"But it looks like it'll go through. It seems to be what Bill wants, anyway."

"And you?" Gus asked.

"I don't know what I want, except I'm worried that if they make the Springs a spa and open it to the public, it'll be Disneyland."

Gus laughed. "Hardly likely. But considering the fi-

nancial alternatives, it may be the best thing for everybody. And then, if you help promote Duration with me,
there won't be a conflict of interest. In fact, as I see it, the
Springs endorsement will be on every package. And the
Springs would, of course, share in some of the profits."

I sipped my wine as Gus examined the cork. "Just one
big happy family."

"Well, look at Nike, for instance. They have the products, the athletes' endorsements, the retail outlets. It's
Marketing One-oh-one."

"Synergy."

"Right. And you and I are going to be an amazing
team. After all, when—excuse me, I don't want to pressure you—let's say *if* we get married, we'll be the biggest
private shareholders."

"Combined, you mean."

"Exactly. We'll have a major power bloc."

"Just what I always wanted to be—a power bloc," I
said. "Actually, Gus, I was thinking of being a bride, not
a bloc. I thought we were discussing a wedding, not a
merger." I twisted my bracelet.

"Our work and our lives have always coexisted,
Jordan," said Gus. "That's what our relationship has been
about."

"You know what? I don't think I want to be part of
anybody's bloc. I think I'm going to vote against this
merger. Actually, I'm going to lobby against it."

"And what about us?" He stared at me.

"I thought we had a relationship, not a business deal.
If we're going to get married, it has to be for the right
reasons. A merger and a product promotion are not the
right reasons, at least not for me. What goes on between

us shouldn't have anything to do with my business decisions—or yours, for that matter."

"Well, of course not, but our lives are totally integrated with our work. It wouldn't make sense to be iconoclastic right now. We're at a crossroads here."

"Tell me about it."

"We have to consider our future, Jordan, the fact that we have the chance to build something together." He shook his head and smiled ruefully. "Sometimes I think you take the opposite point of view from me just to set up some kind of sounding board, to help get your own head straight."

I thought about this for a minute. "It's possible. But I still know what I think and what I want."

Gus looked up and signaled the waiter. "We'd like to order. By the way, just to put your mind at ease, I made a few calls and checked on Anna Martinez."

I looked up from the menu. "And?"

"And she's doing fine. Seems to have handled the move nicely, and she's fitting in on the job. Of course, it's still early, but all indications look good." He put down his menu. "I think I'll have the salmon. How about you?"

"I'll just have an appetizer as a main course, I think. I get up early and put in a big day when I'm working with Jasmine." I described the routine. "But, Gus, I was wondering, if Anna's doing so well and she didn't make that threat to the plane on the way to Malik's memorial, who did?"

"Could be any number of people. You keep personalizing this, but I should tell you, Trent has plenty of people who aren't too happy with him, and any of them could be involved. It could be a corporate thing. He downsized the organization a few months ago and had to let a lot of people go. Strange things have been known to happen after events like that. People get disgruntled, go a little nuts. Sometimes they file nuisance suits, and sometimes they've been known to make vindictive calls. You know, those types who can't see why their jobs were eliminated when the company still keeps a plane. That could be one reason why they would focus on the threat at the airport. I'm going to ask Fisher to look into the people who were let go."

"Fisher thinks all these things are concentric circles, as he calls them—connected somehow."

"The Fish spent too long in the CIA. This isn't the Cold War, it's simple psychology. Now let's get our food. I still have to drive back to LA tonight."

After ten days of working with Jasmine at the beach, I was beginning to think the worst was over. Every day she grew stronger, psychologically as well as physically, and as her strength became more uniform her tennis game improved proportionately. We had a good time, while we were at it, laughing with the Fish and Winnifred every night before going to bed early. Paul, our absentee host, appeared only once, to take Jasmine out to dinner. Aside from that, it was like being at an adult summer camp. We fell into a routine. Kayaking was always the highlight of the day for me. I love being close to nature, and as I paddled the kayak, I felt like a sea animal myself. Many afternoons, as the sun was setting, we saw the pod of dolphins, sometimes as many as twelve or thirteen, paralleling our kayaks as we stroked along the shoreline. We moved Jasmine's routine along, preparing her for Hilton Head, and, watching her on the courts with her coach, Taryn Henderson, a former Davis Cup star herself, it was impossible not to think she would make an indelible impression. I wasn't sure she could win, but I knew she would make a terrific showing, the strongest of her career.

As the time for the tournament came closer, Jasmine's training program intensified and she concentrated exclusively on her tennis, but I continued to go out in the kayak on my own. I liked having some time alone with my thoughts. Every day out on the waves, I debated with myself about marrying Gus and also about the fate of the Springs as a subset of BioTech, because that was what I was convinced it would become. I had the feeling we'd all end up as Trent's employees, and I didn't relish the idea one bit.

About a week before I was due to leave for pre-production meetings at Hilton Head, I couldn't locate Jimmy, so I hauled out the kayak, loaded it into the van, and drove it down to the beach myself. The seas were rough, and it took close to half an hour just to get away from the shore without being beaten back by the waves. Finally, I paddled out to where the big rollers rocked the kayak rhythmically as I made my way along the shoreline. The sun was setting flaming orange. Behind me, I could see the lights of Santa Monica, the "necklace," as the local residents called it.

I was aware of the boat before I saw it—a distant hum of engines, becoming louder as it approached—but I didn't turn my head. There were often boats in the area, but rarely this close to shore, due to the surfers and swimmers. This boat, however, didn't veer off or keep its distance. I turned and saw its bow cutting through the waves, directly across my path; it was a fair-sized powerboat, maybe thirty-five or forty feet, with a flying bridge.

Probably a sport fisherman. I quickly paddled my kayak closer to shore, but the wake of the powerboat was fierce, and I found myself flipped vertical in the water. I held my breath, stayed in the kayak, and paddled myself upright, a maneuver called a kayak roll, which I had learned years ago on a camping trip. Surfacing, I saw the powerboat turn and cut through the waves directly toward me. I waved my paddle, but I could see it didn't help: The boat was going to run me down. It was getting dark, and I was in my wet suit. I knew that if I left the kayak I would be close to invisible in the water. The question was, were they deliberately trying to swamp or run over me? If not, perhaps I would be better off staying with the kayak. In an instant, watching the looming form bear down on me, I decided not to make a riddle of it. I slid over the side of the kayak, dived, and swam as far as I could underwater, hoping the waves would take me in before the current could take me out. In the dark, cold ocean, I swam as if my life depended on it till my lungs felt ready to burst. I broke the surface in the middle of a kelp bed, gasping for air, and in silhouette against the sky I saw the powerboat glance off the side of the kayak, tossing it into a twisted wreck. I gulped in a breath and ducked underwater again, and this time I managed to struggle to the crest of a huge roller and bodysurf to the shore, crashing into the sand and taking in a mouthful of seawater. My lungs ached and I felt nauseated as I lay coughing and dazed in the frigid foam at the edge of the ocean, lashed by incoming waves. It was dark by now, and I scrambled helplessly on my hands and knees, caught in the undertow as it sucked me out with every gathering wave and spit me back onto the sand with the thundering roll of each new breaker.

I wondered if I should swim out past the waves again

and find a better place to come in. But then, there was an equal chance that I would be sucked out into the ocean and, in the dark, drift without being discovered. At least I was wearing the wet suit; otherwise, by now I would probably have had hypothermia, and the sand would have ripped a layer of skin off my whole body. As it was, my palms and knuckles were raw from being buffeted against the shore. It was all I could do to remain calm.

Suddenly, I felt a vicelike grip under my arms, as if all the air was being compressed out of me, and I kicked, clawed, and struggled with all my strength to break free. Salt water and sand stung my eyes as I lost any sense of which way was up, down, or back beneath the waves. Everything was a dark, salty swirl as I felt myself being dragged onto the cold, dry sand.

"That's her!" I heard a voice above the roar of the waves. A blinding light blazed into my face. But the voice sounded familiar. It was Winnifred, dripping wet, her face anxious.

"Turn her over! See if she's breathing!" she commanded.

I lay there, exhausted and unable to move, and retched and vomited seawater. Then someone flipped me onto my back.

"Get a blanket! Hurry!" said a voice.

I felt a hand brush sand from my face. "You'll be fine, dear. We'll get you up to the house and I'll make tea." My eyes burned when I tried to open them, but I could make out Winnifred bending over me again, tucking a blanket under my chin.

"I'm fine," I managed to whisper. I struggled to sit up.

"Jimmy, get her into the car," Winnifred said, wiping my face with her hankie. "I'm sorry, dear, but it's just me and Jimmy. He was showing me how to use the telescope, the smaller one out on the deck off our room, and I saw you out there. I saw everything that happened, dear, with those irresponsible boaters. Goodness, you could have been sliced in half by the propeller! We got down here as quickly as we could, but I didn't have time to find Mr. Fisher or anyone else at the house. Jimmy's paging him now."

Red emergency lights flashed as a lifeguard truck raced up the beach toward us, its bank of floodlights strafing the beach.

"I'm not hurt," I said. "I'm fine, I really am." I stood up rather shakily, my legs more unsteady from nerves than anything else. I squinted out into the darkness, trying to pick out some lights, perhaps spot the powerboat, but I knew it was futile. I wrapped the blanket closer around me. Well, I thought anyone with half a brain who'd wanted to kill me would surely have succeeded by now. If they were only trying to frighten me, they were doing an excellent job. But frighten me about what?

The lifeguard jumped out of his truck and raced across the sand to my side. He was closely followed by a small fleet of emergency vehicles—an ambulance, a police car, and a fire engine.

"All this attention is embarrassing," I said. "Winnifred, was that you in the water? You could have drowned out there, like I almost did."

"Drowned?" she scoffed. "I swam the Channel as a girl."

"What channel?"

She smiled vaguely.

The Fish drove his car directly onto the sand and rushed to my side. He surveyed me, shivering and wet in the blanket. "Good God, Jordan, what were you doing out there, playing Moby Dick?"

Winnifred put an arm protectively around me. "What this girl needs now is a hot shower, and I'm going to see that she gets it. Let's go, dear." She turned on the lifeguard in a momentary fury. "Where were you people? If this were *Baywatch*, you would have rescued her! You would have arrested the driver of that boat! Let's go, Jimmy." Defiantly, she led me back to Jimmy's van as the lifeguard stood by helplessly.

I looked over my shoulder at the Fish. "They've tried to get me on land, via my dog, then air, and now by sea," I said, plucking a piece of seaweed out of my hair.

"That, or you're very unlucky with where you put yourself," he said.

"What do you think I should do now?"

The Fish thought for a minute. "If I were you, I'd stay out of caves."

"I certainly hope you're going to file a complaint." Winnifred bristled. "My dress is ruined."

"And what will they say?" I said. "That it was dark and they couldn't see me. If they even find the boat, that is."

"At least you'd know who it belonged to." She pulled the blanket tighter around me as we walked.

"I suppose they'll have as much luck with this one as with the airplane," I said. "Or the dog food, for that matter. There will be one of two answers: a logical explanation or no explanation."

"Dear, you should just go home and mind your own business."

"Somehow I think that's what they're trying to tell me, Winnifred. But, you know, the funny thing is, that's what

I was doing here—minding my own business. So it must be something more. Maybe I'm overly paranoid, but this seems like a personal vendetta."

As I sat in the car, bundled in the blanket, I rubbed my hands together and realized the bracelet Gus had given me was gone. It must have fallen off in the rough water. Because it was an antique, I knew I wouldn't be able to replace it. Sometimes, when you lose a piece of jewelry, the part of your body that it touched feels naked without it. But I hadn't worn the bracelet for very long, and my wrist didn't feel that way. Not at all.

"Don't worry about the bracelet," Gus said when I called him after a long hot shower and twenty minutes in the hot tub. It had taken that much to get my circulation started again—or at least that's how it felt. "It doesn't matter. I'm just glad you weren't hurt. I'll be glad when we're married and living together once and for all. Then I can keep an eye on you."

"I don't need someone to keep an eye on me. That's absurd."

"Well, that's not what I meant. Of course you don't. Let's put it this way: You seem to have a penchant for putting yourself in situations that are unhealthy. Be that as it may, I think that working with these private clients is embroiling you in their problems, and to a dangerous degree. You've got to draw the line, establish some boundaries."

"It's not Jasmine's fault that a boat almost ran over me. Or a plane."

"It's nobody's fault, I'm sure. But I can't help but worry. I care about you, Jordan. I wish we were working together, like we used to. Then everything made a lot more sense, and we had a lot more fun. Why don't we go to Hilton Head together?"

"I'm doing commentary for the network, and Jasmine's playing. I wouldn't have much time to be a significant other."

"Well, I'm going to be busy too—we're going to be shooting some footage for the Duration infomercial."

"Tournament footage? They let you do that?"

"Actually, the tournament will just be the backdrop. We're going to set up a question-and-answer with some of the top competitors. Informal, after a practice session or warm-up. Paul's set up Jasmine to be involved, in fact; did she tell you? But you and I should be able to find some time for ourselves. And you'll come to the shoot, won't you?" He sounded anxious, as if I might disappoint him, but I knew how important he thought this was.

"Sure I will, Gus. I'll be there."

FOURTEEN

To me, every tournament has its colors. Wimbledon, for instance, is green and purple. And with the Family Circle Magazine Cup tournament, in Hilton Head, South Carolina, the colors I always think of are blue and white. Family Circle magazine has sponsored this clay court tournament in early April for decades, and it's an exciting tradition in women's tennis. For a record eight years, Chris Evert dominated this event. Gabriela Sabatini first made her presence known there as a fourteen-year-old, as did Jennifer Capriati. There could not have been a more appropriate tournament for Jasmine Li to take her place in the ranks of world-class tennis. With her incredible grace, timing, and court sense, I was convinced she had the capability of finally paying off the attention that had first come to her through her looks. More important than that, though, was the fact that this tournament would give Jasmine the opportunity to move through her sadness and depression over Malik's death. In her own mind, Hilton Head had become a kind of break point in her life.

Jasmine flew ahead with Paul and Gus on the BioTech plane because she wanted extra time to become acclimated to the area, and I followed a few days later on a commercial flight. Getting to Hilton Head from the West Coast is always an arduous trek, involving long flights, time zone changes, an airport shuttle, plane changes, and, in my case, the smuggling of A.M. onto the island in my hand luggage. For some reason, the commuter airlines frown on bringing dogs into the airplane cabin, so I've developed a policy of simply not telling them she's coming on board.

I got to the island after dark, picked up my rental car in the little lot across the street from the airport, and took 278 to Sea Pines Plantation, turning in at the Westin–Port Royal, where I'd taken a small apartment for two weeks. I liked having my own place during tournaments—it was easier to handle my laundry that way, and I could stock the kitchen the way I liked it. When I'd been playing, of course, I'd been able to fax my grocery list ahead, the tournament staff would stock the refrigerator for my arrival, and things like laundry were magically taken care of.

I unpacked, settled A.M. in for the night, and went through my messages. There was one from Jasmine's coach, with tomorrow's practice schedule, and one from Gus, who had taken a condo at Sea Pines Plantation. And there was one from KiKi:

The Club will be getting together at nine tonight at the Lobster Trap in Harbour Town. See you there!
KiKi.

KiKi and her Club were an institution at Hilton Head. KiKi had long been a fixture on the tennis circuit. For a number of years, she'd been tour director for the USTA for small events; then she'd been a coordinator with the

Women's Tennis Foundation. Now, officially, KiKi was in charge of player services for the Hilton Head tournament, but in reality her job kept her busy three hundred sixty-five days a year, including and bracketing each tournament and literally taking care of its every aspect— particularly the players. KiKi's Club was quite literally the unseen, often unsung, backbone of the tournament. It was an informal, unofficial organization, but for two weeks every spring, this group of women operated like a finely tuned machine. The Club consisted of KiKi and nine volunteers. These women, from different professions all over the country, saved up their vacation time to converge on the island for the duration of the tournament. Club custom was to convene the night before the nine thousand visitors arrived. They were not part of the sponsor's staff, the players' entourage, or the paid tournament team. The Club mission was simple—two weeks of solid, round-the-clock, twenty-hour days of backbreaking work, benefiting the tournament and the players. But it was work the Club members loved, something they looked forward to all year.

The lineup usually went like this: Ann and Betsy were in charge of courts and setup; Marie and Zelda handled the locker rooms, players' lounge, volunteer café, and medical trailer; Jennifer set up the ushers, umpires, and ball kids; Dorian ran the player porch; Caroline was in charge of player transportation; Dr. Emily Pemberton, aka "Dr. Em," ran the medical services; and KiKi and Rose were in charge of them all.

The Club was a formidable group, as I'd seen firsthand over the years. During the Hilton Head tournament, they ruled supreme. They wore sweatshirts with their own KiKi's Club logo, had their own walkie-talkie radio channel, their own trailer, which they called "the house," and, as KiKi put it, they could get anything in a golf cart. They even had their own yearbook, which they put together every year, post-tournament.

Wimbledon may have its queue, but Hilton Head has its Club, which is just as much a part of this tournament as the play itself. Without the Club, it was unlikely that anything would run smoothly, if at all. Club members arrived at the tournament grounds every day at 6:30 A.M., delivered newspapers to the players and officials, fanned out, each assigned to a specific player, and stayed on the job until the end of the day, however late it might be. Player duties entailed anything from retrieving a lost cat (it was finally located, wrapped in the hotel room draperies) to retrieving keys that had been flushed down an auto-toilet (I never got the details on how this was accomplished). All emergency medical calls that came through the radio came first to KiKi, who would then involve medical services. And Club members in their ubiquitous golf carts escorted all players on and off the courts. At any given time, they could be seen dropping off one player and picking up another, leaving their golf carts running so as not to waste a precious instant of the break-neck schedule.

I had gotten to know KiKi and the Club when I was working for the Women's Tennis Foundation as a physical therapist. They'd made me an honorary member, complete with sweatshirt. I always reserved my first night in Hilton Head for the Club reunion dinner; the only time I'd missed it was when I was in the hospital after my fall.

I pulled on my club sweatshirt and headed into town. Even after dark, Harbour Town is beyond quaint, probably because, although the site is as old as time, the town itself is a relatively new development and was designed from scratch to be tourist-friendly. Just a few minutes down the road from the Sea Pines Racquet Club, where the tournament is held, the town actually is a working harbor, home or visiting port to hundreds of boats and yachts of all sizes and types, especially during the season. The harbor curves in a half-moon shape, cupped in the embrace of the town's waterfront. Small boutiques, souvenir shops, sports shops, ice cream shops, perfumeries, jewelers, beach shops, and every sort of retail venue that a vacationer might enjoy is scattered along the curve, intermingled with restaurants.

In its prime position facing the water, the Lobster Trap was unmistakable, with its huge carved sign featuring a red lobster hanging over the door. Inside, wooden lobster traps, nets, harpoons, life rings, and slowly turning paddle fans hung from the beamed ceilings. Giant picture windows overlooked harbor and channel to the ocean beyond.

"Your group is over there, at the big window table," said the maître d', clearly familiar with KiKi. Everyone knew KiKi; she and her Club were by now island-wide institutions.

KiKi waved enthusiastically from behind a huge mug of beer. As usual, she was dressed from head to toe in tennis memorabilia—her Club sweatshirt, of course, topped by a green Family Circle event windbreaker, a cap from Wimbledon, and on her wrist, I saw as I clasped her hand, a U.S. Open watch. She has a no-nonsense sort of appeal—cropped straight brown hair, lively blue eyes behind glasses, no makeup, and a sunburn.

"You gotta see something. Look at this hand, Jordan,"

KiKi commanded immediately. "Just look at it." She waved her fingers in front of my face.

"It looks fine to me," I said.

"Well, of course it does—*now*. But until yesterday I had this big old wart, and you know me, I'm too busy to get to the doctor, and anyhow I went to the post office to mail some packages for the tournament and this old woman from Daufuskie Island—you know, the wild little island right across the channel here—comes up and out of nowhere she grabs my hand. She says, 'You got a wart.' I say, 'Yeah. So?' And she says, 'Look at me. I know white magic.' And darned if she didn't stare at me like a laser and squeeze my hand like so . . ."—KiKi squeezed my hand in demonstration, practically breaking the bones—"and I kind of shook her off because I thought she was crazy. But then this morning I looked at my hand and that wart was *gone*. I mean G-O-N-E-gone! Can you believe it?" She shook her head in astonishment, paused, and took a gulp from her mug.

I wasn't sure how to react. "That's—amazing," I said.

KiKi forged ahead. "You know everybody, right? Let's see, I took a head count and we're all here except Dr. Em, who's coming in the morning, and Racehorse—her plane was late."

"Racehorse," I knew, was the nickname for Caroline, who was in charge of player transportation, including cars, vans, and personal cars for the top four seeds.

I circled the table and gave everyone a hug. The women ranged in age from their twenties to their sixties, and their occupations and hometowns in the real world spanned the gamut. Ann was a librarian from Phoenix; Jennifer, a real estate salesperson from Palm Springs;

Betsy was a homemaker from New Jersey; Dorian, a graduate student from Seattle; Marie was a painter from Atlanta; "Dr. Em" was a distinguished surgeon from New Orleans.

"Order something," KiKi commanded, thrusting a menu at me. "Relax while you can. Forget about the players; the sponsors and their guests are coming in tomorrow. They've got an L-ten-eleven chartered out of New York, they redid the whole thing in the corporate colors, and four hundred twenty of them are gonna land with all their luggage. They got a couple of the major news anchors, your prerequisite movie stars and celebs, the whole scene. Things are gonna get wild."

I ordered a cup of corn chowder and a salad. It felt good to be out with a group of friends, no pressures and no responsibilities. We spent the next hour or so eating, drinking, and catching up.

"So what do you think about Gus's new sports drink?" asked Jennifer.

"Well, he's working on it," I said. "It's not on the market yet. How'd you learn about it?"

"With all the hoopla here, you can't miss it. Tomorrow night—the night before the tournament opens—BioTech has a big party scheduled, a barbecue over on the Island. They've got some big yachts rented, and they'll ferry people over from the Harbour Island dock. It's going to be a big deal. And they're taping some stuff for TV, I know that. I thought that you might be involved, what with you and Gus—"

"Well, I'm not involved," I said. "This is all just preliminary, for press purposes. I'm here to work with Jasmine. She's going to make a great showing, I think."

"She's really getting to be America's sweetheart," Jennifer agreed. "Losing her fiancé and all—it seems like everybody just adopted her after that."

"Well, she's ready. I think she'll measure up."

"She got here early. Everybody was kind of surprised that she even showed up," said Rose. "After what she's been through, she had a perfect excuse to take a pass."

"Jasmine's not as fragile as she looks," I said. "I think she's going to surprise more than a few people."

We called it a night fairly early. Everybody was tired from traveling, and I still had some calls to make and E-mail to catch up with. And even though I wasn't playing, I still had to be at Jasmine's practice by eight o'clock in the morning.

The next morning, I gulped some herbal tea and a handful of vitamins and fixed a bowl of instant oatmeal from a packet I always put in my suitcase. It was only seven when A.M. and I drove down Lighthouse Road to the tournament grounds, but the place was already a hive of activity. Picket fences were being given a final coat of white paint, and carts loaded with pots of red and pink geraniums were being ferried about for perfect placement around the three courts. The TV towers hovered over the 1,600-seat Stadium Court, overlooking the other courts as well as the sponsor row tents, food court tents, and press tent. I parked and then walked on a carpet of crunchy pine needles over to "the house," where KiKi and Rose were already well into their morning, walkie-talkies and phones clamped to their ears with one hand, dispensing coffee and paperwork with the other. Several dogs ran wildly across the floor of the trailer, adding to the confusion factor and causing A.M. to dive for the safety of my armpit. If there is anything A.M. hates, it's aggressive bigger dogs.

Everyone rushed over to greet A.M.; forget about me. She was always a big star at this tournament.

KiKi waved a handful of messages as she tickled A.M. under the chin. She handed me a walkie-talkie. "Here," she said. "This one's tuned to our channel. You need to stay in the loop."

I clipped on the walkie and went through the messages. One was from the producers of the on-air coverage, with the time and place of our pre-production meeting, another was from Gus, telling me they were going to shoot Jasmine's segment of the infomercial after practice this morning and giving the phone number at his villa.

I crumpled up the message angrily. What did Gus mean, shooting the infomercial segment this morning? Jasmine needed to focus on her game, not spend time filming infomercials. The time before a tournament is crucial, and Jasmine needed to allocate it wisely. After the tournament, or after she'd been eliminated—*if* she got eliminated—that was another story. Right now, I wanted her to concentrate on her game. I grabbed a phone and dialed Gus's number, but there was no answer.

"KiKi, do you know where Gus is shooting that infomercial?" I asked.

"Sure. The production company has a trailer on the grounds, and they're planning on shooting right on the edge of Stadium Court. I think they're doing it today, before the crowds get bigger."

"What time?"

"Any minute. We wanted them over and out as fast as possible."

"Can you watch A.M. for a minute?"

"Sure, but the other dogs might mistake her for a treat."

"Just keep her up on top of the desk. She makes a great paperweight."

I deposited A.M. on top of a pile of papers. "Stay," I commanded, and rushed off to find Jasmine.

"Can I give you a lift?" Ann asked. She was parked in a cart at the trailer door.

"How about a really big favor, Ann. Can I borrow this cart for a few minutes?"

Minutes later, I pulled up in front of another trailer, marked with the sign BIOTECH INFOMERCIAL—WARDROBE AND MAKEUP. I ran up the steps to find Jasmine seated in the makeup chair, covered in a smock, as a makeup artist put the finishing touches on her powder with a puff. Paul Kessler lounged on a couch, smoking. Jasmine broke into a smile when she saw me.

"Hi, Jordan. I'm so glad you're here."

"Hi, Jordan." Paul yawned sleepily.

"Jasmine," I said, planting myself in front of her, "get out of that chair and get onto the practice courts, where you belong. Paul, you have to get her to practice."

She looked puzzled. "But Jordan, Gus said this was what you wanted. He said—"

"Never mind," I muttered. Gus! I couldn't wait to get my hands on him. I rushed back out of the trailer and hopped back into the cart, weaving my way through the fast-growing crowd to the edge of Stadium Court. I saw cameras and equipment, a crew running around in jeans and sneakers, with phones clipped to their belts, laminated passes looped around their necks, and then I saw Gus, holding a clipboard and leafing through a script with Trent and a production assistant with a digital stopwatch.

"Jordan." He beamed when he saw me. "Great. I knew you'd be here."

"Yes, *I* can be here, but Jasmine absolutely can't be here. What are you thinking of? This girl needs to keep her mind on the match. This is a huge distraction—makeup, learning lines. Find somebody else."

Gus came over to me, took my arm, and guided me a few steps away. He smiled at me, but his voice was tense. "Jordan, Jasmine and I both thought you wanted this for her. For us, in fact."

"Your timing stinks, Gus. Later. Not now."

"This was the only time we could get access to this location, Jordan. You know better than anybody that the networks will take over the area, and when the tournament starts it will be impossible. Let me recap where we're at. Jasmine will be on camera in five minutes. She will be paid a great deal of money for what you consider to be a diversion. This isn't about me or you. Be supportive of your client. Why upset her now, before she goes on? She's not a professional actress, and she's nervous enough. All you're going to do is make her look bad if she's flustered or blows her lines. Do you really want that?"

"All I know, Gus, is that she came here to accomplish an objective, and this is not taking her toward that objective. I think you should bag it. Get somebody else."

"In the next five minutes? Be realistic, Jordan." He tapped a pencil against his clipboard. "Well, there is one option."

"Great. What is it?" I was relieved that we weren't going head-to-head on this.

"You."

"What?"

"You. You do the interview. We've talked about it enough. You've said you're considering it. Well, now would be perfect timing. You step in and do the interview and the testimonial."

"Me? I've never tried the product. It wouldn't be honest."

"I happen to have some right here." Gus tossed me a bottle, and I caught it.

"Careful!" screamed a voice from the sidelines. "Put down that bottle, please! That's the hero product! The one with the color-corrected label, the one we're going to use in the shot!" A frazzled young man in a work shirt and jeans materialized and grabbed the bottle from my hand. "Take this," he said, brusquely thrusting another bottle at me.

Gus and I stood staring at each other.

"Well?" Gus said. "Are we doing this together—or not?"

I felt trapped. There was no good decision, and no way I could back out of the infomercial without blatantly refusing Gus. Maybe Gus was right. Maybe I was just being stubborn, being overtly independent. "Will I have time to really use this stuff before the infomercial runs?" I asked, wavering.

"Sure. Lots of time. We still don't have full approval, so it won't go on the air for a while."

"Okay," I said. "I'll do it, if you let Jasmine go practice."

Gus broke into a broad grin and hugged me, but the hug felt empty. "Great, Jordan. This is terrific." With his arm still around me, he turned to the crew. "Guys, Trent, there's been a little change. Jordan's going to do the infomercial. Somebody get her a script."

Trent let out a whoop and applauded.

Just then a cart raced up and an official in a tournament jacket leaned over. "Sorry, guys, but I have to tell you— you've been bumped out of this location."

"Now?" Gus motioned to Trent, who hurried to try and neutralize the official, without success.

"The network needs this space. They're doing some pre-match stuff. You've got to leave. Sorry."

"Who can I talk to about this?" Trent fumed. "I have clearance. This is going to cost six figures."

The official shrugged. "All I know is, you've got to move out."

"This is an outrage," Trent said, his voice scorching.

"Do I have to call security?" the official said.

Trent stiffened. He seemed calm, but a muscle in his cheek twitched spasmodically, and he picked at the buttons on his shirt. His left foot tapped impatiently in the gravel. "No. We'll be cooperative. But it's still an outrage and I fully intend to find out exactly why this misunderstanding occurred and who's responsible." He turned to Gus and me. "I guess that's it. We have to regroup. I'm going to talk to the location people, see if we can find another place to set up." He walked off. I could see by the pitch of his shoulders that he was set for a confrontation. One thing about tennis, it teaches you to read body language. A few feet away stood the hapless director, wearing a resigned expression, clearly aware of what was coming.

Gus just stood there, shaking his head. "What next?" he grumbled.

"Next is, I take Jasmine to the hotel courts for practice." Luckily, Hilton Head has no shortage of tennis facilities.

Gus thrust a heavy package at me. "Take this. It's samples of the complete Duration system—the drink, the bars, the powder, the supplements. Try everything and play a few matches. Then you'll be ready when we finally get back in front of the cameras. I think you'll be pleasantly surprised."

"Fine."

"And the barbecue is tonight. It's a Gullah barbecue, a real island specialty."

"I know. I got your message. But what's a Gullah barbecue?"

He laughed. "To tell you the truth, I'm not sure. It'll be a surprise. I'd pick you up, but I have to get there early."

"In that case, I'll go with Jasmine."

"See you there. The first boat leaves from Harbour Town at six."

I had Jasmine out of makeup and onto a practice court by ten-thirty. She was practicing her serve, and looking very good, when the Fish appeared, outfitted in a velour jogging suit, the height of fashion about twenty years ago, and a Hilton Head baseball cap. "The trouble with you," he said, "is you're never where you're supposed to be, and if anybody's with you they're never there either."

I had to smile. The Fish always knew exactly where everybody, including me, was at any given time. He made a point of it. This was all posturing. "So where were *you*? You were supposed to be guarding Jasmine."

He wiped his brow. "I had some catching up to do with an old buddy of mine, Hank Murray. He's the director of security for Sea Pines Plantation. We go way back to the CIA together."

"An old CIA buddy? Here on the plantation?" The Fish's contacts never ceased to amaze me. The fact that the Fish had supposedly been in the CIA, in itself, never ceased to amaze me. When he first told me about his CIA involvement, I doubted it, but whenever I checked anything out, the Fish's stories were always confirmed, and this was no exception.

"We were at the Pentagon together too. Office of Special Investigations. Worked on the Black Programs together. But Hank had to scale back. The guy never saw his family. Now that he has a wife and kids, this is the way to go."

I kept one eye on Jasmine as she practiced her overheads. "Well, it's hardly the same as the CIA," I said. "A resort—nothing probably ever happens here. Maybe a few tourists lose their wallets, or somebody steals a golf cart—"

"Oh, you'd be surprised. Besides, Hank isn't entirely out of the loop. It's a funny thing. It's a very difficult network to get into, and it takes a long time in your career to build the skills you need. They don't want to throw that away. He still dips in and out. Him and me have a lot in common. We both have very open minds and very closed mouths. But you'll meet him tonight. He's coming to the barbecue—working it, of course, not as a guest. The security's going to be incredible."

"What did you two talk about?"

"I briefed him on the Jasmine situation, and on the death threats and Anna Martinez. He's distributed a picture of her to all his people and to local law enforcement, just on a watch basis. I told him to keep an eye on you, too."

"I wish you'd mind your own business," I said irritably.

"If I did, you'd have died more than once."

"Well, just keep him out of my hair. That's all I need,

some half-baked, excitement-starved Barney Fife island security guard getting overexcited on my behalf."

The Fish picked his teeth. "There is absolutely no resemblance to that scenario. For one thing, Barney Fife had one bullet and an unloaded gun. Hank Murray uses semiautomatic weapons. When the need arises, of course."

"Now I'm really reassured."

"Hold off judgment till you meet him. Besides, this is a long tournament and we're dealing with twenty-two thousand people here on the island. Anything could happen. If you're lucky, things'll be boring."

I pointed to Jasmine. "Look at her. She looks great out there. The cross-training paid off. She's significantly equalized her strength. And with her grasp of the court, she could clean up at this tournament."

"She's a good kid. I hope she does," said the Fish.

"Any further news of Anna Martinez?"

"Funny you should ask. She's not going to be here. She had a sudden assignment come up—in Germany. She's out of the country."

"Did she actually go?"

The Fish nodded. "I checked with Passport Control. My buddy Duane at the State Department. Good guy." He squinted at the bag I was holding. "Is there food in there? You holding out on me?"

I opened the bag and pulled out a bottle of Duration and a bar. "Health food."

He made a face. "Not up my alley."

"I guess I should try it. I'm doing the testimonial."

"Caved in, huh?"

"Well, it was becoming ridiculous. I think I was disagreeing just to disagree." I peeled back the wrapper and munched the bar. It wasn't bad, sort of like chocolate-covered granola.

The Fish scrutinized the label. "Can this stuff actually get you to have more energy in a match?"

"So they say. Gus is a very serious scientist. He's thorough. It would have to work. They gave me some backup paperwork to read—it looks like a lot of boilerplate. But then, even a teaspoon of honey or an electrolyte drink will give you some kind of energy boost. This is just packaging. But I suppose it's no different from any of those other products out there. It's mostly hype."

"And you're becoming part of the hype?"

I stopped chewing. It took a minute before I could answer. "Well, we'll see."

Jasmine wrapped up her practice and changed into her warm-ups. I gave her a hug. "Malik would be so proud of you," I said.

She smiled. "It feels good." A group of young girls swarmed up for autographs.

"I'll see you at the barbecue," I said. The crowds were growing, I noticed, as they always do right before a tournament. People seem to materialize from nowhere until, suddenly, a tournament town is alive with tennis and the people who love it. This particular crowd seemed friendly and supportive, young girls and someone they could idolize. Jasmine was indeed the perfect product spokesperson. She had a big endorsement future ahead of her. I glanced across the tennis court and my eyes froze.

Anna Martinez. She was standing by a fence, and she was staring at Jasmine. The woman was wearing sunglasses, but I knew it was Anna. I reached out and grabbed the Fish by the sleeve. "Look," I whispered. "Over there." I didn't want to alarm Jasmine. "Isn't that Anna Martinez?"

He squinted. "Could be. Or maybe not."

"Let's find out." We started across the court, but as we took our first steps, the woman turned, ran, and disappeared into the parking lot. The Fish and I followed. We stood scanning the cars and people cramming into the lot. "She could be anywhere," I said.

"Or anyone," the Fish noted.

"I know it was Anna. She's not in Germany, she's here. And she's watching Jasmine. What does that mean?"

"Unfortunately," said the Fish, "it means absolutely nothing. It's no crime for a fan to watch a celebrity player at a tournament. Even if it is her, she'd actually have to try to harm Jasmine or somebody else before the police would step in."

"But what about your buddy Hank Murray? He's not with the police."

"Right. He's private security. I'll brief him, don't worry. If it's the Martinez woman, she won't get within a mile of Jasmine—or you. Did it ever occur to you that maybe she was watching you, not Jasmine? I mean, you two were standing together, and she was wearing sunglasses. How could you tell who she was watching?"

"Oh, God, you're right."

"Look, Jasmine's going back to the villa to change right now. I'll have one of my women guards stay with her, and you and I can swing by and let Hank in on this latest development."

"I thought you didn't think it was Anna."

"Just a precaution."

Within half an hour, we were with Hank Murray, near the entrance to the Sea Pines Plantation development office. Hank was tall, with dark hair salted with gray, a mustache, and a strong chin. He was dressed in an immaculately pressed white shirt and a tie, more like an executive than a law-enforcement officer. And he seemed like an executive. His office was bustling with subordinates, checking in on the telephone, handing him messages, jockeying paperwork. Everyone called him "sir" or "chief." The office was simply decorated, with basic oak furniture, a set of bookcases, and a big map of the area and a brass barometer on the wall. On Hank's desk were a computer and a bronze statue of a horse and rider.

"So are you guys still involved in all these national security affairs, or is my friend Mr. Fisher just trying to impress me?" I asked jokingly.

Murray reached into his pocket and flashed a laminated badge with the insignia of the Department of Defense. At least it looked authentic. "We're not dead yet," he said. "Got to have some excitement when you work on an island. Actually, I don't work on the whole island. I got seventeen square miles, and fifty in security."

"Sounds like enough per square mile," I said.

He shrugged. "Adequate. Now, what brings you back here, Fisher? I thought I got rid of you." He grinned.

"The person I told you about, Anna Martinez. You have her picture. She may not be in Europe. We may have seen her on the island a few minutes ago."

"The one who was threatening people?"

"That's the one."

"She make any threats here?"

"No."

"But she was staring. It gave me the creeps," I said. "I think she's going to do something."

Hank nodded. "If she's on the island, we'll find her. And keep an eye on her." The phone buzzed. "Excuse me. This is my urgent line." He picked it up. The conversation consisted of two words: "When?" and "Where?" Then he hung up. "Here we go. One of the workers keeled over down at the stadium. They've got him at the medical trailer."

"Who was it?" I asked, wondering if it was anyone I knew.

"Rusty from the chicken concession."

"Rusty? I know Rusty." Everybody at the tournament knew Rusty; he was a fixture. Rusty and I were old buddies. He had even given me his secret recipe. The secret was olive oil in the marinade.

"Well, they got a problem if it's serious," said Hank. "Rusty's doing the barbecue tonight on Daufuskie. No Rusty, no chicken. And Rusty, he's not in good shape to begin with. Had a heart problem this year. Surgery, some sort of valve or bypass thing."

"Poor guy. And is it serious?"

The phone buzzed again. Hank grabbed it, listened, and hung up. "He's coding. I'd better get over there."

The Fish and I followed the security cars, their sirens wailing and lights blinking, cutting through traffic back to the tournament grounds. We arrived as Rusty was being loaded into the ambulance. He looked as if someone had drained the blood out of his body. Dr. Em was assisting the head tournament doctor as he climbed into the ambulance. She slammed the doors, and the vehicle took off.

"Em, what happened?" I asked. "Will he make it?"

She shook her head. "Can't tell. He was apparently nauseated; then he went down with chest pains. Then he coded on us. If he makes it to the hospital, the next few hours are critical."

I noticed she had a bottle of Duration in her hand. "Did Gus give you that?" I asked.

"No, I took it from Rusty. He was drinking it while he was setting up his stand, and he had it clutched in his hand. I had to pry it out of his grasp." She looked at the bottle. "What is it?"

"A new product Gus is working on. A sports drink." I took the bottle and looked at it quickly but closely. "What's in this?" I wondered. "Maybe Rusty is allergic to something." But there was no ingredients label, probably because the product wasn't on the market yet. I remembered, then, the poisoned dog food on my patio. The thought made me shiver, but I didn't want to cause a general panic by blurting it out. I put the bottle in my jacket pocket.

"Rusty was in terrible shape," said Hank. "All he ate was chicken—with the skin. The guy was a walking heart attack."

"I wonder how Rusty got a hold of this test bottle of Duration," I said. "It's not available to the public."

A young man in an apron, who had been standing by, watching tensely, spoke up. "I was working with Rusty. He picked it up over there where they were shooting that commercial. Somebody on the crew gave it to us. Said it gave you energy. We had a long day, so he wanted to try it. I had some too. It's good stuff."

I took Dr. Em aside. "Listen, Emily, it's probably nothing," I said. "But just to be thorough, can you have your lab at the hospital check this drink out—maybe analyze it? In case Rusty ends up being allergic to something, then we'd know. Or—well, you never know—what if there was some poison involved?"

"Poison!" whispered Em. "Do you want to call the police? What made you think there could be poison?"

"Somebody tried to poison my dog, so it's on my mind. It's crazy. And also very unlikely. I mean my dog and Rusty—they have nothing in common. I'm paranoid. I'd just like to double-check without making a big deal. If I involve the police or Hank Murray, either this will get out of hand or they'll think I've lost my mind. But in case we can help Rusty, can we do this just on the QT? Okay, Em?"

She nodded quickly. The Club stuck together. "I'd have to send it FedEx today," she said. "That would take too long. But, you know, maybe I can get something sooner. I have an associate in Charleston—that's just a short drive. We can messenger it there."

"Perfect."

The young man stood quavering, wiping his hands continuously on his pin-striped apron. He had a thin face and bad skin, the kind of acne that leaves scars when you're older. "This is bad, real bad. I got twenty-five hundred pounds of chicken to cook and no Rusty. What am I gonna do? He never even told me the recipe."

"The secret is olive oil," I said.

FIFTEEN

By the time I got to the pre-production meeting for the U.S. Sports coverage, I felt like I'd lived a lifetime in a morning. The network had a small trailer community set up on the tournament grounds behind the grandstand, and I stepped carefully through the spaghetti bowl of cables that snaked across the ground. The behind-the-scenes part of the tennis world is far less glamorous than what you see on TV or from the stands. As I made my way to the trailer, I remembered the year I placed second in this tournament. The awards ceremony was, as always, held in the middle of the Stadium Court. A gleaming silver tray was being awarded to me, and Seranata Aziz, who had won the tournament in a close match, was to receive the traditional championship cup. As the sponsors from the magazine gave the preamble and introductions, Seranata and I stood out of sight, beneath the bleachers, awaiting our turn to come out on the field, anticipating the usual applause. We were standing together quietly—neither of us had much energy left for talking or joking—when suddenly someone high in the stands decided to dispose of their extra-large soft drink. The liquid showered down some ten feet directly onto

263

our heads, drenching us both. We barely had time to mop our faces and comb our fingers through our newly sticky hair before we had to walk onto the court for the awards presentation in front of the live and TV audiences. I hope people watching the awards presentation that day attributed our noticeably damp appearances to the exertions of a brutal match.

The pre-pro meeting was like old home week. Shauna and I hugged, happy to be working together again. Jon Wetherill was sitting on the edge of a desk in the trailer, dressed in the coat, tie, and loafers I supposed he'd been born in, and Harrison Barber was on the phone.

"Haven't seen you in a while, Jordan," said Jon. "What've you been up to?"

"Doing some training. I haven't been on camera for a bit—hope I don't make any mistakes," I joked.

Harrison shot a look from his phone conversation. "Nobody makes any mistakes—not on this team," he said pointedly, then resumed his phone call without missing a beat.

"Did you see Paul Kessler today?" Jon asked.

"Yes, in fact. Earlier today. He was with Jasmine."

"Weird guy," said Jon. "I saw him at a restaurant last night and he was nice, and then this morning he mouthed off at me. Go figure."

"He had a bad day," I said. "But that doesn't mean I don't think he's weird too."

We went through the notes for the live and prerecorded coverage. "We're going to kick off tomorrow with an interview with Billie Jean, a kind of perspective piece on women's tennis. Then you and Jon'll be doing the post-match interviews," said Harrison. "The usual point-counterpoint thing. Now, Jasmine Li is the one the crowd is rooting for at this tournament—first comeback since the fiancé's death. And she's your client. Can you give us anything exclusive to work with?"

"We can talk about her pre-tournament training, maybe."

"Anything more personal?"

"Well, she wants to dedicate her play at this tournament to Malik."

"Bingo. There we go. Christy!" he yelled. A young production assistant scurried to his side. "Tell graphics we'll use the montage, the one we cut for the engagement. Any local stories? Local color? Island stuff? I mean, beyond the historical and the tourist promos."

"First casualty of the tournament: One of the food vendors keeled over and was rushed to the hospital," said another assistant.

Harrison shook his head. "I don't think anybody cares."

"There was a report of a couple of rogue gators," Christy volunteered. "It was in the paper. I guess it's mating season; they can get very aggressive this time of year. A woman was walking on the golf course, picking up balls with a ball collector, and an alligator chased her. And a tourist was feeding another alligator on Shipyard, and it actually attacked her. It had to be whacked off her with a grappling rod, and then they shot it. Then there was a dog that was killed in its yard, on a chain. They think a gator did it." She read from her notes. "Local law enforcement and Fish and Game have them under control, but I did a little research. Gators are very common here but mostly they leave you alone. Unless provoked.

Then—get this—here's how they do you in: They clamp their jaws around you, drag you to water, and hold you down until you go limp. Then, once they've drowned you, they go in for the kill."

"That's just plain ugly," Harrison proclaimed. "Our viewers are looking for relaxation and entertainment for God's sake. They don't want to hear that some oversize reptile with a brain the size of a grape is rampaging through town. Keep trying to come up with something. Okay, people, we'll be setting up in the tent tomorrow at eight A.M. Jordan and Jon, if you could be wardrobed and through with hair and makeup—"

We nodded.

"Everybody have their passes?"

"I need tickets. My parents are coming," said Christy.

"Tell Jeremy. Okay, then, that's it. See you people tomorrow."

The meeting broke up and I put a call in to Hank Murray. He was out of the station. I got on the walkie and called KiKi. "Any word on Rusty?" I asked.

"Well, he won't be making that barbecue tonight, but he'll pull through. They're running tests."

"Thanks, KiKi."

Next, I called up Dr. Em on the walkie. "Did the lab call back?" I asked.

"We should have something by late today or early tomorrow," she said.

Finally, I paged the Fish. He called back immediately. "Guess what? I think you were right about Anna Martinez. She did leave the country, but she came back the next day. So watch yourself. She's a loose cannon."

"Well, then, I guess I'll see you tonight. I want to drive my own car to the dock. Call me if you hear anything."

"Jordan, Jordan, do you copy?" I heard KiKi's voice over the walkie-talkie.

"Yes, KiKi."

"Jasmine is looking for you. She needs to talk to you right away. She's over at the players' lounge."

"I'll be right there." I hoped Anna Martinez hadn't gotten to her. And where was the Fish?

The players' lounge was actually located in the Heritage Club, at the entrance to the tournament grounds. Traffic was building now, so it took me almost half an hour to make my way there. Security was in effect. I signed in and showed my pass at the entrance, and a guard punched the pass. I walked into a huge skylit room with a view of the pool and the condos beyond, framed by pine trees. Up the stairs, a quiet area had been set aside for players and their guests. It was very much a plush living room atmosphere, with rose velvet couches, a big-screen TV, a simple buffet, and a small bar. People sat in clusters, talking softly in English, German, French, and Spanish. Staff members in black slacks and white shirts circulated politely, removing dishes and glasses. Jasmine sat on one of the couches, looking like a frightened bird. She was holding Stanley, her rubber penguin, as if she were a little girl with a security blanket; beside her was a woman I had last seen at the memorial service for Malik—his mother, Doris Evans.

"Jas, what is it?" I greeted Mrs. Evans and sat down as Jasmine motioned me closer.

"I have to ask your help," she whispered. "You're the only one I can trust. Something's happened." She looked around the room to be sure nobody could overhear. "Doris and I, as you know, were going to set up a special

268 Martina Navratilova and Liz Nickles

fund in Malik's name. Scholarships for kids. We were so excited." She glanced at Doris.

Doris spoke quietly. "My son died young, but he left a sizable estate. Plenty to set up a fund. But when we started asking questions today, Mr. Kessler said there wasn't enough money in the account to do it. He said there were a lot of commissions and taxes and unexpected expenses."

"I wish I could help," I said, "but I really am not a financial person. You need to talk to an accountant, not me."

"I suggested that," Jasmine said. "And Paul got so angry. He accused me of not trusting him, of not appreciating what he'd done for me and for Malik. I've never seen him like this."

"Who's in charge of the finances?" I asked.

"When Malik died, I gave Mr. Kessler power of attorney. It seemed like the thing to do," said Mrs. Evans. "After all, he's a respected businessman."

"What kind of expenses were there?" I asked.

"Paul said there were administrative expenses. Office expenses."

"Malik had an office?"

"No, so Paul had to build one."

"What? Where?"

"Well, it was already built, but he remodeled it. In LA."

"Who's in the office?"

"Paul. It seemed like it was necessary. A place to run the foundation that was separate from Paul's main office."

"Jasmine, I think you're going to have to hire an independent financial person and get the books audited."

"You don't think—that Paul spent all Malik's money?"

"I don't know. But you have to find out, Mrs. Evans."

She shook her head. "He did so much for my son. He'd been managing his money all along, so it was only natural that he continue to manage it after his death."

"I wonder if any money was missing before he died, and if Malik found out," I said.

Jasmine's hand flew to her mouth. "You don't think . . ."

"Take it easy, I'm not accusing Paul of anything. I just think that if a lot of money is unaccounted for—how much, would you guess?"

"Six or seven million," said Mrs. Evans. "But that's just based on what Malik said he had. I never saw any actual figures. Paul Kessler had all the paperwork."

Now it was my turn to gasp. "Six or seven *million* in expenses and administrative costs and taxes?"

"I don't know anything about finances," Jasmine said. "What am I going to do?"

I thought for a minute. Then I had an idea. "You know, maybe *you* don't have to do anything. There is another party that will be extremely interested in that money, and you won't even have to pay to get them involved down to the last penny."

"I want to do right by my son," said Mrs. Evans. "Who are these people?"

"They're the Internal Revenue Service. And with minimal prodding from the right source"—I happened to know that the Fish had friends in high places at the IRS—"they would be more than pleased to audit Malik's estate. And believe me, Paul Kessler does not frighten the IRS."

"The IRS," said Jasmine, mulling it over. "Of course."

"They come in," I said, "and let the chips fall where they may. If Paul's not guilty of anything, it'll come out. If he skimmed from the estate, you'll get your grounds to at least sue for recovery and damages."

Jasmine sagged on the couch. "Let's do it. Doris?"

Mrs. Evans nodded. "I never thought I'd welcome an IRS audit," she said. And we all had to smile, in spite of the situation.

"But I still can't forgive Paul," Jasmine said. "I trusted him."

"And I still wonder if Malik knew anything," I said.

"How will we find out?" Jasmine asked.

"Dates of transactions would help. Once we open this up, everything should become clear. But, Jasmine, there is absolutely nothing you can do about this right now. I will alert someone who can help. Your job now is to do what you set out to do, to win this tournament. You need to get your focus back."

"I don't know if I can," she whispered. "I feel so betrayed."

"Well, then, show him. Show Paul you don't need him. Show him you can do this on your own. It's going to be you, alone, out on that court—not him. Show him you can do this, take care of yourself, on court and in your life."

She sat up straighter and nodded slowly. "You're right. I can do this. I can't believe that Paul actually took money from Malik, but if he did, if he failed Malik or used him, I won't let it stop me. I will be strong. I must be strong. I'll win this tournament, and I'll donate the prize money to Malik's fund." Her eyes had a resolve I had never seen in them before, not the will of a contender or the grief of a lover; all girlishness was gone now, stripped away and replaced by a single-minded sense of purpose, as if she had been placed on this earth to do just what she had said.

Doris and Jasmine hugged. "You'll always be my daughter," Doris said. "I'm so proud of you. You're one fine girl, and my son knew it."

I put my hand on Jas's shoulder. "See you tonight," I said. "Or maybe you're not up to going to that barbecue?"

She sat ramrod straight, her face like stone. The sweetness was gone now, strangled out of her expression by a new wariness. "Of course," she said. "What do *I* have to hide? But how should I act with Paul?"

"Act normal for now," I said. "Smooth things over for the moment, if you can. It's best to catch him by surprise—if there's anything to catch. And Doris," I said, "I have to ask you. After your son's death, were you going to sue the Springs?"

She looked puzzled. "No. For what? Why would I?"

Parking in Harbour Town during the tourist season is always a feat, but I managed it by trailing a couple with ice cream cones back to their car and appropriating their space as soon as they pulled out.

As promised on the invitation from BioTech, the boat was waiting at the end of the dock. She was an impressive gleaming-white yacht, about eighty feet long, called *The Victory Lane*. About fifty people milled around on the deck, enjoying drinks and appetizers that were being passed around by a crew in immaculate white pants and T-shirts. A combo played softly on the upper deck.

Gus stood flanked by Paul, Trent, and Jasmine. He was holding a glass of champagne, and at that moment, I thought, he had never looked more successful and satisfied with life. He spotted me immediately and came over with a glass of champagne and a kiss.

"I'm so glad you're here to see this," he said. "Isn't it great? Trent thought of everything."

I grabbed his arm. "Gus, I have to ask, just quickly. Is there anything in the drink that could cause an allergic reaction? One of the food vendors was drinking it just before he passed out. He actually went into cardiac arrest."

"Jordan, you know anyone can be allergic to anything. There are people who are allergic to sunlight, for God's sake, or dust. It's a case-by-case scenario. I have no idea." Still, he frowned. I could tell the question bothered him.

"What is it?"

"How'd some local food vendor get hold of a confidential product in limited production? That's what I don't like. We've been extremely careful about who got samples of the test product. Only endorsers or potential endorsers should have it at this point."

"Somebody on the set today, I think."

"I'll speak to Trent right now. That absolutely should not happen. Wait here." He made his way back to Trent, and I could see them conferring.

The boat started to move. We pulled away from the harbor to a spectacular view of the town and the island. It was sunset. The weather was chilly but springlike. I spotted the Fish, clinging to a rail, his eyes glued to Jasmine, his face drained of blood.

I rushed over. "Are you all right? What's happening? You didn't eat any shellfish, did you?"

"Seasick," he whispered.

"But we're only two feet from the dock and the ocean is calm," I pointed out.

"This was why I never went into the Navy," he said. He closed his eyes. "God, please let it be over soon."

"You're in luck," I said. "This is only a fifteen-minute trip. And when your stomach can take it, I have to talk to you about Paul Kessler."

His eyes flew open. "I'm feeling better already. What?"

"According to Jasmine and Malik's mother, a large portion of Malik's estate, which was being managed by Kessler, is unaccounted for. Paul is giving them the runaround. And of course they don't intimidate him at all. So I was thinking: You know how the IRS is partial to auditing high-profile estates . . . and you have lots of friends at the IRS—"

He held up his hand. "I work for Mr. Kessler. That would be highly unethical. I could not be a party to this."

"You couldn't?"

"No, I couldn't. But you can call them. Or his mother can. I'll give you a name. As for me, I don't want to attract attention to myself. It—wouldn't suit my purposes."

"Exactly what purposes are those?" I asked. Now I was suspicious. With the Fish, things were rarely as they seemed. In fact, I now knew—he had virtually told me, in his Fishlike way—that things were definitely *not* as they appeared, at least as far as he was concerned. "You're here on a job, aren't you?" I asked. "You don't really work for Kessler, do you?"

"I certainly do. Do you have any Dramamine? I need Dramamine."

"You have to take it before you get on the boat, if you want it to work. It's too late. Stop changing the subject. I don't think you're sick at all. You have to tell me who you work for, because if you're going to defend Kessler, we have a problem, and there's a lot at stake. Maybe even lives."

"Don't look so serious, Jordan. People will start staring."

I smiled a phony grin. "How's this? Okay. Who do you work for?"

"Let's just say that my employer has a great interest in knowing what's happening with Paul Kessler."

"One of his competitors?" Then it dawned on me. "It's the government. Of course. He's under investigation, and you're doing the investigating."

The Fish sighed. "You never know. Let's just say, there are certain irregularities, and large sums of money are leaving the country that have a way of turning up in off-shore and foreign accounts."

"Paul Kessler's money?"

"Many people's money."

"His clients?"

"Well, nobody's been able to prove anything. So a person is innocent until proven guilty. But because Malik's mother and Jasmine put their trust in you, we may have the toehold we've been looking for. Sometimes people aren't as careful when they're dealing with dead people's money. I think we may be looking at such a case. Dead men tell no tales, as they say—but their relatives sure do."

"No wonder he figured he could afford to buy out the Springs. He has his own way of fund-raising, I guess."

I looked over at Paul, who was exuberantly welcoming sponsors. Jasmine was playing her role, smiling and being charming. Her heart had to be breaking, but you would never have known it. I knew she would help us however she could. I had great admiration for what she could do on the tennis court, but I admired her for this kind of courage even more.

There was a large contingent from the Springs on board: I spotted Bill, of course, and Ginny Jennings. Across the deck of the boat, I was surprised to see KiKi, dressed in a cap and windbreaker. I waved, and she made her way over, a process that took three times as long as it should have because everybody wanted to say hello to her.

"I didn't know you were coming," I said. I was genuinely surprised. During the tournament, KiKi usually swore off all social events.

"Well, as you can see by the way I'm dressed, I wasn't planning to come. We had some players who were invited—Ramona Cerutti and Carolee Ashford and a couple of others—and traffic was a mess, so I drove them down to the dock in my cart, and one thing led to another and here I am." She grinned. "Hey, if it gets too late, I can always swim back."

"Daufuskie Island—isn't that where the white witch who cured your wart lives?"

"Sure is. A lot of weirdness over there, if you ask me. The natives speak their own language—it's called Gullah, and it's a mixture of English, African, and French. They believe in evil spirits; in fact, they paint their houses blue to ward them off."

"A white witch would fit right in."

"You said it. *We're* the outsiders. The island isn't very big, but it's been inhabited for nine thousand years, maybe longer. Native Americans lived there, and the Spanish, and some British privateer types. There was a lot of action on Daufuskie during the Revolutionary War and the Civil War. There's still some fascinating ruins and architecture on the island—a winery, a schoolhouse—but if you ask me, the best thing about Daufuskie is the deviled crabs. Best in the world."

The Fish perked up. "Did somebody say crabs?"

"Off limits," I snapped.

"Jordan, come over here and meet my friend Arnold from Nike," Gus called out. "And Walter from *Sports Illustrated*." Clearly, this event was packed with corporate brass. It was equally obvious that Gus and Trent hoped to make a major impression on potential investors and opinion leaders. This barbecue was intended to kick off Duration with the best possible impression.

The boat was pulling in at the dock as I joined Gus. "So how do we get to the barbecue?" I asked.

"The old-fashioned way." He pointed, and I saw a long lineup of horse-drawn carriages. "Trent's people thought of everything. There's even going to be a concert by some gospel singers during dinner. Admit it, Jordan, maybe being affiliated with BioTech isn't all bad. Now come with me and let's ride together with the people from the *Times*."

"Just let me check on Jasmine."

"Jordan, can I see you for a sec?" It was KiKi, holding out her cell phone. "Dr. Em's been trying to reach you. She called me."

I took the phone. "Emily—anything from the lab?"

"Jordan, they found something. That drink isn't poisoned, but it's really supercharged. The levels seem all out of proportion, and they've related toxicity to it. The potassium alone could cause somebody to get hyperkalemic. The vitamin A level is suspect, too. Usually, you know, they don't put much vitamin A in drinks, because you can't be sure what other supplements people are taking."

"But what's in *this* drink?"

"They told me the bottle they tested had forty percent of the usual therapeutic dose of thirty to sixty thousand milligrams, which is on the high side to begin with, but if you also took supplements it could put you over into toxic time: rough dry skin, maybe aching joints, even intercranial pressure that results in headaches, irritability—it comes on gradually. And they're checking on the electrolyte balance."

"Who's affected by this? Anybody?"

"Well, it can be asymptomatic until cardiac problems intervene. Like I said, maybe you're taking supplements. And then, certain people are affected by too low or too high a level of potassium. You can cause a ventricular arrhythmia, which, as you know, is a prelude to a heart attack, and then fibrillation and ultimately an arrest. The heart muscle, in particular, doesn't work right when there's too much potassium. Someone with a bad heart, like Rusty, would be at an especially high risk. So would someone whose heart is bad but who doesn't even know it—maybe a mitral valve prolapse, something that can cause problems, and you might not even know you have the condition. Maybe someone who is otherwise very infirm, or very young, or—"

Very young. "My God." My blood chilled. I walked quickly to the stern of the boat, where the crowd had cleared out in the crush for the dock. "Em, do you think this is the case with all the product they made or just this one bottle? I mean, did somebody doctor this bottle?" I was thinking of A.M., of the dog food. Horrible as it was, I was actually *hoping* that just this one bottle had been tampered with. Because any other thought was too awful to contemplate. "I mean, his assistant had also had a bottle. Nothing happened to him."

"Maybe it was just one idiosyncratic bottle. Or maybe Rusty's heart problems made him more vulnerable. The fact is, under the right circumstances, this shouldn't kill anybody. But that's assuming you're in good shape, with a certain level of tolerance, and no heart or other hidden circumstances, and you're not taking other supplements that could increase the levels even more."

"Did you contact the hospital with this information?"

"That was my first call."

I had to ask. "Em, could this drink *cause* a heart problem, like a faulty valve?"

"Cause a biological problem? No, I don't think so. But if someone already had a heart problem, even an undetected one, or if someone was already taking other medications or supplements—that's the real area of concern."

I couldn't listen anymore. "Thanks, Em," I whispered, and turned off the phone. Then I got sick over the rail of the boat.

"Now who needs Dramamine?" said the Fish, materializing at my side with a handful of paper towels.

"I wish that was all I needed," I said. My knees felt as if they had dissolved under my skin, and my head pounded viciously.

"So what was that all about?"

"The Duration bottle that Rusty drank had toxic levels of additives. I have to talk to Gus." I broke away from the Fish and hurried off the boat. The crowd clogged the dock, but I shoved my way through till I found him.

He was so pleased to see me. "There you are, Jordan. Perfect. Your carriage awaits."

"Gus, we have to talk."

He smiled. "And we will. But first we have to get to the barbecue. Come on, there are people waiting for us."

"No, we have to talk now."

"Jordan, you look terrible. What's wrong? Do you have a fever?"

"Yes. Now listen to me," I whispered. "I need to know what's in the drink. What's in the Duration formula?"

"I gave you a press kit. The ingredients are listed."

"That food vendor drank a bottle of Duration, and it nearly killed him. There was a potentially toxic level of potassium and vitamin A and God knows what else in it." I watched Gus's face closely, but he seemed only puzzled.

"I don't understand how that could happen. We won't let this get by us, believe me. I'm very concerned, of course. But a complete investigation is required. We can't jump to conclusions standing here without all the facts."

"What are you going to do about it right now? This minute? There's a man in the hospital."

"Jordan, let's face it, we are on an island in the middle of a very important event, it's almost dark, and the only way back to the mainland is by boat. We can't do one thing right now. When this event is over, we'll get to the bottom of things. I'm sure there is a simple explanation and, if not, we'll still insist on answers."

"Gus, I saw Anna Martinez today."

"You did? How is that possible?"

"She's here, that's all. She left the country for Germany, then came back, and she's here."

"Oh, God."

"Gus, do you think she poisoned that drink?"

"I really don't know. But it's one possibility. I'll alert security immediately. That woman is so unbalanced."

"You thought you neutralized her by getting her a job with Filament. Maybe not."

"Neutralize is a poor choice of words, Jordan."

"What did you owe that woman then, to get her a big job in a new place, move her there. . . . Gus we have a lot to discuss."

"And we will. But not now. This is an important event, and we have important guests. It's not the place to be arguing off in a corner."

"I guess some things are more important, at least to me."

His face hardened. "Here we go again. Suit yourself." He turned and walked away, then climbed into a carriage.

Ginny Jennings saw me standing there alone. She put her arm around me. "You look so low. You two are really the battling Bickersons these days. Well, come with me."

"I have to go back. I can't stay here."

"Well, then, we'll go back."

"This is a dock," I said. "There have to be some smaller boats for hire. Let's find ourselves a little private transportation."

*   *   *

Actually, Gus was right. There was very little I could do at this hour.

Ginny and I rounded up KiKi, and the three of us managed to get a ride back to Hilton Head with some fishermen in a Boston Whaler. "You've got to be careful in these things," KiKi said, as we sped back toward the lights of Harbour Town. "The water's deceptive out here in the Calibogue Sound. The currents are incredible. When the tide is moving, you can almost see a river running through here. And the bottom is irregular. You never know how deep it really is."

Back on dry land, I went immediately to the security office to see if I could locate Hank Murray. He was at home eating dinner with his wife and kids, but one of his assistants put me through to him.

"Well," he said, "the first thing I'll be doing is notifying the local authorities. This goes beyond a Plantation security problem. The next thing somebody needs to do is confiscate all of that product and examine it."

"Oh, my God," I said. "I wonder if they're giving out samples at the barbecue."

"I'll send a man over there right away."

"What about Anna Martinez? She may be involved."

"Nobody can link her to this directly, but since she wrote threatening letters and faxes, we can give the police a reason to pick her up for questioning—if she surfaces. But you gotta remember, tomorrow's the official opening day of the tournament. There's going to be a mob scene. It won't be easy to find anybody who doesn't want to be found."

"But we need to talk to her."

"You get her to come out, we'll talk."

I went back to my room and settled in uneasily to go

over my script for the next morning's live interview with
Billie Jean King. Suddenly, an idea occurred to me. I
picked up the phone again and left a message for Billie
Jean to call me as soon as she could. Then I fell into a
fitful sleep, knowing that at least I had a plan.

SIXTEEN

I was on the set, sitting in the wicker chair in my familiar commentator's blazer, waiting for Billie Jean to take her seat across from me on the couch. It felt good, comfortable, to be back; I was no longer the new kid.

"You'll be live," said Harrison as a sound technician clipped a mike to my lapel. "So remember, no accidental swearing, like you did at Wimbledon that time."

"Very funny. I'm a pro now, remember? But Harrison, there is one thing."

He groaned. "No surprises, okay? Surprises are for birthday parties, not live interviews. We only have a four-second delay here."

"Well, it's newsworthy."

"Don't scare me like this."

Billie Jean took her place on the couch and was miked as we spoke.

"Thirty seconds," announced the assistant director, calling the countdown.

"Jordan," said Harrison, his voice a cross between a scolding and a warning. "The script. Stick to the script. There's a TelePrompTer. There are rules—"

"Ten seconds!"

And I was on. Looking into the camera, I stuck to the

script and gave my usual intro. "Hi, everybody, I'm Jordan Myles, live from the Family Circle Magazine Cup at Hilton Head Island, South Carolina. We're looking forward to some very exciting tennis here, in one of the country's most beautiful natural settings, where the top competitors in women's tennis have gathered to battle it out in a tournament that's rich in both history and tradition."

Billie Jean and I went smoothly through the preliminaries, and she did a lively recap of the past winners.

"You almost won this tournament yourself, didn't you, Jordan?" she asked. As we had mutually agreed the night before on the phone, that was my cue.

"Yes, Billie Jean, I did. And I have a lot of respect for this tournament. Which is why I've chosen this particular time to announce that I am personally setting up a scholarship in the name of Celine York, a little girl who passed away earlier this year but who many of us in tennis feel should be remembered."

Across the set, I thought I heard the sound of Harrison Barber choking, but I continued.

"I'd like to dedicate this scholarship fund of ten thousand dollars to her. The money will go to the young woman player each year who demonstrates both potential and humanitarianism, as voted on by a panel of her peers and fellow players."

"That's a wonderful idea, Jordan, and I'm sure the sport of tennis will benefit as well," said Billie Jean. Then we continued with the interview as scripted.

When it was over, Harrison Barber limped forward with a makeshift ice pack clamped to his forehead. "You're trying to finish me off, Jordan. What was that all about?"

"I want to set up a fund, and I thought this was a perfect time to announce it." That was true. But I also had another purpose. Whether it worked or not was a matter of wait-and-see. I anticipated that Harrison, the network, and Gus would all be on my back about this, but it was something I felt I had to do, for many reasons.

I unclipped my mike and took the expected messages from the production assistant. They were from names I recognized as people upstairs at the network—but, surprisingly, no message from Gus.

Billie Jean and I walked out of the set and into the food court area. We were immediately surrounded by autograph seekers. Someone thrust a paper under my nose. I was about to sign it, when I realized there was writing on it already. It said, *We must talk.* I looked up into the face of Anna Martinez. She was wearing a scarf and sunglasses, and tears were streaming down her cheeks.

"You understand," she said.

I took her to what I thought would be a quiet place, Em's medical trailer. Emily was busy bandaging a blister, so we went in the back, to the examining room. Anna sat on the cot.

"I saw your announcement on television," she said. "I was watching you."

I had sensed she would, that if she had taken the trouble to come here, she would miss nothing. I had sensed, too, that my announcement would bring her forward. "Anna, I am happy to do this for Celine. She was so young, and she loved tennis so much."

"Yes. She wanted to be a tennis player, like Seranata. Artie was going to teach her."

"I want you to think, Anna. Did Celine ever drink from

a bottle like this?" I showed her a picture from the press kit of the Duration bottle.

She shook her head. "No. I never saw such a bottle before in my life. Never."

Then it occurred to me. As a test product, there was a different bottle months ago. Hadn't I been at the presentation when the design agency showed the new label? Of course she wouldn't recognize the bottle I had with me. "Any unusual drink? Maybe something she got from Artie?"

"No. But I can tell you, she did drink something of Seranata's—something in a plastic squeeze bottle. She drank it only because Seranata, her idol, drank it. So she thought she should too. My baby was like that."

"Seranata had a drink?"

"Yes, because Artie gave it to her. It did nothing bad to Seranata. But something happened to it afterward, I am sure. Someone got into it, put something terrible in it. I have thought it over and over. This drink is where they put the poison, I swear to you. When we were not looking. This is what I have been saying. But it was something different, not that bottle you showed me. I don't know anything about that bottle you showed me. The bottle my baby drank from, it had no label at all. This bottle in the picture looks very fancy. At the Garden, it was just a plain plastic squeeze bottle, like the kind you take to the gym."

At last, something made sense. When you eat or drink or even show any kind of product during a tournament, unless the sponsor has particularly paid to have its label shown, you must obscure the label, to honor agreements with sponsors who *have* paid for the privilege. If Seranata had any kind of nonsponsorship drink, she could very well have transferred it to another container. For a match, she might have had several such containers. It was quite possible that the little girl picked one up. Or was given one.

"Do you believe me now?" Anna pleaded.

I held her in my arms as she crumpled and sobbed. "Yes," I whispered. "I believe you." And, unfortunately, I did.

As I stood there, I felt more conflicted than ever. I desperately needed to know how the Duration drink formula had become so unbalanced—and why. But I wanted to find out without compromising Gus's chances for success. As I was all too aware, negative information like this could destroy any hope for the success of a product, much less a new one in the launch phase, when the public is forming an impression. Many millions of dollars had been spent; many more were at stake. And Gus had gambled his entire career and professional reputation on Duration. It was his baby, and I didn't want it to be stillborn.

On the other hand, there were lives involved. There had *been* lives involved. And illnesses, and deaths.

My mind whirled like a kaleidoscope. Maybe if we worked together, I thought, we could salvage the situation without compromising anyone's safety. Maybe it was all a fluke, or a random act by a crazed lunatic, like that time when somebody in the Midwest poisoned the Tylenol on the store shelves. It was desperate, selfish thinking, and of course I knew it. What else would you call it when you find yourself hoping for this kind of tragic explanation? I knew I couldn't be objective. Gus wasn't just a client or an associate; he was my alter ego, my lover, the man I might marry. I needed an outside, unbiased sounding board, someone who didn't have a sentimental bone in his body.

I needed the Fish.

While Jasmine was at practice, it took minimal convincing to get the Fish to join me for a walk on the beach behind my hotel. He arrived carrying a kite, complete with tail and ball of string, wound around a fishing-reel type of device.

"Diversion," he explained. "Clears the mind. We did this all the time in the CIA."

The image of a bunch of undercover agents flying kites was beyond my imagination, but then, with the Fish, it was better to go with the flow. As we walked to a good place to catch the wind, I told him about Anna Martinez and my conversation with her. "All she wanted was for someone to take her seriously," I said.

"She still could be a wild card. Do you think somebody poisoned the kid?"

We walked onto the beach—wide, broad, and gorgeously unspoiled for as far as the eye could see in either direction. It was a beautiful day, perfect for kite-flying, and A.M. scampered at my feet, thrilled to be in touch with nature for the first time in weeks. "I don't have any opinion. But I'll tell you what I do know, what I've learned that really scares me. You know, the purpose of a drink like this is to hydrate the body for duration play. What you drink during breaks in those long matches is crucial, because you're losing electrolytes while you play. The wrong proportion of minerals or vitamins or electrolytes can cause any number of problems—say, nausea, headaches, arrhythmia of the heart. Dr. Em went down the laundry list. And the thing is, some of those

symptoms sound like the complaints I heard from
Tanner; he was complaining of a splitting headache when
he left the court. And Malik had dizziness and nausea and
a headache. For that matter, so did Paul Kessler. And the
Schidors. I think we need to know exactly who was given
the product to sample. Specific names and dates."

A gust of wind came up. "I'll stand here and you run
with the kite," said the Fish, unraveling some twine. "I'd
run, but I got bunions. So who would have the list from
the sampling program?"

"Trent . . . Gus."

"So ask them."

"I intend to."

I ran down the beach with the kite, into the wind,
holding it high above my head until it gave a tug. I let go,
and it swooped low for a minute, then sailed aloft, high
and free.

I was still in my shorts and windbreaker, my backpack
slung over my arm, when I located Gus at lunch in the
sponsors' tent. He was sitting at an empty table, but there
were jackets and papers at the other places.

"Gus, I've got to ask you something important."

He looked up from his plate of salad and barbecue.
"Where've you been? Caught in a wind tunnel?"

I patted my hair haphazardly. Maybe I should have
combed it or braided it. "More or less."

"And where'd you disappear to last night? We missed
you."

"I felt sick. Listen, Gus, I actually spoke to Anna
Martinez—"

"You did? When?"

"She's here, like I thought. I smoked her out. And, you

know, underneath all her craziness there is a grain of fact.
I think we can get to the bottom of this whole thing. Do
you have a list of who got samples of the Duration
product?"

"Not the total list. But probably some of the names."

"Was Malik on it?"

"Yes, he was. We wanted to get as many of the top
players as we could."

"And were the Schidors? And Tanner?"

He raised his eyebrows. "Where are you going with
this, Jordan?"

"I think we need to know if we can relate people in the
sampling program with the people who got sick—or
worse. Was Seranata given samples?"

"I really don't know. Trent was in charge of the list. It
was a marketing issue."

"But you were the liaison. You're the one with the
relationships with the players and their people. I know
how organized you are. You must have some records."

"Whatever I do have is in my files back at the Springs,
in boxes, ready to be shipped to my new office. It's
impossible to access right now."

The rest of the group arrived back at the table with full
plates and took their places.

"Jordan, won't you join us?" It was Trent, flanked by
the man from the *Times*, five or six people I didn't recognize, and one person I did—Sunday Stanley. I had to
admit, Sunday looked sensational. She was wearing a
pink cashmere jacket, tailored and tapered to show her
small waist, a matching pink cashmere turtleneck, tight
white slacks, and high-heeled sandals, through which
peeked pearly pedicured toenails. Her red hair was pulled
smoothly back into a simple ponytail. A Chanel purse

dangled from her shoulder on a slim gold chain, and she wafted an expensive spicy scent. As far as jet pilots went, Chuck Yeager she wasn't. She slid into a chair beside Gus, picked up a piece of cornbread from her plate, and deposited it on his. Then she licked her fingertips.

She said nothing—in fact, didn't even look at me—but there was something about that gesture, something intangibly proprietary that maybe only another woman's intuition would pick up. *Sunday Stanley is a charter pilot,* I reminded myself. *She's used to airplane meal service. Like when the flight attendant offers you the sourdough or whole wheat roll.*

"Our guests have been seated. Would you like to join us, Jordan? We can pull up another chair."

"Your guests?" I looked pointedly at Sunday.

"We'll have to resume our discussion at another time, obviously." He swiveled in his seat. "I see an empty chair at the next table."

"Thanks, but no thanks. Lunch isn't on my diet."

I walked across the tournament grounds to the Club's trailer, where KiKi gave me a small table to use as a temporary headquarters. I dialed Winnifred. I had pleaded with her once again to visit her sister while I was gone, but if past history set any precedent, she would have ignored me and would be there to pick up my phone at the Springs.

The phone rang, and sure enough, she answered. I could tell that Winnifred was eating while she was talking. It didn't matter. Thank God she hadn't listened to me and left town. There was nobody else who could do this.

"Winnifred! Great, you're there. Now listen closely—"

"Jordan Myles," she interrupted, "you really should check in more often for your messages."

"Okay, I'll try. Winnifred, here's what I need. You know they're moving Gus's office to his new setup in LA?"

"Yes, I've passed by and seen Judy packing him up. I think everything is ready to move right before he returns from Hilton Head."

"Is the office locked?"

"Probably."

"Can you get the key or get in?"

"Do you need something?"

"I need a file."

"Well, that should be no problem. I'll just ask Judy. That secretary of his keeps impeccable files. I've been reading her tarot cards, you know."

"Actually, I'd rather Gus didn't know I'm looking for this file, so maybe you'd better not go through Judy." I felt uncomfortable saying this, but it was true. Judy had been with Gus for years. If Gus told her to bar the door, she would do so with the fierceness of a barracuda, no matter what was going on in her Major Arcana.

"Which file, dear?"

"I don't know how it's labeled, but I need the files that list the tennis players who were involved in the Duration sampling program. It might be labeled ENDORSERS or TESTIMONIALS or TEST PROGRAM or something along those lines."

"Are you sure there is such a file, dear?"

"Yes, because he told me there was, and that it was in his office."

"If the file exists, I will find it."

"How will you get in his office without Judy or security being involved?"

"Well, dear, I fully intend to involve security."

"What?"

"I'm having a little romance with one of the guards. Eddie."

"You and Eddie?" I was stunned. Eddie was in his fifties and competed in senior bodybuilding tournaments. Winnifred was closer to ninety and was—well, Winnifred.

"Well, we don't discuss it. It started when I brought him homemade sticky buns—you know, those decadent little rolls with caramel and brown sugar and cinnamon and pecans swirled in them? Now he comes around every day when his shift starts, and we have a cup of tea. I can tell when a man is interested."

"And what if Eddie isn't interested in opening that office for you?"

"Why wouldn't he be, dear? I brought a cheesecake today. Real graham cracker crust. Eddie is into carbs, you know. Besides, didn't you leave something there that you urgently need? And if not, I do have my hairpins. Low tech, but highly effective."

"Winnifred, you amaze me."

"You young girls today—you're so liberated, you're helpless. Like an entire generation of turtles on their backs."

I held the phone away from my ear as the decibel level rose. "Don't yell into the phone, Winnifred. I can hear you fine. Now, if you find this file, fax it to me here immediately, okay?" I gave her the fax number in the trailer.

"Bye-bye, dear. Kiss our little puppy for me. Dogs' mouths are much cleaner than humans', you know." The phone clicked as she presumably went off to pick Gus's lock with a hairpin prior to serving up her famous cheesecake.

As I hung up, KiKi tapped me on the shoulder. "Bad news from the hospital, I'm afraid. Rusty didn't make it. I thought you'd want to know."

My head dropped into my hands. "I feel worse than awful about this, KiKi. You can't imagine." And she couldn't. Nobody could. The entire web of suspicion that, for me, now surrounded the potential victims of the Duration situation was, at this point, beyond comprehension.

KiKi put a reassuring hand on my shoulder. "There was nothing you could do about it."

As far as she knew, that was.

"Listen, Jordan," she said, "I've got to dash out of here to pick up Cecile Normand for an awards presentation on center court. They're presenting a special award for work in breast cancer awareness to Cecile, co-sponsored by the magazine and BioTech. You know, she put on that marathon and raised a ton of money in Aspen. It's one of the first events of the tournament. Your friend Trent is presenting the check for twenty thousand dollars to the new foundation that BioTech is setting up for cancer research. Why don't you come with me? All the players are going to be lining the court to show their support."

"I had no idea BioTech was doing this."

"Really? There's been a lot of press."

It was not only a generous charity effort but also a brilliant PR move to enhance their image among women. I figured that if Trent was making the presentation, the entire BioTech cabal would be there. Including, of course, Gus. I tucked A.M. under my arm and took off with KiKi in her golf cart.

KiKi picked up Cecile at the entrance to the players'

lounge, and we sped to center court. I'd known Cecile for about ten years. She was a large-boned freckled brunette, a powerhouse on the court and off, who was devoted to women's issues and causes and a great political advocate. I congratulated her on her award, and she gave A.M. a reunion pat, but our main concern was negotiating the glut of people that now surrounded the entire tournament grounds so Cecile wouldn't be late for the on-camera presentation. Unlike, say, the U.S. Open, at this tournament everyone was polite, although the crowds were out in force now and getting around was next to impossible. Bumper-to-bumper traffic that would rival anything on Park Avenue at rush hour clogged the artery into the tournament and Harbour Town, and it took us a good thirty minutes to make the round trip from KiKi's trailer to the players' lounge and back to center court.

"It's only going to get worse," said KiKi. "The sponsors and the press are all on the island now, and the celebrities are arriving. But that's good. We love crowds. It means the tournament's a success."

KiKi expertly swung the golf cart into an area at the entrance to center court. Security guards, tournament officials in suits, and Gus and Trent stood in a cluster, waiting to walk out with Cecile. The Fish, uncharacteristically in a suit himself, stood off to the side, wearing an earpiece, looking very Secret Service. He gave me an imperceptible nod. I could see Jasmine and the other players lining the perimeter of the court, with Chris Evert already at the microphone, ready to announce the presentation; she was always generous with her time, especially at this tournament, which she had won so often before her retirement. Scanning the packed stadium, I noticed some familiar faces. Bill had taken a box, and he was there, sitting with Evie, Ginny Jennings, and several clients and guests. In the BioTech box, I spotted Paul Kessler, Doris Evans, and, I noted with particular interest, Sunday Stanley, who appeared to be becoming a fixture on the BioTech scene.

My walkie-talkie crackled on the Club channel, and I grabbed it as I heard my name. "This is Jordan."

"Jordan, Rose. Do you copy?"

"I copy, Rose."

"You got a two-page fax here marked urgent from your secretary, Winnifred. She also called to say you should receive it immediately, no matter what you were doing. She was most emphatic. Should I have a runner bring it to you?"

It could only mean one thing: either Winnifred's hairpin or her cheesecake had met with success. "Thanks, Rose. Yes, I'd really appreciate it if you could get that fax over to me right away."

The magazine publisher, the official host of the tournament, was welcoming the crowd now from a microphone in the middle of the court, flanked by key sponsors. Trent was announced and walked out to applause, holding a silver plate. The publisher held an envelope, which would no doubt be the check. After his brief introduction, Trent began to run through Cecile's accomplishments and her charitable contributions, including the organization of a women's marathon to raise funds for breast cancer research. What she had achieved was inspiring, but I couldn't focus on the speech; I was scanning the crowd in the opposite direction for a golf cart.

Finally, it came. Astrid, Rose's teenage daughter, swung through the crowd and, with a wave, handed me an envelope. In return, I handed her A.M. "Would you mind baby-sitting?"

Astrid beamed as the dog jumped into her lap. She had known A.M. since she was a little girl.

My hands clenched the envelope as I ripped it open. In the background, I heard applause as Cecile walked on court, but it was like listening to the sound of the ocean through a conch shell—something that sounds far away and not quite real. I scanned the two-page list quickly, my eyes flickering between the papers and Gus's face as he stood there, an arm's length away. There were dozens of names listed alphabetically; in fact, most of the top names in tennis. Beneath each star's name was the name of a contact person—coach, trainer, agent, or PR person. Since Seranata Aziz's last name started with an *A,* her name was near the top of the list. Under it, marked with an asterisk, was the name of Artie Lutz. The Schidors were on the list, and Tanner Axel, and Malik and Jasmine, with Paul Kessler's name asterisked beneath theirs. I was on the list. It was like the membership roster of an exclusive club you would never want to join. I quickly folded up the list and stuffed it into my backpack. My fingers touched something hard—Winnifred's little revolver, still snuggled under my T-shirt and hair brush. I resolved to give the revolver to the Fish for safekeeping and snapped the backpack shut.

Gus came over and stood beside me. "She'd be a great person for the Duration campaign, don't you think?" he said, indicating Cecile, who was now accepting her check to a standing ovation. I found myself clapping automatically.

"No, I don't, Gus. Nobody else is going to be part of that campaign, not if I can help it."

"What are you saying, Jordan?"

"I'm saying that you chose certain high-profile players and their coaches, trainers, and agents as part of a sampling program for this product, and then you gave them a product that caused serious harm and even death to some of them." I couldn't believe I was saying this, now, but there was no good time to say it, and it had to be said. "Do you have any idea what was in that product?"

"Of course. It was my formula, and it was perfectly safe. Don't you think I'm as concerned as you, more so? My reputation and my entire career are at stake." His voice was condescending.

"Then let's go together and put this on the table. Let's talk to Trent. Let's get the BioTech lab involved. If the formula got tampered with on the line, let's trace it. And let's recall all those samples."

"Recall them? You realize that would kill the entire launch?"

"Better than killing *people*, don't you think, Gus? What kind of overdose did you pump into that drink? Were you that desperate?"

Gus's jaw was set. "Everyone who was in the sampling program was in great shape physically. Nothing in the product would harm them. If some of their levels were elevated—"

"Some! What if some people who got the product weren't in such great shape? What if they were a little child with a heart problem? Or an out-of-shape coach? Or what if they were in great shape but they took a ton of other supplements that put them over the top, things that made toxic levels in their systems?"

"You know I would never do something like that."

"Well, maybe Trent would. He had an awful lot at stake, Gus. Not just a product—a huge acquisition."

I could see Gus knew exactly what I was saying. I could see he'd thought the same thing. "The FDA regulates these things very closely," he whispered.

"That's when you're on the market or going to market. But not in the trial stages, when you're not even in an official test market. We both know that. You made these people your unwitting guinea pigs. You banked on the fact that they were athletes, in good physical shape, that their tolerance levels were high. You oversaturated the formula with energy-boosting additives so they'd be sure to really feel a difference from the product. Then they'd do the testimonials, and you could always readjust the formula for the mass market."

"How can you accuse me of doing something like that?" Gus said angrily.

"Well, if you didn't do it, who did? Because that's the only explanation."

"Boy, you're on a real witch-hunt, aren't you? Excuse me. I have guests. We'll discuss it later. Right now I have to go to the box."

"You know I'm right. I learned everything from you, Gus, so you must know what I know."

He looked at me with a faint smile and left.

Two minutes later, he was in the box, sitting next to Sunday Stanley. Looking at them, it was like a curtain lifted: I knew. I just knew. This was not a pilot-passenger relationship. Those two were having an affair. Gus revealed nothing, but Sunday's entire body language was directed toward him. I watched her brush something off his shoulder. She was a bit too proprietary and protective, and her body had a tilt—toward him. I was watching myself be replaced. Except deep inside I knew I'd already made my exit.

Sunday Stanley had been in the closest proximity to Gus, Trent, and all the other important people at Bio-Tech. It would be fascinating, I thought, to know what she knew and what her role had been, beyond flying the plane. You don't get into a courtside box just by perfecting your takeoff, I thought. She seemed to have become a much more critical member of the BioTech team than your average pilot. Then there was the little issue of my near decapitation by the jet in Santa Monica. Some pilot certainly went over and above the call of duty, risking his—or her—license. Who would do that, and why? Over in the box, Gus leaned toward Sunday, speaking to her. She nodded, folded up her program, stood, and left the box.

I reached into my pocket and handed the Fish the fax from Winnifred. "Can you ask Hank Murray to contact the authorities and make sure the BioTech plane doesn't leave the island?"

"We can slow them down, but without a good reason we can't ground them."

"Well, we may have a good reason." I took off to follow Sunday. It was time for some girl talk.

SEVENTEEN

I trailed Sunday through the food court area until I caught up with her. "Hi, Sunday. Can we talk a minute?"

"Oh, Jordan. Actually, I have to be somewhere." She kept walking briskly.

"Where are you going?" I trotted alongside her.

"The airport. I have to check my plane, file my flight plan."

"That wouldn't include trying to shear a couple of inches off somebody's head, would it? Just kidding."

She stopped in her tracks. "I understand you were involved in an upsetting incident, but that's no reason to be hostile with me."

"Well, while we're talking hostile, what about that boat?"

"Boat?"

"The one in Malibu that tried to run me down in the kayak." I was guessing, but I wanted to see her reaction.

"You have a problem, lady. You're sick." The way she was looking at me, she seemed to really despise me, so I decided to go for it.

"You know, Gus gave me the most beautiful bracelet. A sort of pre-engagement gift, actually."

Her face didn't move, but her eyes widened. "Pre-engagement?" She looked involuntarily at her left hand, and then I saw an antique amethyst ring in a gold filigree setting not unlike my bracelet. I wondered if Gus had gotten a volume discount.

"Well, we haven't set the date, but depending on the product launch and the merger. . . . Well, I'm sure he'll let you know. We may want you to fly us on our honeymoon."

"I don't do personal trips. And I don't like being manipulated."

"Really? That little buzz in Santa Monica seemed pretty personal and manipulative."

"I wasn't flying that plane."

"Then who was? One of your buddies that you scammed into doing it?"

"This is grounds for libel, you know."

"You'll find a surprise at the airport. BioTech is under investigation. Somebody tampered with the Duration formula for the sampling program, and the police and the FDA are very interested in all parties involved. People have died."

Sunday put her hands on her hips. "You know, I don't understand you, Jordan. If you're so close to Gus, why aren't you helping him? Instead of having these paranoid fantasies."

"Is that what you think? Well, yes, Gus and I are close, but that doesn't change the fact that a child died, and some friends of mine as well."

"Do you believe someone with Gus's sense of values would have done that?"

Applause burst from the stands behind us. "No, but nobody stopped it either. And, if you're enabling this in any way, you are in big trouble and I'm going to make it."

"You're harassing me. And I can't believe your attitude toward Gus."

"What could you know about me and Gus?"

She whirled away, and I watched as she cut behind the tents toward the parking lot.

The minute Sunday was out of sight, the Fish materialized. "That's too bad," he said. "I thought I was going to see a real catfight."

"She's not worth it," I said.

"The doc left the stadium right after she did. Think they're going to hook up?"

"We better get to the airport. What if they take off?"

"You know what? I think they're about to be grounded."

One thing about a small island—the airport is usually of equal scale. The Hilton Head airport parking lot is about the size of that of your average supermarket, and the car pickup-and-return area is even smaller. The Fish and I easily spotted Gus's rental pull in. Not that he was trying to hide anything, I told myself. I caught up with him before he reached the terminal.

"Meeting a sponsor?" I asked.

"Jordan! Actually, I have to make a quick trip back to LA. Just a one-day turnaround, I hope."

"You didn't mention it. Lucky you've got access to that corporate plane. But isn't this going to screw up your plans?"

He shouldered his carry-on. "I don't see why. The press conference isn't until tomorrow. And we're still regrouping on the infomercial. Well, I'd better be going."

"Gus, what's your exact relationship to Sunday Stanley?"

"She's a company pilot—and a friend. You know that."

"What kind of friend? Are you having an affair?"

He stared at me. "Would it honestly matter to you?"

"It might. She doesn't seem to like me very much. I get the feeling she'd really like me out of the way."

"Jordan, why are you doing this now? You really know how to pick your time, don't you?"

"What better time? Although, come to think of it, there's a man in the morgue who would have preferred that we had this discussion much earlier. As for me, I've loved you for a long time, and I suppose I still do."

His eyes could have melted me—in other circumstances.

"But that doesn't alter the reality of the situation. Either through carelessness or by design, you allowed a formula that could harm people out of the lab. Me, I can't live with that. I know what you thought, Gus—that these were healthy, strong athletes whose bodies could handle it. In fact, not only could they handle it, but they'd feel a burst of energy like nothing they'd ever felt before. You counted on that. It would translate to a big endorsement lineup. And it worked—in the controlled environment of the BioTech lab. But this is the real world, Gus, and it's not made up of control groups and lab specimens."

"I can't get into this now, Jordan. Except to say you're wrong. There's so much about this that you don't understand."

"I admit I'm not a scientist. But I understand this: You've got three-year-old kids out there, and people with defective hearts and clogged arteries, and people with hidden aneurysms, and even athletes who are already taking God knows what other kinds of supplements. Was the formula I had tested an isolated accident? An example of sabotage? Or was that the way you planned it?"

"I hope you're not suggesting that I, or BioTech, was planning to harm anybody. Nothing could be further from the truth."

"But all the people who were hurt were people on your sampling program or individuals who had access to those people, isn't that the case?"

Something flickered across Gus's face. Was it remorse, sadness, or just dissatisfaction with a problem that he couldn't handle?

"Gus," I said quietly, "I have the list from your sampling program."

He hardened. "If you went into my files, that's confidential information."

"You're talking about a technicality when people's lives are literally at stake. I feel terrible about this, Gus, and I know you must feel worse. But you have to face up to it. We need to find out if it was an accident of individual incidents or whether the formula was spiked on purpose, for greater impact in the sampling phase. Were you planning to scale back the proportions when you launched on the mass market? Was that it?" I was begging for him to prove me wrong.

"Don't answer her."

I had been so engrossed in my confrontation with Gus, I hadn't noticed Sunday Stanley approach.

"Who do you think you are, the police? You think you can stand here and interrogate this man like this, whip him mentally and emotionally? I don't think so." Sunday's voice was edged with disdain.

Gus reached out for her arm. "Sunday, let's just get to the plane."

"I wondered where you were. So I came to look. We'll get going—in a second." She turned back to me. "You seem to make a hobby of tearing Gus down. It's not enough to be totally nonsupportive, to stand in the way of everything he's trying to do—oh, yes, I've heard—now you have to be accusatory. Well, he may be nice about it, but I've had it. Your little insecurities are destructive. Nobody wants to hear about them."

"I don't think your plane will be taking off today, captain," I said. "And what do you have to do with any of this?"

"Sunday," Gus said, trying to cut her off.

She planted herself protectively in front of him. "Can't you stop causing problems? Can't you see you're making him miserable?"

"If I stopped causing problems, as you call it, that would be convenient, wouldn't it," I said. "Is that why you tried to run me down in a plane and in a boat?"

She lifted her chin. "I won't dignify that paranoia with an answer. I don't have to talk to you, and I don't intend to."

"Oh, I have no doubt you despise talking to me," I said. "But on the other hand, you can't help yourself. You can't resist the chance to come out in the open with your hostility and jealousy."

"This is a pointless conversation. I have to be somewhere," Gus said. "Let's go, Sunday."

Over at the entrance to the airport, I noticed that Hank Murray and a group of security and police cars had pulled up to the curb. I pointed to them. "Before you go, there are a few people besides me with some questions—unless they're throwing you two a shower."

I heard it before I saw it—a screech of tires, and a car

tearing wildly through the parking lot. Brakes squealed, a door slammed, and, in one motion Anna Martinez flung herself out of the car and onto Gus. She was like a possessed wild animal, clawing, screaming, flailing. I saw a glint of flailing metal—a knife.

"You! You are the one who killed my child! You poisoned her!" Anna screamed as she pummeled Gus. Hank's security men launched themselves toward us, but they were across the parking lot. The Fish, who was closer, rushed over, but before anyone could reach her, Sunday had managed to throw herself between Anna and Gus, and the two women fell to the ground in a heap, their limbs thrashing. Suddenly I saw Anna's arm, over her head with the knife. I lunged forward, all my weight on one leg, and planted my foot on her wrist. Anna squirmed and shrieked, but I stayed firm; with my other foot, I kicked the knife out of her hand. It looked like a kitchen knife, a paring knife, as it clattered across the pavement and skidded under a parked car. The parking lot swirled into a frantic melee of people screaming, cars honking, and sirens erupting. Anna thrashed wildly, trying to wrench her wrist from under my foot, but I grabbed a car door handle and hung on.

"He's getting away! That murderer! He's getting away!" she shrieked. "I'll kill him! Let me go so I can kill him!"

The Fish grabbed Anna under her shoulders and flipped her over, her face to the ground, holding her hands behind her back. Only then did I realize that I had been so focused on Anna and the knife, and keeping her down, that she was right: Gus had slipped away.

One of Hank's men helped Sunday to her feet. Her

hands were deeply cut, and there were slashes in her pink jacket.

Anna continued to moan. "Mr. Big Shot Scientist. He thought he'd get rid of me, send me away to Siberia. Came to my house. Made the big pitch. What did he think, that I was stupid?"

"Anna!" I yelled at her. "It's me, Jordan."

"Jordan, Jordan," she cried. "Help me."

"Anna, you don't know that Dr. Laidlaw poisoned your daughter. There's no proof of such a terrible thing."

She lay there, her eyes closed now. "Artie told me," she said. "He killed himself because of it. That Dr. Franken-stein convinced him to get Seranata to try his drink, to keep it with her when she was on the road. He said the company would pay Artie a lot of money. But my baby got it instead. She always wanted to do everything Ser-anata did. And then she died. Artie knew it. He told me. And he killed himself. He loved my baby. He thought it was his fault; he couldn't live with it. But the person who should die is that doctor." She fell into sobs as Hank Murray leaned over her and took her from the Fish.

"The doc ran off someplace," said the Fish. "But it's an island. I'm not too worried. They've already secured the bridge to the mainland. He's not going far."

"But why would he run?" I said. "It's not like him."

"Really?" said the Fish. "What *is* like him?"

Of course, the Fish was right. I'd been with Gus so long and so intimately. I'd worked with him, loved him, hated him, almost married him. And I still didn't really *know* him, any more than he had ever really known me.

"This is all your fault," muttered Sunday Stanley.

"Let me see those cuts," I said. "You could bleed to death."

She stared at me, her eyes filled with hatred. "*You* forced Gus to do this," she said. "You pushed him and nagged at him until he had to leave his own company to get away, and then you refused to help him with his new business. After all he did for you—he told me, you know." She licked blood off her hand, smearing it onto her cheeks, but it continued to drip onto the pavement, making dark, winelike stains.

"So," I said. "You thought you'd just get me out of the way so Gus could fulfill his destiny—which was to be with you. Was that it?"

"He didn't realize. He was blind to it, he couldn't see how you were standing in his way. But now look. I was right. You've ruined all our lives—including your own. You selfish bitch!"

I turned to the Fish. "It was her—at the airport, at Malibu, probably even at my house, poisoning the dog food." I realized with a chill that, through Gus, Sunday had access to my schedule, even my keys. If she was sleeping with Gus, he probably told her everything, or at least his version of everything, and she added her own spin. "As the company pilot, she had access to corporate conversations and even documents."

"Do you think she knew about Anna Martinez?" asked the Fish.

"Probably. I think she figured that any threats, like the bomb threat at the airport, would be attributed to Anna."

"Well," said the Fish, "you were a fly in the ointment. She couldn't manipulate you. And if she couldn't scare you out of the way, I wonder what she would have progressed to next." The Fish looked at Sunday as if he had a microscope and she were under a slide. He was always

fascinated by the criminal mentality—as I was repulsed
by it.

"I wonder why Gus wanted to marry me, especially
with this woman in the picture," I said.

Sunday stared at us venomously. "Gus never loved
you," she seethed at me. "For him, it was business. It was
all about the stock. You flatter yourself. You and your
love affair with yourself."

"And let's not forget, if you're married to someone
you can't testify against him," the Fish added pointedly.

"Where is Gus now, do you have any idea?" I asked
Hank. The sheriff's men had arrived and were taking
Anna into custody and putting Sunday in an ambulance.
"And what's going to happen to Sunday?" I asked.

"Threatening airline personnel and equipment is usually a federal offense," said the Fish. "We'll start there
and work our way up."

I looked down and noticed that a cut had sliced
through my pants leg, and I was standing in a pool of
blood. "Oh, my God!" I hadn't even felt it, but now the
cut started to throb. I quickly rolled up my pants leg. The
cut ran vertically along my right leg from below my knee
to my ankle. It wasn't deep, but it was messy.

"Maybe you better go to the hospital yourself," said
Hank, as he frowned with concern at my leg.

I took off my sweater, wadded it up, and held it hard
against the cut. "It's superficial. It just needs a little pressure. They can clean it up later. Right now I have to find
Gus." Dreading the prospect, I picked up my backpack
from where it had fallen on the pavement.

"That's not your province. Let us do that," Hank said.
"It's opening day of the tournament, one of the busiest
days of the year. We got people coming in for the golf

tournament that follows it, too. This island is swamped with humanity. All you have to do is walk down the street, and you're hiding in a crowd. This road only goes three places. There's the bridge—that's blocked. There's Harbour Town. And there's in between, which includes both sides of the island, but already there are roadblocks in place. We've got fifty in security for seventeen square miles of the Plantation, plus now the state is here. He's not going to get far, believe me. But we have to have a formal complaint filed. Are you going to file it?"

"I guess I am," I said. That simple phrase was the hardest I had ever spoken.

"So he's going to make a run for it, rather than face charges? But we don't have any charges yet. He should get legal counsel."

"I don't think he's running away," I said. "It's my feeling that he's running *to* something or somebody. He was trying to get back to LA and I think he still is. He may be meeting a lawyer, but I feel he's looking for answers that are physically there to some questions he can't resolve. In the lab or in his records. Gus is not a man without a conscience." I remembered the hours and hours of conversations with him, when I was in the hospital, after my fall, when we talked about the human spirit, the two sides of everyone's nature, how we each combine light and dark, harboring the capability of both brilliance and destruction. He had loomed so large then, leaning like a lifeline over the side of my bed, as I lay there after my fall, my tennis career destroyed, with no hope and no prospects. He had given me back my dignity, my faith in myself, my future.

No matter what he had done, now I owed it to Gus to do the same for him.

* * *

The first thing I did was send out an all-points bulletin—
not to the police but to the Club. The sheriff's department
and the security people, the authorities, all go through
official channels. They deal with what is happening on
the surface. They travel on paved roads. The Club, on the
other hand, was adept at the way things needed to be
done now. Club members could find anyone, anywhere,
any time. Period. Their island network was unsurpassed,
and their means of transportation circumvented even the
worst traffic jams. If anyone could locate Gus on opening day of the tournament in a massive crowd, I'd bet on
the Club.

"You really think these women can find him?" asked
the Fish dubiously.

"One of the players lost a contact lens once and
couldn't go on court until she found it. All they knew was
the lens was *somewhere* on the tournament grounds.
We're talking about a tiny little contact lens, and a couple
of thousand feet trampling over it."

"They found it?"

"Well, actually, no, but they found an optometrist in
town who replaced the lens on an emergency basis in less
than thirty minutes. But another time they did locate
A.M. after she got loose from her carrier."

"There's a record for you," said the Fish with a snort.

A voice over my walkie. "Jordan? KiKi. We spotted
him. He's on Lighthouse Road in a white Saab, heading
toward Greenwood Circle. They have a roadblock at the
circle. The police have probably ID'd him too."

"I'm going there now. Come with me," I said to the
Fish. "Gus is heading toward Greenwood Circle. Do you
think we could get a police helicopter?"

"There are no charges filed, Jordan. It would take too long to authorize."

"Then let's take your car."

We'd been on the road about ten minutes when KiKi came back on the radio. "He pulled over and got out of the car. The traffic is really thick now—people pouring in and out of the tournament grounds, people heading back to their hotels, people going to Harbour Town. He just slipped into the crowd."

The Fish and I had just passed the fire station. "Where would he go?" I asked KiKi.

"There's a bike path that parallels the road, and he could always cut across the golf course by the lagoon. He's got the fire station ahead of him, the roadblock at the circle, and golf courses and lagoons on both sides."

I could see the golf course. "Pull over," I said to the Fish. As soon as the car slowed down, I leaped out and ran up to an elderly couple in a golf cart. "Excuse me, this is an emergency!" I yelled. "I need to borrow this golf cart!"

The couple stared at me. The man gripped the wheel, giving no indication of letting go.

Suddenly the woman broke into a smile. "Jordan Myles! Fred, look, it's Jordan Myles, from TV!"

He squinted at me. "Oh, yes. Yes, you're right. It is! Jordan Myles! My daughter loves your show."

"Thank you, but right now I really need to borrow this cart."

The woman yanked at her husband. "Get out, Fred."

The two of them climbed out of the cart, still smiling. "Imagine that," said the husband. "Jordan Myles borrowing our golf cart."

"Thanks!" I jumped into the golf cart and headed

across the course toward the lagoon, which was rimmed by pines and palms. It was a peaceful spot, but I felt anything but tranquil as I veered across the grass.

Then, as I looked ahead, I saw Gus. He was walking rapidly in a crowd of tourists, wearing sunglasses and a cap, but there was still something intangible between us that made me look immediately at him. In the same way, he felt my gaze, looked up, and veered into the shadows of the trees, at the edge of the lagoon. I stopped the cart, got out, and raced over to him. He didn't try to outrun me, but he kept walking. Thunderclouds had moved in, and it was starting to rain. The tourists were clearing out of the walkways and bike paths, making for cover, as a spit of lightning cracked the sky.

"Where are you going?" I said quietly. "Everyone is looking for you."

"I have to get back to LA," he said grimly. "You have to help me. I have to talk to the head of R and D at the lab."

"Research and development? Why now?"

"The formula for Duration. I think they misinterpreted it."

"Well, somebody obviously did something to it. Do you think or do you know?"

"I gave them several levels to work with. I'm not sure what they finally used. That's what I need to find out."

"Does it matter? The end result was the same. People died. You put lives at risk. You have to face your part in this."

"Oh, God, it all seemed like the right way to go: the product, the formula, all the new opportunities. I'm sorry, Jordan. I believed in what I was doing."

"There is no 'sorry' and no excuse, Gus. Anna Martinez was right. At the very least, you looked the other way. You chose not to see, not to question. You are as guilty as if you did poison those people. They were your friends; they trusted you."

"And I trusted *you*," Gus said bitterly. "You who couldn't wait to one-up me, to show me for a fool. You used me, Jordan. You used me to get your footing after the accident, and then you stepped all over me on your way to what you perceived as the top, shallow though it was. So you won't help me now, any more than you would then."

"That's how you saw it? So you had to do something bigger, better. But who tried to use whom? You wanted me for that infomercial so you could tap into the women's market, and I had the credibility and the name recognition. Except I didn't go for it."

"You didn't go for anything that wasn't on your personal agenda, Jordan. At least recognize that about yourself."

"And Sunday Stanley? Whose agenda was she on?" I knew it was a mistake to bring up her name, but I couldn't help myself.

"At least she believed in me," Gus said. The phrase landed between us with a thud.

My mouth opened, but no words emerged. I had no comeback because that, at least, was true. Somewhere along the way, deep inside, I had stopped believing in Gus. Maybe it was when I started believing in myself. Maybe it was when I began to travel a different path, maybe when he did. Regardless, once we began to diverge, neither of us could really continue together. It had all been over for us a long time ago. I just hadn't wanted to admit it. It was somehow comforting to nurture the image of the all-powerful Gus, father figure, teacher, and mentor I could go to for all my problems, and there he would be, with the solutions. It was just one big, destructive fantasy. Gus was right. In that, I was as guilty as he had been. Neither of us had been able to face reality.

"Let's go talk to the authorities, Gus," I said. "Why make this worse? And look. You're bleeding."

Dark patches of blood were seeping through his jacket in several places, mingling with the rain.

Gus's face clenched as he dabbed at his wounds. "It's superficial. I'm not going to let BioTech use me as their fall guy," he said. "There are some answers, and I intend to get them." He reached out and touched my cheek. "We could have done it together, Jordan," he said.

"No," I said. "We couldn't have."

Gus reached out and hesitated, and I thought he was going to touch me again. Instead, he collected himself, like an animal about to take off at a wild gallop, and, after the briefest pause, lunged at me in a fury. All the hostility and frustration we'd felt toward each other came boiling to the surface, and I recoiled, pulled my arm back, and smashed him in the face with my hand, which was wrapped around my walkie-talkie. I could feel bone crunching beneath my knuckles as my punch connected and the planes of his nose collapsed under my closed fist. The forehand smash. Once, that had been my specialty; apparently, it still was.

The force of my own blow threw me off balance, and I slipped on the wet grass and fell to the ground. When I scrambled to my hands and knees and looked up, Gus had vanished. I sat on the grass, staring at my bloody knuckles, unsure if it was my blood or his.

I heard splashing in the lagoon and realized that Gus was in the water, probably trying to find a shortcut by swimming to the other side, and I scrambled to get closer as thunder rumbled overhead.

The Fish suddenly caught up and pushed me down. "Get out of the way!" he yelled. "Hank and his guys are right behind me. They'll handle this."

I looked up and to my horror saw the back of a large alligator thrashing in the shallow water, struggling with Gus, dragging his body into the pond.

I staggered to my knees.

"He was running, and he must have stepped on a nest with hatchlings," said the Fish, breathing hard. "That thing came out of the edge of the water. Looked like a log to me. You couldn't see it. And then it just grabbed him."

"I didn't even see it." It was agonizing, just sitting there. The water churned and foamed, a demon's brew.

The Fish shook his head as we stared, riveted, at the horror in the lagoon. "Hank told me they can outrun a human in a fifty-yard dash."

I couldn't let this happen. I yanked off my backpack, tore it open and pulled out the gun. I clicked off the safety, took aim instinctively, and fired once, then again, praying I would hit the animal, not the man.

The thrashing suddenly stilled in the water. With a rush, six or seven uniformed men descended on the lagoon, and I watched numbly as they surrounded the shallows. Two men waded cautiously into the lagoon and, using nets and grappling poles, hauled something to the surface that I realized was Gus.

"He was trying to get to LA," I said to the Fish. The

rain was teeming down now, drenching us, and my teeth were chattering with shock. "He was trying to convince himself that he's not to blame. He thinks the R and D people will prove him right. They have exact formulas for the samples." I was talking to hear the sound of my own voice, as if that could restore normalcy to the horror of the moment. As soon as they laid Gus on the lagoon bank, I saw his white face. One of the men was already administering CPR. Suddenly, Gus coughed, and I saw his chest begin to move. "Oh my God," I whispered. "I didn't shoot him, did I?"

Then I saw that his left leg below the knee and most of his left arm were missing.

EIGHTEEN

By the end of the tournament, the stakes had been higher than anyone could have imagined. Anna Martinez was arrested and put under observation for mental competence. Sunday Stanley was arrested when I filed a complaint against her for attempted murder—of me—and an infatuated fellow pilot and habitué of the Spitfire Grill admitted he'd tried to "buzz" me as a little joke she'd asked him to play. Trent was placed under investigation, and BioTech production was immediately shut down by the FDA.

"Thank God we hadn't announced the merger," said Bill, clenching his jaw in relief. We were sitting in the players' lounge with Jasmine and Ginny Jennings. "I think we can skip the formality of the shareholder vote that we'd planned for after the tournament."

"I won't miss being involved with those corporate vipers." I shuddered.

"So far, we've kept this very quiet, and I want us to all keep it that way," Bill added. "Gus Laidlaw had left our employ when this occurred. I want to keep any association away from the Springs. And now that I've named Jordan executive vice president in his place, she is placing renewed emphasis on our physical conditioning program. We're getting back to basics, which is where our commitment has always been."

"I don't think the investment community is going to focus on anybody but BioTech," said Ginny. "They were the rah-rah boys. It was pretty publicly known that Jordan had refused to do an infomercial for them."

"*I* didn't refuse," said Jasmine sadly. She was still in her warm-up outfit. On court she was invincible, winning every match, her steely concentration matching her grace and coordination, as if the relief of finding some answers to Malik's death and all the threats and deceit that had followed had freed her up for the game of her life. The press and fans literally swarmed about her now, as she approached the finals as the favorite. The players' lounge was one of the few places she could sit without being accosted for autographs or interviews.

"I blame myself. God, to think that drink contributed to Malik's death."

"It wasn't just the product in his case, though," I reminded her. "He was taking all those supplements. The drink just put him over the top, and he got into a weakened condition."

"But Paul Kessler had him drink that stuff. And I bought into it."

"Even Paul didn't know what the combination of the drink and Malik's supplements could do. Paul's a bad guy, but he wasn't part of the Duration scam. He was drinking the stuff himself. It was an argument that went too far, with both of them affected by the drink."

In the course of the investigation, Paul had admitted under oath that he and Malik had had an argument about the misappropriation of Malik's funds, and the argument had continued on the hiking trail. Paul had shoved Malik,

and in his weakened condition Malik had lost his balance
and fallen. The Palm Springs district attorney was charg-
ing Paul with involuntary manslaughter, which, knowing
Pinocchio, he would probably beat, with the help of his
high-priced lawyers and his claim that the effects of
drinking Duration had put him on an emotional seesaw: a
variation on the Twinkie defense. However, it was less certain that he would be successful at manipulating the IRS.

Gus, in his own way, was a survivor, but to me it
would have been better if he had been less strong. I
doubted that he would thank me for the shot that saved
him. If he were in a position to voice a vote, death would
no doubt have been his preference. But he was not given
that choice. I was planning to visit him in the hospital in
Charleston as soon as my tournament responsibilities
were over. Of course, he wouldn't know that I was there.
Gus couldn't move, not because of the trauma of his
missing limbs, but due to brain damage from the lack of
oxygen when he'd been dragged and held underwater. At
this point, doctors were unclear about what, if any,
capacities would ever be regained. There was not even
any point in prosecuting or even implicating him for his
role in the Duration saga, although the Schidor brothers
were threatening to sue.

It was ironic, I felt, that so brilliant a man had, in the
end, been outsmarted by a creature with a brain the size
of a grape. But then, as Paul had pointed out, primitive
animals have finely honed instincts, and Gus had been
intellectual, not instinctive. I knew I would always be
conflicted about Gus, but I also felt I owed him something for all the efforts he'd made in my own rehabilita-
tion. Whatever duel had been going on between us, he'd
ultimately won.

Because now I could never abandon him. Never. Any more than I could ever love him again.

Ginny had promised to come with me. She'd been a true friend, propping me up through this, letting me know there was someone who cared. When I went back to the Springs, I planned to sell my house and move into Ginny's place with her. My own home had too many memories of Gus. Ginny and I planned to take a vacation, maybe to Paris, or Rome, or some other highly urban environment. The more steel, cement, and pollution the better.

I didn't want to see any wildlife, not for a long, long time.

If you liked Jordan Myles in KILLER INSTINCT,
don't miss her earlier adventures:

THE TOTAL ZONE

and

BREAKING POINT

by Martina Navratilova
and Liz Nickles

"An inspired behind-the-scenes look at the
world of tennis, with intrigue and suspense
thrown in for a grand slam."
—CLIVE CUSSLER

THE TOTAL ZONE

The First Jordan Myles Mystery

Tennis-champ-turned-sports-therapist Jordan Myles helps players achieve the Total Zone, when mind and body are in perfect harmony and winning is a sure thing.

Teenage tennis phenomenon Audrey Armat comes to Jordan to achieve the Zone, but when she suddenly vanishes into the dark shadows of the international tennis world, it's up to Jordan to find her.

THE TOTAL ZONE

by Martina Navratilova and Liz Nickles

Published by Ballantine Books.
Available at your local bookstore.

BREAKING POINT

A tennis promoter's assistant plunges to her death at a gala reception in Paris—and Jordan Myles, women's-tennis-champ-turned-sports-therapist, is convinced it was no accident.

While searching for clues, she clashes with several tennis personalities, but when someone tries to run Jordan off the road, she knows she's on to something more than sinister. Now she prepares to face off with a killer opponent in a game of sudden death....

BREAKING POINT

by Martina Navratilova and Liz Nickles

Published by Ballantine Books.
Available at your local bookstore.

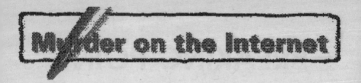